You Can Trust Me

GINA BLAXILL

SCHOLASTIC

To Hugh, who should read more fiction.

Call log, 1 November, 19:11

OPERATOR: Hello? Are you still there?

GIRL'S VOICE: Yes.

OPERATOR: Don't worry, whatever you say is completely confidential and anonymous. Take your time.

GIRL: I. . .

OPERATOR: There's no pressure to tell me what happened if it's too difficult. You can talk about how you feel instead, or just ask questions.

GIRL: [heavy breathing]

OPERATOR: We won't say anything to the police unless you want us to.

GIRL: [hangs up]

ONE

Mum swings the car through smart iron gates on to a tree-lined tarmacked driveway. The last house we passed was a few kilometres back, and there are no street lamps down the narrow, winding country lanes. I can't even hear any traffic. The sign we've just passed says STILLWATER HOUSE. We're definitely in the right place. So where is everyone?

I double-check the address Esme texted earlier. When I glance up, I see a huge manor house looming at the end of the driveway. Tudor, I think, and despite the jitters that set in the moment we left home, my stomach does an excited leap. The large decorative chimneys are a dead giveaway, as are the gable roof and low arch over the entrance. It all reminds me of places I used to visit with Dad.

There's no way the New Year's party is somewhere this glamorous. And yet I can see teenagers walking past a line of parked cars in a field to the side, and hear the faint beat of music.

Mum laughs as she parks up. "Your face is a picture, Alana! I take it this isn't what you were expecting."

"Esme said it was something else, but I didn't think... Mum, this is ridiculous. Why didn't you say anything?"

"I thought it would be a nice surprise."

"That's one way of putting it." I'm unable to keep the smile off my face. Whoever owns this place is probably a millionaire, maybe even aristocracy. I knew there would be seriously well-off kids here tonight – while my new school, Fairfield, is a regular comp, the party's being hosted by someone from the local eye-wateringly expensive boys' private school, St Julian's College. According to Esme, Fairfield and St Julian's kids mingle all the time outside of school. "Everyone knows everyone else around here" were her exact words. It's miles from what I'm used to, that's for sure.

"Are the nerves more or less bad now you've seen the house?" asks Mum.

"Still present." I wet my lips, wondering what the hell I'm going to find to talk about with these posh guys. I grew up in a three-bed terrace in Essex. "I just want to fit in, that's all."

"You'll make friends no problem," says Mum. "Why

don't you find a way to talk about modelling? I bet the other girls would like to hear about that."

"Mum, no! If I go round saying I was a model they'll think I'm a total show-off. I'm not, anyway, not any more. I'd rather forget I ever did it."

"OK, OK, just a suggestion." Mum glances at her watch. "Look, love . . . I get that walking into a room of strangers is tough, but you already know Esme. She'll look after you. I'm sure you'll have a great time." She smiles. "And you look lovely."

I draw a deep breath, then get out of the car. "OK. I can do this. See you next year."

Mum gives me a thumbs up. "Enjoy yourself. I'd have loved to party here when I was sixteen. If you get a chance, ask about Stillwater's history. Some of it's gruesome, but there's the fair share of ladies-in-waiting and military commanders too, all your kind of thing. The estate was private back in my day but I still heard all the stories."

She drives off before I can ask more. It's easy to forget Mum grew up nearby. That explains the book she gave me about Suffolk folklore for Christmas. I did think it a strange gift coming from her – Dad's the history teacher. Man, he'd love this place. Tudor England is his thing. I'd send him photos, if we were actually talking.

I psych myself up as I follow a group round the side of the house through an immaculate garden lit by a trail of lanterns. There aren't lights in the windows of the manor house so the party must be in another building – a sign tells me we're heading in the direction of THE GREAT BARN and GARDENS, away from THE STABLES HEALTH CLUB and THE ORANGERY CAFÉ. Maybe this is one of those estates which welcomes visitors, though I can't see any indication that the house is open to the public.

I feel a bit nauseous, but it's the good kind, like you get when a roller coaster is climbing upwards. Once I find Esme, everything will be OK. She sounded a little off when we messaged earlier, but that could be because I heard about the party from a guy I bumped into in the village shop rather than her. I can't believe she wasn't going to invite me. I've only seen Esme once since we arrived two weeks ago – the Morgans were away over Christmas – but we were so close as kids, almost like sisters. It's true that we've drifted apart but it's not like we ever lost contact. She can't have changed that much, can she?

The music turns out to be coming from a converted barn a short walk from the house. Taking a deep breath, I step inside – and only just manage to stop my jaw from dropping. Whatever I expected, it wasn't this. Everything in the barn screams slick, like how I imagine a high-end club. Apart from the beams across the roof, the vibe in here is modern. At one end is an actual, real bar, staffed by hip guys mixing cocktails. At the other end is someone who must be a professional DJ, judging by the decks and speakers. Lanterns and fairy lights hang from above, creating an atmosphere that's both intimate and fun. And is that a photo booth in the corner? The French windows on the opposite wall open on to a decked outside area where a few girls are already dancing.

This is amazing! There are fifty, maybe sixty kids here. Esme's nowhere to be seen. My stomach does a scary plunge. Brilliant – I'm going to have to butt into someone's conversation. It's either that or standing here looking stupid. Then a voice says, "Hi, New Girl. You made it."

It's Henry, the boy from the village shop. We only chatted briefly but I'm so relieved to see a familiar face that I give him a big smile.

"Hi. Don't tell me you've already forgotten my name."

Henry smiles back. His teeth are dazzlingly white, so much so that I wonder if he's had them bleached. His hair looks high maintenance too, and I can tell his glasses are expensive. Must be one of the St Julian's boys. At least his jeans and polo shirt are casual – I was almost expecting boys in bow ties and tails. Like almost everyone else here, he's white. Just another thing that's not what I'm used to.

"Course not. Alana. See? I was listening. Let's get you a drink."

None of the boys back home had such slick manners. I follow Henry to the bar. There's a queue but Henry catches a member of the staff's eyes instantly. I ask for a lemonade and immediately want to kick myself for being lame. I don't like the taste of alcohol, but I could have chosen something fancier like a mocktail.

"So," Henry says. "How come you've moved a term into the year?"

"We had a nightmare selling our old place. I really hope I've not got tons to catch up on."

"You'll be OK. You seem smart enough."

"I'd better be." I pull a face.

He laughs, placing a hand on my shoulder and guiding me away from the bar. "Smart or not, you look great. I'm sure I won't be the only one telling you that tonight. You must get a lot of attention from guys."

I almost spit out my drink. Is he joking? The only attention I normally get is: *She'd be hot if there was half a foot less of her.* For some reason, my height intimidates boys. Is it the lipstick? Tonight's my first time trying such a bright colour. If it gets this reaction maybe I need to wear it more often. "Er, thanks."

"Oops, am I embarrassing you?" asks Henry. "Sorry. Not my intention."

"It's fine," I say quickly. It's not Henry's fault I'm not used to taking compliments. You'd think modelling would have helped with that.

I glance around, but I still can't see Esme. My eyes fall on a group of giggling girls who look away so quickly I'm sure they were whispering about me. My palms turn clammy. Have they clocked my accent, my clothes? I don't sound that Essex, but it's enough to stick out. And I thought my tartan dress was a good choice – it has pockets, and is just about long enough for my legs – but judging by the number of girls in jeans it's over the top. Or is it my make-up? Does it scream trying too hard?

"Ignore them," says Henry. Hoping my cheeks aren't burning, I turn back to him. To my surprise – and delight – our chat reveals that he likes nineties Britpop, just like me. I'd always thought I was uncool for liking the same music as my dad, but Henry's even familiar with female-fronted Britpop like Sleeper – what are the chances? Maybe I was wrong to assume I'd have nothing in common with the private school boys. Another of my favourite bands is doing a reunion gig on TV tonight after the New Year's countdown, and we talk for a while about that.

By the time I spot Esme, standing by the doors to the terrace, my cup is almost empty. She catches my eye and waves. I wave back, and interrupt Henry talking about his school rugby team.

"Sorry, I've just seen my friend."

"Who? Oh – Esme Morgan. I didn't realize you knew her."

Something about the way he says that bugs me a little – as though he ought to know, even though we've only just met. "Yeah, our mums are best friends. Until a couple of years ago, Esme used to stay with us during school holidays while her parents were working abroad. Um, anyway, it was really nice chatting. I still can't believe you actually listen to Sleeper! Speak to you later, maybe?"

"Definitely," Henry calls after me.

Esme gives me a big grin as I join her. She looks no different from the last time I saw her just over a week ago – same pale, freckled skin, curvy figure, snub nose. The only change is her hair, now a brown almost as dark as mine rather than her natural ginger.

"Alana!" she says. "Sorry I was late. Diana escaped and it took ages to find her."

"Diana?"

"My new kitten – named after Wonder Woman. I'm glad you found someone to talk to."

"I can't believe you didn't tell me where this party was. At least the only person who saw me gawping at the house was Mum. It's incredible."

"Tell that to Xander. It's his party. And he likes praise. Not sure where he is right now. I'll point him out later. And I knew you'd dig Stillwater." Esme's eyes sparkle. "I mean, you are the girl who used to have a poster of Prince Rupert of the Rhine on her wall, so. . ."

"Hey! Prince Rupert was cool. He used to ride into battle with his poodle under his arm. After the civil war he became a scientist, artist and tennis player. . ."

"I hate to break it to you, Miss History Nerd, but he's also been dead for four hundred years. So you should probably stop crushing on him."

"And otherwise he was the perfect guy." We both laugh, and it feels so comfortable that the worries I had about it being weird having Esme in my life again fade.

"It's good to see you," I say. "I like the new hair."

She pulls a face. "Really? My friend persuaded me it'd be a good idea. Normally she's totally on point – she's a beauty vlogger – but this time, ugh. Big mistake."

"It's not bad, honestly. You can dye it back, right? I'm looking forward to meeting your mates. They look really fun on your socials." I pause. "You don't mind me being here tonight, do you?"

"Why would I mind?"

"Over WhatsApp you sounded a little . . . not yourself. And you didn't mention there was a party, so. . ."

"That's nothing to do with you." She glances over her shoulder, fiddling with her necklace. Her smile is gone. I open my mouth to ask if she's OK, but Esme speaks first.

"So, Henry. It looked like you two hit it off."

I peer at her. "Yeah, he's nice. You don't like him?"

"He's all right. Bit full of himself, but all the upper sixth guys on the St Jules rugby team are. They won the league last year, and pretty much boss everyone else. Henry must've split with his girlfriend again if he was chatting to you." Oh. Maybe that's why those girls were whispering. Esme pauses. I get the impression she's picking her words carefully. "Alana . . . look after yourself tonight, all right? Sometimes parties here get a bit . . . out of control. You know. Full on."

No surprises there, given the open bar. I give her a reassuring smile. "I'll be fine."

"Good," she says quickly. "This party should be OK. There aren't any boys from outside town and they're the ones who. . . Anyway. Never mind. How's your brother? Still uploading videos of your cat on YouTube?"

I frown, but before I can speak, a group of girls have

joined us. Esme introduces everyone. The only name that sticks in my head is Marley, Esme's best friend. The way she slings her arm round Esme and giggles about the bad dye job she did on Esme's hair makes me feel a little sad. I've always hovered at the edge of big groups – someone you'd invite to a party, but no one's first choice to sit next to in class, or confide in, or even message. Judging by how quiet my WhatsApp has already been, those friendships aren't going to last now that I've moved.

One girl asks me which subjects I'm taking. When I mention my favourite is history, she giggles.

"There's plenty of that around here! Have you heard of the Witches' Pool?"

An "umm" goes round the circle, followed by laughter.

"Not yet," I say. "I'm guessing it's some kind of pond?"

"Yeah, at the bottom of the hill, by the woods," says Esme. "Honestly, it's the creepiest place. Hundreds of years ago the lord of the manor drowned his pregnant lover there, supposedly because she was a witch. Other people have died too – young women, many accused of witchcraft, but probably murdered by their husbands and fathers and lovers." She lowers her voice. "Every time there's a new death, a blue anemone appears nearby . . . or so the legend goes."

I raise an eyebrow. "People aren't drowning witches there now, though. At least, I hope they aren't."

Marley laughs. "Course not. We're not that backward here, babe!"

"We could creep down there later on," suggests one of the others. "Full moon tonight. If ever there was a night for ghosts. . ."

"You mean werewolves, hon," says Marley. "Get your paranormal creatures sorted."

Esme glances at me. "The Witches' Pool is known as a bit of a suicide spot these days," she says. "People treat the place like it's spiritual – they tie little notes to the trees, like it's a cemetery."

The girl who suggested going to the pool leans closer, speaking in a hushed tone. "And if you stand there long enough you can hear the dead calling from beneath the water. . ."

Even though I don't believe that for an instant, a shiver goes up my spine. "Eww."

"Tell me about it!" says Esme. "Hey Lana, do you remember that horror film phase we went through when we were ten? Why did we think terrifying ourselves every night was a good idea?"

"Oh God," I say. "The one with the killer bees was the worst! Mum was so angry we got hold of that."

"Ugh, yes. That buzzing haunted my childhood." She imitates it, which sets the other girls off.

Time passes as we chat, and I start to feel more relaxed. Esme makes sure I'm included, and her friends are chatty and down to earth. I worried they might think some of my interests nerdy – people back home did – but apart from some light teasing, no one bats an eyelid. Someone fetches me some kind of fruity drink. I take a sip and nearly gag. It tastes like it has half a sweet shop in it.

"Don't you like your punch?" Esme spots that I'm not drinking. I shake my head. "If it's non-alcoholic I'll have it," she says, and holds out her empty cup. Grateful, I pour the liquid in.

"Thanks. You're not drinking either?"

"Nope. I'm finishing a course of antibiotics. Plus, well, I'm not in the mood."

I hesitate, then lower my voice. "Are you sure you're OK, Esme? You seem . . . not yourself."

"Fine, I told you." But she doesn't meet my eyes.

It's approaching half eleven when I feel a hand press into the small of my back.

"Alana." It's Henry. With him is another boy, big, stocky and fair skinned, wearing a camouflage-print T-shirt. "You getting on OK?" He leans close and whispers in my ear. "I was thinking, we could go and watch that gig together later. There's a cinema room down the corridor."

The other boy distracts me from answering. He slaps Henry on the shoulder, letting out a low whistle.

"Bro! You weren't exaggerating. I think New Year's is about to knock Halloween into second place for my favourite celebration. This is going to be epic."

And he gives me a look that's almost . . . hungry. Like he knows something good is coming his way. I stare back, but he's already swaggering away with a "Laters, matey." Henry rolls his eyes. There's a smile playing round his lips too. One I suddenly don't like. His hand slides down my back, then lifts before I can step away.

"I'd better keep him out of trouble. Can I get you another drink? I noticed you finished your punch."

I shake my head, watching as he walks off. Does he think I'm into him? I thought our chat was friendly, not flirty. My brother aside, I don't have much experience talking to boys, let alone dating. I look at the others – and give a double take, because Esme's gone deathly white. For a moment, she stands as though frozen. Then she pushes past me and into the crowd. Mystified, I watch as she disappears into the corridor.

"Did something happen?"

"She's drunk too much, probably. I'll check she's OK." And Marley's off before I can point out that Esme isn't drinking tonight. I start to follow, but one of the other girls jumps in, asking how far I've got with a Netflix series I mentioned earlier. Out of the corner of my eye I catch sight of Henry's friend. He's watching me, grinning. Quickly I turn back to the girls, fingernails digging into my cup.

Look after yourself, Esme said earlier. The way she fiddled with her necklace, and seemed so lukewarm about the party over WhatsApp. . .

Thinking back now, her words feel sinister.

What exactly did she mean?

TWO

Half an hour later Esme still hasn't returned. I look for her as we crowd out on to the terrace to count down to midnight, but it's too busy to see if she's here or not.

"Three . . . two . . . one. . . Happy New Year!"

Everyone cheers and applauds and starts hugging, and two of the girls I'm with kiss. Right on cue, there's a whistling from the direction of Attlingham, the nearest town, and fireworks burst above us in brilliant colour. Everyone oohs and aahs, then laughs. One of Esme's friends whispers something in my ear about wishing there were sparklers, even though it makes her sound about five. Her girlfriend raises her glass, saying we should toast to a new year and new friends. They grin at me and I grin back. In this moment, it feels like I belong.

It's too cold to stay outside for long. A few people leave when we go back into the barn, but most start dancing. The music is louder now, the DJ pounding out banger after banger. I close my eyes, enjoying the feeling of my hair bouncing on my shoulders and the swish of my skirt. When I open them, Henry's there.

"The band's about to play," he says. "Let's go."

It takes me a second to realize he means the gig we were talking about earlier, and that his hand is on my arm. I shake my head, stepping away. "Thanks, but I'll watch it on catch-up."

"You've got to watch live! They're going to start doing New Year's speeches here soon and that's boring as hell."

"Is anyone else coming?"

"Sure, we won't be alone." Henry doesn't even blink, and suddenly I doubt myself. Perhaps he is only being friendly. We have a shared interest, right? No one's warned me off him. Henry doesn't go to my school but it mightn't be the smartest move to be stand-offish. And if people I don't know are going to make speeches, I'd rather watch the gig.

As I follow Henry away from the dance floor he takes out his phone. I see him type a quick message before he slides it back in his pocket. Over his shoulder he calls, "Sure I can't get you another drink?"

"No, thanks. I'll have something later, maybe."

"Feeling a little drunk?" Henry smiles knowingly. I shrug, not wanting to look uncool by admitting I've been on soft drinks. Henry takes me out into a small, dark hallway at the end of the barn. Cool air hits my bare arms, and I feel them goosepimple. The music dies away as the door swings shut behind us. All of a sudden it's very, very quiet. . .

I hesitate. Even though we aren't far from everyone else, it feels it. "Maybe I should find Esme. . . I haven't seen her since before midnight, and—"

"She'll be fine. Come on."

Still uncertain, I follow him into a room at the end of the passage. It's the size of a large lounge, with an enormous screen and several plush sofas. Henry relaxes into one, placing his phone on the armrest. He downs the rest of whatever he was drinking, and I suddenly wonder how much he's had. I hover by the door.

"So who else is coming?"

"Friends of mine." Henry picks up a remote. "They're getting drinks. You feeling OK? Not too tipsy? Take a seat."

Why does he keep asking if I'm drunk? Leaving the door open, I perch at the end of Henry's sofa, hoping the distance between us makes it clear I don't want him to touch me. The gig pops up on the screen. The band kick off with my favourite song, but as the minutes pass it becomes harder and harder to enjoy the music. Henry keeps glancing between me and his phone. He's not even watching the TV. And whoever's joining us is taking a long time to pick up a cocktail.

My heart beats a little faster. Even though my dress isn't that revealing, his eyes make me feel exposed. The edge of the sofa digs into the backs of my thighs, and I realize I've been sitting so still my muscles have tensed. Did Henry lie about there being other people? But then, why is he just sitting there? He doesn't seem shy, or under-confident. If anything he's looking pleased with himself.

Very pleased with himself.

Anger bursts inside me. Why the hell did I let this guy take me here? To be polite? Because he's rich, and probably popular? Screw this. I'm about to leave when there are footsteps outside. Startled, I wheel round. It's a boy, though I can't see him properly in the dark.

"Finally!" Henry says. "Oh. Just you?"

"He'll be along in a minute, I bet. Not that we need to wait." The boy's voice pulses with excitement. "You're not gonna keep this crappy band on, are you?"

"As mood music? Yeah, right!" They both laugh. The other boy steps inside and the door closes with a soft click.

They're going to lock it. The thought comes from nowhere. Frightened, I leap to my feet. Henry looks shocked, and the other boy says, "What? She's supposed to be—" but I'm gone before I can hear the rest of the sentence.

Outside I almost collide with someone standing by the door. He – I think it's a he – immediately retreats into the shadows. I hurry down the passage and back into the main room, skin prickling all over.

While I've been gone, the crowd in the barn has thinned

out, and the music is even louder. More time has passed than I realized; it's quarter to one. I watch two girls dance round a spilled drink, feeling dazed. It's so . . . normal. Did I overreact just now? Could it have been some weird joke? Perhaps the boy who came in really did want to watch the gig, and the third guy he mentioned was bringing the drinks. . . No. That can't be right. He called the music "crappy". Henry turned the TV off. And their reactions when I left. . .

My lip wobbles. Suddenly I want to cry. I feel small, vulnerable, out of place, and all I can think about is going home. I'm supposed to be sharing a taxi with Esme, booked for half one. I'd better find her. I walk through the room and out on to the terrace, but Esme isn't there, and her friends haven't seen her. Starting to feel anxious, I take out my phone. And my stomach flips over.

Three missed calls from Esme, and a message.

Esme: Whatever you do, don't go off alone with Henry.

I stare at the letters on the screen. My heart thuds. The timestamp is just before midnight – around twenty minutes before I did exactly what Esme warned me not to. Earlier, she'd said Henry was all right. Did something change her mind?

I have to find her. I dig out my coat from the pile in the corner of the barn and step through the main door on to the gravel path I walked up earlier. It feels eerie standing in the darkness alone, and I hug my arms around myself, wishing I'd brought a thicker coat. I walk round the barn and into some walled gardens, but no one seems to be about. When I ring Esme she doesn't pick up.

Where the hell is she? I don't want to have to get the taxi alone and leave her. Might Esme have gone to the Witches' Pool? She did say she sometimes went there in the dark. And her friend, the one keenest on creepy stuff, is missing. She could have left, but perhaps they're together?

Hoping it's a short walk, I set off. I should be heading in the right direction – this path is taking me downhill, parallel to the woods Esme mentioned. I try ringing her again. A few seconds later I think I hear a faint ringtone coming from the trees. But when I shine the torch from my phone up and down, there doesn't seem to be anyone there. I guess it must be the music from the barn.

The path winds downhill for what feels like ages. This is a stupid idea. Esme would never have come this far from the party. I'm about to turn back when a little copse looms up. Through the trees my torch picks out the gleam of water.

The Witches' Pool. I've found it.

"Esme?" I call.

Silence answers. My voice sounds tiny in the vast blackness. Being here alone is majorly creeping me out, even with a full moon, but curiosity makes me walk to the edge of the pool. It's larger than I'd imagined, more of a lake than a pond. All around – on the branches of evergreen trees – little scraps of paper flutter in the breeze.

Messages to the dead. I shiver.

How many women have died here over the centuries? There could have been hundreds of witches – lonely women whose only crime was to be a little strange. And since then? Something must draw the desperate and desolate to plunge into the dark water. Perhaps they come because being here makes them feel less alone, if there really is whispering from the depths of the pool. All I can hear is the breeze shushing through the trees, but on another night. . .

I'm being silly, of course. The dead are just that – dead. No ghosts or hauntings, even if this place does feel like it comes from another century. I give the pool a final sweep with my torch – and for a second my heart stops, because floating there is a body.

THREE

Fear shoots through me, and I almost scream. I edge closer to get a better look. It's a girl, lying face down. The skirt of her dress drifts round her legs, her hair fanned out. She isn't moving.

For a moment, I stare, repulsed and transfixed. Then I snap to life. I kick off my pumps, discard my coat and bag, and plunge into the pool. Icy water swirls around my ankles. I suck in a sharp breath and force my feet forward, praying the mud below stays firm. By the time I reach the girl I'm waist-deep, almost paralysed by the cold. I grab her under the armpits, hauling her backwards. She's much heavier than I expected. One step – another – keep going – I'm in the shallow water when there's splashing from behind. A boy appears next to me.

"What happened?"

"I don't know," I gasp. "She's unconscious."

Together we pull the girl out, laying her down on the grass – and then I really do scream, because Esme's face stares back at me. Her lips are a funny blue colour, skin impossibly pale. She doesn't seem to be breathing. Instinctively I press my fingers against her neck: no pulse.

"Oh God," I whisper. The boy pushes my hand out of the way and takes her pulse himself.

"Shit," he says. "Shit, shit, shit."

My whole body is shaking, my breath ragged. I almost say *what do we do* but I realize I know: CPR. Mum taught me this ages ago. *Tip back the head. Clear the airways. Pinch the nose. Rescue breaths, then chest compressions. Repeat until help comes.*

As I grasp Esme's chin the boy puts his hand over mine.

"I'll do it." I clock his accent: American. "Your teeth are chattering."

He's right so I don't argue. He leans over Esme and starts the rescue breaths. To my relief, he knows what he's doing. I pull my coat back on and grab my phone. The screen shows a small circle with a line through it – *emergency calls only.* My fingers are shaking so much it takes three attempts to punch in 999. As I press the phone to my ear, I spot blood on Esme's temple. There's a wound on the side of her head; small, nasty-looking, almost like a puncture.

An operator's voice comes down the line, asking which

service I require. "Ambulance," I gasp, and explain. By the time I hang up, the boy has done several rounds of CPR so I take over. I force myself to focus on counting compressions rather than on how Esme's cold, wet skin feels against my lips. By the time we switch again, I'm beginning to panic. Surely she'd have started breathing if this was going to work? Esme's body suddenly buckles. She splutters up water, then sucks in a deep breath. Both the boy and I freeze. For a long moment, Esme remains motionless. Then her chest falls before she takes another breath.

"It worked!" The boy looks shell-shocked. I lean forward, patting Esme's cheek.

"Esme? Can you hear us?" I ask urgently, but she doesn't respond. Together, we roll her into the recovery position and pile our coats over her, though his is only a leather jacket. Underneath, she looks tiny and bedraggled.

We stare at Esme, neither of us speaking. Then the boy says, "You'll get hypothermia if you stay here. Can you make it to the barn?"

I don't know if my legs will take me all that way. They feel like overcooked spaghetti. I open my mouth to say the ambulance will be here soon but suddenly I'm not sure. Will they be able to find us with the directions I gave? The Stillwater Estate must be vast. Maybe there's more than one pool, one wood. Dread grips me as I picture paramedics bumbling around in the dark, too far away to hear us shout. Every second counts. A couple of coats aren't going to warm Esme quickly enough, not out here.

"Forget me getting hypothermia," I say. "We need to get Esme somewhere warm, wet clothes off – crap, is it even safe to move her?"

"The closest place is the barn. The others can bring blankets from the house."

"That'll take ages!"

"We really need that ambulance. Like, now. But tonight will be hella busy. Did they say how long it'd be?"

I shake my head. A helpless moment passes as we look at each other. Then the boy climbs up.

"Screw this. We'll take her to the hospital ourselves. My car's not far. And if the ambulance shows first, even better."

I realize this could be the decision between life and death. But I nod.

The boy manages to bring his car right to the edge of the Witches' Pool. It takes less than five minutes but feels like for ever. He hefts Esme into his arms and I help him position her across the back seat. It's only when he starts the engine and we're bumping across the grass that I realize I didn't think twice about getting in beside him, or pulling on the hoodie I found on the passenger seat. Does anyone else know what's happened? I open my mouth to ask, then grab on to the door as the car lurches forward. "Hey! Careful."

"Sorry!" the boy says. "Oh crap!"

The engine splutters, then cuts out. The boy turns the key in the ignition, swearing under his breath. I glance back at Esme. *I hope we're not making a terrible mistake.* The car stalls again. Something inside me snaps.

"I thought you said you could drive!"

"I can!" the boy yells back. "It's only first gear I screw up, and if you hadn't noticed, this is a stressful situation—"

He stalls a third time. I dig my nails into the side of the seat.

"Are you drunk?"

"What? No! You think I'd be able to do CPR wasted?" Finally he gets the car moving again. I glance over as he pulls on to the empty main road and we gather speed, hoping I'm right to trust him. Even with the heating on full whack I'm shivering.

"Do you need directions? I can get a map on my phone – oh, wait. My bag's gone. Must've dropped it. Where's yours?"

"My jacket."

Our coats are still piled over Esme so I swivel round so I can reach. Ten minutes later we're pulling up by A & E. Esme's still unconscious. Inside the hospital things happen quickly; there are receptionists, doctors, stretchers, hurried explanations, and Esme is rushed off.

The nurses check us over too, though the boy was only in the pool up to his knees. My dress mostly dried off in the car and though my body temperature is still low, they seem happy that it's returning to normal. I cup my hands gratefully around the hot drink a nurse brings me. I know I've been lucky.

Slowly, my muscles relax. The waiting room is dazzling white, too bright after the darkness of the country lanes. From further down the corridor I can hear a phone ring and two drunk dudes arguing. Everything smells sterile, right down to my polystyrene cup. Now I don't need to do anything, I'm feeling dizzy: part relief, part exhaustion.

I glance over at CPR boy. He's drumming his fingers on the side of his chair, looking pensive. I wasn't paying attention earlier, but he's quite good-looking in a scruffy kind of way, with tousled brown hair long enough to tie back. There's a shadow of stubble on his jaw, and his skin's several shades more tanned than mine, suggesting he's been somewhere warm recently. Even though he's wearing a roomy sweater I can tell he's strong and sporty. No wonder he carried Esme so easily.

And he's tall. Like, really tall. I sit up straighter. "What's your name? I never asked."

"Liam. Alana, right? I saw you talking to Henry earlier."

There's something loaded in the way he says Henry's name, but I'm too tired to work out what. And I don't even want to think about the cinema room. "Do you think we need to wait around?"

"Not sure. Esme's doctor will want to talk with us, I guess, though if they call the cops I'm bailing."

"Police?"

"She didn't wind up in the water by magic, unless you believe ghosts pulled her in. It looks like she was attacked."

He's right. I've been so focused on getting here, then

warming up, that it hadn't occurred to me to wonder how Esme wound up in the water, far away from everyone else. "But Esme can swim. I know she can. We did a summer club when we were eight. She was good."

"Maybe she was unconscious, then. She could have passed out. Fallen in."

"Or been knocked out." Uncomfortably, I remember the mark on Esme's temple. "No one would walk away and leave her to drown, though, right?"

Liam shrugs. He's picking at the skin around his nails, but absently, as though not fully aware he's doing it. Some of the cuticles are bleeding.

"I was wondering," he says.

"What?"

"If maybe she took something."

"As in – drugs?"

"Yeah. Last I saw her she was pretty wasted. That's not so strange, but the way she was acting. . . She said she felt sick, and she was kind of, I don't know. Not making sense."

"When was this?"

"Just before the fireworks."

I purse my lips. Esme rushed off at about half eleven. She was tipsy, maybe, but that was all. Then I remember: Esme wasn't drinking.

If that's true. . .

She shouldn't have been tipsy at all.

"Were there drugs?" I ask.

"I guess. Aren't there always drugs at parties?" Liam

looks uncomfortable. I want to tell him Esme wouldn't have taken drugs, that she's always been a rule follower, but I don't really know her that well any more, do I? I wonder out loud, "Why did she even go to the Witches' Pool by herself? The barn wasn't so hot that you'd go that far to cool off. How come you were outside?"

"Went for a walk." Liam checks his phone. I can't help thinking he's done it to avoid making eye contact. He must have been very close to the pool – he came to help so quickly.

A doctor appears before I can ask. He wants us to explain what happened again, and doesn't do a good job of hiding his frustration when we're vague. I feel guilty I can't be more helpful.

When the doctor leaves, Liam gets up. He's very pale now, hazel eyes troubled. When I ask if he's OK, he says, "It's sinking in. You know – everything. That pool. . . It's where. . ." He checks himself, then gives me the world's most unconvincing smile. "I just want to get home. Where do you live? I'll give you a ride. Assuming you're not traumatized by my sucky driving, that is."

Liam stalling his car isn't the part of tonight I'm going to have nightmares about. "Thanks, but no. My mum will be along soon. She works in the ICU. One of the nurses said she'd tell her what's happened."

I don't add that I badly want to see Mum, hear her say we did the right thing not waiting for the ambulance. Even if it's a lie. Liam hovers by the chair, then, reluctantly, says he'll wait. He starts picking at his nails again, and I have to look away to prevent myself from stopping him.

A few minutes later Mum appears, reassuringly calm in her spotless nurse's tunic. After asking how I am, she tells us that Esme's in a room with her parents. Her voice carries the same detachment as it does when she talks about her own patients. Even before I ask if Esme is going to be OK I know her answer will be professionally mechanical: it's too early to say. I'm close to tears as we leave the hospital, waving goodbye to Liam in the car park. I don't know Esme's dad very well but her mum's a lot like her, always warm and upbeat, bringing out Mum's fun side, which sometimes I forget is there. I picture Laura and Doug in the converted almshouse I was looking forward to visiting, being awoken by the phone shrilling with terrible news. . .

We get home. The cottage feels cold and unwelcoming, and somehow not very homely. My brother Seb's asleep on the sofa in front of a wildlife documentary, pizza crusts on a plate on the floor. I close the door to avoid waking him and watch as Mum hangs her bag on the end of the banister, half impressed, half annoyed that she can act normally.

"Was taking Esme to hospital ourselves the right thing to do?" I ask in a low voice.

"You should get to bed, Alana. We can talk about this in the morning."

"Mum. I need to know."

Mum gives me a hug, the sharp edge of her ID badge digging into my arm. It doesn't feel as comforting as it should.

"No, but it won't have harmed her. So don't feel bad." A pause. "You did well tonight. Saving Esme was very brave."

I don't feel brave. I always imagined saving a life would feel good, but all I can fixate on is everything I could have done differently. What if I'd searched for Esme sooner? What if I'd stopped her going outside, even? "Do you think she'll be OK?"

"Alana, I told you. A lot will depend on the next few hours."

"But she's not going to die. We saved her, right?"

There's a pause. I can tell Mum's deciding whether to sugar-coat this. "These things are unpredictable," she says eventually. I catch a tiny wobble in her voice. "You really need to get to bed. Do you think you can sleep? God, that bloody cat's meowing. He'd better not have killed something. The sooner we get a cat flap put in the better."

I let Mum go to let Bruce in. For a second, I think about ringing Dad. It would be so reassuring to hear his voice... But no. He'll be asleep, or out at some party with *her.* And I'm doing just fine without him.

Somehow I manage to sleep. By the time I wake up, still wearing Liam's hoodie and last night's dress, it's midday. Mum promised she'd let me know if she heard anything so Esme must still be the same.

Far too on edge to snooze, I shower, change and go downstairs to make myself a sandwich, bare feet cold on the stone floor. I eat staring out of the kitchen window across the small, colourless back garden, and the muddy fields beyond that belong to the farm down the lane. I wonder what will grow there when the weather gets warmer, and if Esme will be better by then. We'd started making plans over WhatsApp. She'd promised to show me the cat shelter she volunteers at and teach me to decorate cakes so I can surprise Seb on his birthday, and I'd persuaded her to take a beginner's archery class with me at a place I found online. *I'll be the (useless) Prim to your Katniss but if you want to try it that badly, I'm game*, she'd written, and it had made me laugh.

I should have spent my time with Esme last night, not a creepy boy who played a sick joke I don't even understand. I feel so stupid. I *knew* something was off. Why didn't I trust my instincts? When I think about that second boy coming in, and the way they called me *she*, as though I wasn't there. . .

My hands tremble as I add my plate to the pile of washing-up in the sink. I want to believe it was just drunk boys messing about. Yet Esme's missed calls suggest otherwise. Was that why she had rushed off, the colour really drained from her face?

Would she have got so agitated over nothing?

The message, too, had sounded serious. Like a warning.

It wasn't a joke, a dark voice in my head whispers. *Something was wrong. You were in danger.*

I'm washing up when Seb appears in his pyjamas, an old pair with stars on which he's clung on to so long you can't tell what colour they're supposed to be. The legs end way above his ankles. His hair, the same dark brown as mine, is tufted up from sleep, making him look younger than almost fifteen.

"Your heart stops," he announces. "That's what ultimately kills you when you drown, according to Google. You breathe in water, it floods your airways, falling oxygen levels make you unconscious, then the heart struggles. And without oxygen, none of our cells can get the energy they need to survive."

I squeeze the scourer, not replying. After a moment, Seb says, "You probably didn't want to hear that. Sorry. I was only trying to understand what happened. Mum told me. I should have asked if you were OK first. Are you?"

I sigh. Normally, I like the way my brother focuses on facts, getting straight to the heart of things. It seems a lot smarter than the way my brain bounds about, getting excited and distracted by whys and what ifs. Unfortunately, people at our old school didn't see Seb's autism so positively.

"What are her chances of recovering fully, then?" I ask. "Mum won't say. I'm guessing you googled that too."

"It depends on what exactly happened. You're lucky the CPR even worked. It often doesn't. She can't have been in the water very long. That's good, because it decreases the amount of water she can have swallowed, and the chance she'll wake up brain-damaged." I wince. "And another thing. . ."

Seb stops. Outside, gravel crunches. When I go to the window I see a man and woman climbing out of a car.

The police.

"You'd better fetch Mum," I say, and go to let them in. The male officer – fifty-something, white, balding, overweight – introduces himself as Inspector Harcourt, and his younger colleague as Constable Mills.

"Is Esme OK?" I ask nervously as I show them into the sitting room. "I'm guessing you're here about last night. She's not. . ."

I can't bring myself to say *dead.* After a horrible pause, Harcourt shakes his head, and says there's no change. Mum hurries in, hair wet and wearing no make-up, looking flustered, Seb behind her. Harcourt tells us he's gathering statements, so I explain about looking for Esme and what happened when I found her. He asks about the party beforehand, but to my relief, he's mostly interested in how much alcohol there was, or if I saw anyone using drugs. I avoid mentioning Henry. What happened is far too embarrassing to bring up in front of strangers, or Mum, for that matter. Then Harcourt says there's been a new development.

"The hospital ran blood tests on Esme." His voice sounds very serious now. "They found GHB in her system."

He looks at us expectantly. Those letters mean nothing to me but Mum sucks in a breath.

"What is it?" I whisper.

After a moment, Mum says, "Liquid ecstasy. It's a date rape drug."

FOUR

The police watch me closely as Mum's words sink in.

"Your mother's correct," says Harcourt. "GHB, or gamma-hydroxybutyrate, is a class B drug, often slipped into drinks and used for the purposes of date rape. It's colourless, odourless and very difficult to detect both when it's consumed and afterwards because it leaves the system so quickly. Victims feel confused, disoriented and weak, with little memory of what may have happened. Hence, vulnerable to sexual assault."

I stare at him, stunned. I thought people used date rape drugs in bars and clubs. Older people. Dangerous people. Not teenagers at house parties. But then teenagers can be dangerous, can't they? If I hadn't escaped the cinema room when I did... Quickly – and to my relief – Harcourt adds, "Esme hasn't been sexually assaulted, but we do need to determine if she was given GHB with the intention of rape. That's very serious. It may have been the effects of the drug that caused her to lose consciousness in the water."

After a few more questions and reassurances, he and Mills leave. I watch them back out of our drive, feeling rattled.

One – or more than one – of the boys I met last night is a wannabe rapist.

Was that what Henry and his friend intended to do to me in the cinema room?

The afternoon drifts by. I talk to Seb, but he tunes out when I start repeating myself, and Mum has gone to see Esme's parents before her shift starts. She's made me promise to be extra careful.

"I'd imagine whoever drugged Esme will be too scared to even think about trying anything on right now, but even so, please watch yourself." Almost as an afterthought, she adds, "It's OK if you're scared. You know you can talk to me about anything, right?"

I'm not so sure about that. Sympathy isn't Mum's strong suit, and she's so tough that it makes me feel ashamed when I'm not. Like my height – Mum never got why hitting six feet at thirteen made me self-conscious and awkward. Dad was the one who encouraged me to turn it into a positive and try modelling. Like *that* turned out well.

I wander round, unable to focus. I must be wrong about the cinema room. I wasn't drugged. Esme was the one targeted. Whatever Henry was up to, I can't bring myself to believe it was *that*. Everything turns round and round in my head and I end up walking into the village to distract myself. Apart from the shop, the next most exciting thing here is the postbox. No one seems to be around, which is probably why the chatty old shopkeeper comes outside and collars me.

"I hear the Witches' Pool has claimed another victim," she says. "You were there, weren't you?"

She must have overheard me talking to Henry in her shop the other day. I tell her what happened. She clicks her tongue against the top of her mouth, eyes sad.

"Such a pity. So soon after that teacher too."

Teacher? When I ask, the shopkeeper is only too happy to explain.

"Thea Keats taught English at St Julian's last year. She was renting a cottage on the Stillwater Estate and often came into the shop to say hello. Struggled from the moment she arrived, poor thing. Fresh out of university, no experience of fee-paying schools, softly spoken, pretty. . . Those sixth form boys made her life hell. They're polite and charming on the outside, but I know bullies when I see them. The kind of boys who like keeping girls in their place." She glowers. I'm impressed by her unexpected feminist cred. "Anyway, Thea must have decided she couldn't cope and walked into the pool."

I remember the icy water swirling around my legs and wince. "That's horrible. My friend said it always seems to be young women who drown there."

"Mostly. Not always. There was a man fairly recently, from the next village, but that was a good five years ago now, and he was in his forties. Before then . . . so many dead women. Not all suicides either, if you ask me." She sighs. "Look out for yourself, dear. The less you have to do with those boys the better."

I bet she's talking about Henry and the rugby team. I say goodbye and loop round the green before heading home, deep in thought. The bullying probably wasn't the only reason Thea Keats killed herself but it sounds like a big factor. Was this the kind of thing Esme was thinking of when she told me to be careful?

It's only after it gets dark that I remember my missing phone. I can't believe I forgot; shows how super weird today's been. I could cycle over to Stillwater, but the narrow country lanes Mum drove down last night freak me out even in daylight, and it isn't fair to leave Seb by himself when he was alone last night.

Instead, I curl up on the sofa with the laptop, wishing this place felt more homely and less remote. The leather sofas from our old house look out of place with the beamed ceiling, old-fashioned fireplace and uneven brick floor. Despite the rooms being small, it still feels empty. At first, I loved the idea of living in a cottage this old and creaky. It looks idyllic from the outside, exactly the kind of place you imagine finding in the English countryside. My enthusiasm faded when I discovered how low the door frames are. Avoiding accidentally knocking myself out is a daily problem.

Normally I spend my time online reading blogs – things like The F-Word, and Scarlett Curtis, sometimes historical conspiracy theories and trivia – but tonight I can't focus, and I don't feel like scrolling through updates from my old friends either. I find myself on Esme's page. The comments people have started leaving immediately make me feel queasy – *miss you babe, can't believe what's happened.*

They make it sound like she's already dead.

I look at Esme's profile picture. It's a head-and-shoulder shot from before she dyed her hair. She's cuddling her kitten, wearing a flour-covered, fifties-style, cherry-print apron. Over the photo is some text: *Cake for Cats, 20 Dec, 2–4 p.m.* Must be a charity bake sale. When we were little, Esme wanted to be a vet. She isn't taking science subjects so that dream has probably died, but it's nice to see she's still passionate about animals.

Round her neck is the pretty gold collarette necklace hung with ornate blue teardrops she wore last night. It looks antique, but actually came from a market stall. She told me that when I admired it.

And yet. . . I frown. I'm almost certain Esme's neck was bare when I pulled her from the pool. Did it fall off while she was being attacked? Or did someone take it?

I click on Esme's followers. There are several faces I recognize. Would it be weird if I messaged them? Henry doesn't follow Esme. Neither does Liam. Is he at St Jules, or Fairfield Comp? I never asked.

I search around for them. Liam doesn't seem to do social media, but I find Henry. His page is full of rugby pictures, dumb political quotes and selfies of him posing with a blonde girl whose name is Faith. They're clearly an item, or they were until two days ago when the last photo was uploaded.

"Brilliant," I mutter. So Esme was wrong – Henry hasn't split with his girlfriend. No wonder those girls were so cold yesterday! Someone could have said. How was I supposed to know? Henry wasn't acting like he was coupled up.

I'm about to fetch a drink when I hear scuffling outside. Bruce hunting, no doubt. He'd better not bring in any half-dead "presents" – and then I go still, because Bruce is sitting in the armchair opposite me, ears pricked up.

Someone's there.

It's too early for Mum. It's too late for anyone else. The noise comes again. My heart thuds. I'm not normally jumpy, but the cottage next door is a rental, empty at this time of year, and the farm is half a mile away.

Crunch. This time, I'm sure it's footsteps on gravel. I stay where I am, not moving. When a couple of minutes pass, I edge into the hallway. It's silent. I wait another minute, then inch open the door on the latch.

No one's there – and on the step is the bag I had last

night. And a flower. I look up, but no one's there. I grab it and go back inside. A quick search of my bag reveals nothing's missing. My phone is dead, but boots up when I stick a charger in.

I sink down at the kitchen table, very glad Seb's upstairs. Anyone could have found my bag by the pool before the police arrived, but why didn't whoever brought it back ring the bell? How do they know where I live? There's nothing inside with my address on it.

And why the flower? Stalkers in creepy films leave flowers on girls' doorsteps. Not people in real life. I remember Esme talking about the pool: *every time there's a new death, a blue anemone appears nearby.*

This flower is blue. When I Google "anemone", sure enough, it's a match.

Involuntarily, I shiver.

FIVE

On Tuesday school starts. Before the party I was looking forward to making a new start, but now I wish the Christmas break was longer. The anemone haunted my dreams, so I'm tired as well as on edge. It has to be a really sick joke. And yet it doesn't feel like one. It feels threatening.

The air is clogged with unappetizing drizzle. It feels like a bad omen. Seb is even more anxious than I am, constantly fiddling with the stiff collar of his new uniform. I wish I'd thought to wash the synthetic new-clothes smell out. As a sixth former, at least I can wear my own clothes. Today I'm playing it safe in jeans and a check shirt.

Mum planned to drive us to school as it's our first day, but she also had a night shift, so I switch off her alarm. There's no point in her overstretching herself and burning out. Mum can't do everything, however determined she seems to be to try. We've left it too tight to cycle so we catch the bus, which we've used to get to Attlingham, the nearest town a couple of times already. There isn't an official stop so we wait at the side of the main road and I stick out my arm when the bus rolls out of the mist. It's old and creaky, with threadbare seats and so little legroom I'm forced to pivot my legs into the aisle. I can't get used to needing wheels to get everywhere. Back home I could walk to school, the shops and my friends' houses, down well-lit streets that didn't freak me out. Here, I'm starting to feel trapped.

My new school sits in the centre of Attlingham, which has a population of only six thousand. From the outside, Fairfield Comp is nothing like my previous school: single storey, with big draughty windows and a flat roof. Inside, though, it feels familiar, with the same green plastic chairs, desks in rows, and long locker-lined corridors lit by skylights. It could do with a refurb – some of the lino flooring is peeling away – but immediately I feel comfortable, like I'm in the real world again. From the back of the sixth form block, you can see the partially ruined Attlingham Castle – and, beyond, sitting proud on the hill at the edge of town, the towers of St Julian's College.

When Seb and I report to the school office, we're

handed timetables, and Seb is taken off by his form tutor. I feel a stab of guilt as he disappears. Seb finds change difficult. I wish I could stay with him. I'm introduced to the head prefect, Ursula, a pretty Black girl who wears round glasses with tortoiseshell frames. She gives me a quick tour but I can tell she's preoccupied. I look around for Marley and Esme's other friends, or Liam, but everyone is a stranger. When Ursula hands me over to a couple of other girls from my year I brace myself for a chilly reception, but word has got round about me dragging Esme from the pool and they're all over me. The questions and congratulations soon make me squirm. I've no idea what to say. These girls seem more interested in gossip than Esme being in hospital. It's a relief when lessons start. At least in English all I need to think about is Shakespeare.

At break I tag along with a group from my last class to the canteen. Everyone is still talking about the party and whether the curse of the Witches' Pool has struck again. The blue walls are the exact same shade as the anemone lying in the kitchen bin at home.

A hand settles on my arm.

"Hey, Alana." It's Marley. At the party, the thing about Marley that stood out was her incredible eye make-up – figures, given she's a vlogger. She's toned it down today but her liner and sleek ombre bob are still on point, lip gloss well chosen for her rosy skin. Her black ribbed roll-neck jumper and cord skirt are equally stylish. "How's it going? Sorry, I meant to grab you first thing, and make you welcome. I started here a year after everyone else, so I know what it's like to be the new girl."

"It's OK," I say quickly. "Today isn't exactly an ordinary day."

"Yeah, understatement. All I can think about is Esme." She pauses. "Thanks for saving her."

I shift my weight from one leg to the other, feeling awkward again. Thanks to Mum, and visiting Laura and Doug yesterday, I probably know more about Esme's condition than her friends do, even though Mum won't allow me to visit the hospital. She's still in a coma, and, while she's comfortable, the big concern is how lack of oxygen has affected her brain. Mum refused to be drawn about her chances of waking. I wish she'd let me see Esme, but Mum is adamant it's a bad idea.

"Listen, I have to shoot," says Marley. "But if you don't have lunch plans, the gang are heading into town. The stuff they serve here is pretty rank. Fancy joining us?"

Grateful to be invited, I tell her I'll be there. Sure enough, at half twelve Marley and Esme's other friends are waiting by the exit. We follow a stream of sixth formers to a café called The Hideout on the sleepy town square. For no obvious reason it has a retro school gym theme, the shiny wooden floor painted with netball markings and soft drinks served in milk bottles.

"Best café in town, hands down," Marley tells me as we queue. "It's not as hip as the owners think but at least it feels like something out of the twenty-first century. Plus there's a Fairfield discount. That red velvet cake is to die for. So says Esme, anyway."

Her face clouds over. We order paninis and fries and settle at a raised table at the back, perched on an old gym horse. Before I can ask Marley how she's doing, another girl says, "Uh-oh." I follow her gaze. The glass café door swings open and a group of boys stride in. Most of them are wearing sports kit, even though their legs must be cold in shorts. The crest on their track tops identifies them as St Jules students. They're joking with each other, and radiate confidence.

This must be the upper sixth rugby crowd – the ones Esme said were full of themselves. At the front is a blonde boy with stylishly messy hair, a Supreme sports bag slung over one shoulder and a pair of high-end headphones around his neck. He's very good-looking, and I'm pretty sure he knows it. Next to him is Henry, his arm round the girl I saw in his photographs. Even though I knew I'd come face to face with him at some point, my stomach tightens. Following them are several others, including Henry's weird friend. They have a similar look: strong, fit, polished, and they're all, excepting one mixed-race guy, white. A couple dump their bags on a table by the window. The two girls sitting there immediately move.

"Bastard," Marley mutters. Her anger seems to be directed at the blonde boy, who she's giving a real death glare. He's noticed. I watch as his mouth curves into a half smile. "Striding in here laughing like my best friend isn't in hospital! I bet he knows exactly how she wound up in the pool."

I blink. "Him? Why?"

"It was his party. Nothing ever happens around here without Xander Lockwood being at the centre of it." Her hands ball into fists. Alarmed, I glance back at the boys – and catch Henry looking directly at me. His face is expressionless, but the intensity in his eyes makes my whole body tense, and I have to look away. When I peek up again, he's studying the chalkboard menu, arm still round his girlfriend. But Xander – the blonde boy – is coming over. Marley goes rigid. I half-expect her to fling her panini at him. Instead she takes off, disappearing outside. Xander raises his eyebrows.

"Was it something I said?"

I glance at the other girls. One giggles nervously. Not able to bear the silence, I speak up. "She's upset about Esme."

Xander looks me up and down. Then he extends his hand, smiling. His teeth are Hollywood perfect. "We haven't had a chance to say hello. I'm Xander. Welcome."

None of the boys at my old school would ever greet another teenager like this. Very aware of the eyes on us – and how cuttingly posh his voice is compared to mine – I take Xander's hand, dropping it as soon as I can. "Alana."

"I would say I hope you enjoyed my party, but I'm guessing what happened by the pool ruined your night. How is Esme?"

"She's still in hospital. No change."

"Right. Well, see you around, Alana. Have some coffees on me, girls. You look as though you need them."

He tosses a twenty-pound note on the table and rejoins his friends. They burst out laughing, and I wonder if Xander's made some comment about me. I didn't like how he said my name, or the way the other girls fell silent. Was that because he's good-looking? Or are they afraid for some reason?

No one touches the twenty. Someone mutters about not wanting to upset Marley. In the end I slip it into the charity collection box on the counter. We head back to school in silence. The vibe within the group isn't comfortable like it was at New Year's. I hope the funniness isn't anything to do with me. Before I can ask if someone should check up on Marley, the head teacher enters the busy reception and calls for silence. All sixth form girls are to go to the hall immediately. The police want to speak to us.

Five minutes later I'm sitting on a wobbly plastic chair along with thirty other girls. The atmosphere is close, apprehensive, the only sound a few whispers. From the grave looks on the faces of the head teacher and Harcourt and Mills, I can tell something has happened.

"Ladies," the head teacher says. "I know you've all heard the terrible news about Esme Morgan. This is Inspector Harcourt. He'd like to have a word."

Harcourt takes the stage. He's sweating, and I can see tiny pockets of skin where his shirt strains at the buttons over his stomach. He's older than I thought; maybe even close to retirement. "You may already know that on Friday night Esme was given a date rape drug, probably via a spiked drink. She also had a head injury which was unlikely to have been caused by accident. Unfortunately, we have to conclude that someone attacked her."

The hall goes silent.

"Our working theory is that this is a date rape attempt that went wrong. It's possible Esme somehow stumbled into the pool and lost consciousness. However" – his expression hardens – "given the distance involved, that seems unlikely. And whoever drugged and attacked her would have known that she'd be unable to pull herself out of even shallow water. So, until we have reason to believe otherwise, we are treating what happened as suspicious."

I stare at Harcourt, only dimly aware of the gasps around me. What he's saying is crystal clear. At best, this is assault and almost manslaughter. At worst. . .

It's attempted murder.

"We've had a word with everyone who attended the party now." A pause. "I'd like you all to think very carefully. Have any of the boys – either from here, or St Julian's College – made you feel unsafe, or vulnerable, or given you unwanted attention, face to face or online? Have you ever been aware of them using drugs? Anything, however small, we need to know. You can speak to us in confidence today, or later with your parents, if you prefer. We'll be in the conference room until four."

More murmurs ripple through the crowd. The head teacher reminds us the school counsellor's door is open, then asks if we have any questions. No one does. We shuffle out of the hall. The others must be feeling even more dazed than I am. Everyone knows each other in this neck of the woods. To think that a boy you've grown up with could have done something like this. . .

A nasty thought slips into my mind. I stop walking, and the girl behind bumps into me.

Oh, no. Oh, no, no, no.

The drink I gave to Esme. The drink I didn't like the taste of. The drink that somehow made Esme tipsy, even though it wasn't alcoholic.

The drink I'm suddenly scared was spiked.

The drink meant for me.

SIX

Constable Mills doesn't say much as I speak. She sits across the table from me in the room the police have been given for interviews, occasionally sipping a glass of water. Harcourt is behind her, listening, which doesn't make me feel very comfortable. If they were going to do the whole "girls will be more likely to confide in a female officer thing", he shouldn't be here at all. The teacher next to me, Mrs Stannard, the deputy head, doesn't talk either. No one has turned on the light, and even though we're by the windows, the low ceiling makes the room feel oppressive. The sickly-sweet smell of cleaning products hangs heavy in the air.

"Let me check I've understood." Mills sounds nervous; not used to taking the lead, probably. "You think Henry spiked your punch, which Esme drank, and that's how she came to have drugs in her system. And the other boy who entered the cinema room was involved too."

It sounds so horrible said out loud. I fold my hands on my lap, then, realizing they're clammy, unfold them. "I know it sounds odd, but Henry was pushy about getting me into the room, then shocked when I walked out. So was his friend. There was a third boy coming too. They said so, and I bumped into someone outside. And" – I slide my phone across the table – "Esme sent me this."

Whatever you do, don't go off alone with Henry. Mills looks at the message for what seems a long time. Then she takes a picture of it with her own phone and hands it back. "Why do you think Henry would have drugged your drink, Alana?"

I don't want to answer. I can feel myself starting to sweat, even though it isn't especially warm. Suddenly I'm grateful for the murky light.

"Isn't that obvious?" I mumble.

There's a scraping sound as a chair is pulled back. Harcourt comes into view. He gives me what I think is supposed to be an encouraging smile.

"Can you describe the boy who came into the room, Alana? And the one in the corridor?"

I hesitate. I *think* the guy who came in was Henry's friend, but I can't be sure. As for the boy outside. . .

He could have been anyone. If it even was a boy. I didn't really see. No longer feeling so confident, I admit, "Not in any detail. It was dark. And I'm new, so. . ."

Henry would have seen me as an easy target. No friends, grateful to be spoken to – that's why they picked me. Henry must have thought it would be easy. Did he intend to do this the moment he met me in the village shop? Did he and his friends plan it together? What state would I have been in if I had drunk that punch? I picture myself sprawled across the sofa, the TV screen swimming, confused and scared. The boys coming over.

I feel even sicker. I want to cry when I remember how I tried to convince myself it was a joke, even though I knew it wasn't. Rape is such a scary word. It makes you think of older guys, losers, outcasts. Not teenage boys with ordinary lives and A-levels to sit.

Does this make Esme drowning my fault? If she hadn't been drugged she could have run away from her attacker, or pulled herself from the water. . .

Suddenly I really want to go home. Not to the cold, creaky cottage, but home home, in Essex, where I felt safe.

"Can I go?"

"One second, please," says Harcourt. "This drink. Can you remember who gave it to you?"

"One of the girls, I think. It was just handed to me. Maybe Henry slipped something in it when they weren't looking." I lean forward. "Esme was fine. She wasn't drinking. Then she suddenly seemed tipsy. What if the drug was kicking in? That punch never left her hand, and she didn't have anything else afterwards."

"OK. And to get this absolutely clear – in the cinema room, you walked out, and neither of the boys touched you? Not even Henry, before the other boy arrived?"

His tone isn't accusatory, but there's scepticism in his raised eyebrows. My face gets even hotter. I can't bring myself to tell him about Henry's hand sliding down my back. I'll sound like a pathetic diva. "Not really."

"Could he have got the wrong idea? Taken you going with him as encouragement, even if it wasn't meant that way?"

I stare at him. Is he serious? This is what I'm supposed to do every time I speak to a boy – tell him I don't fancy him, *just in case*?

I find my voice again. "Maybe I wasn't clear, but he spiked my drink. I don't know how, but he did."

"We'll look into it."

Will they? Harcourt just checked his watch. I lean forwards. "He must have! Esme warned me about him. Maybe he and his mate realized she knew and then attacked her, I don't know."

Neither Harcourt nor Mills says anything. Feeling small, confused, somehow dirty, and hating it, I glance away.

"What's happened is frightening, I understand." Harcourt's voice adopts the kind, patient tone you might use with a toddler. "You feel vulnerable, especially as a new girl. Finding your friend in the pool was frightening. But it could just be that whatever went on between you and Henry was a simple misunderstanding."

"Why did he insist on me going into the cinema room? Why did his friend come in? Why did Esme warn me?"

"Like I said, we'll have a word with Henry. For now, try not to worry."

"You don't believe me."

"I didn't say that."

"Why would I make something like this up? I want you to catch whoever did this, and—"

"Alana," Mrs Stannard says gently. "All Inspector Harcourt is saying is that it's easy to get confused, especially at a party where people are drinking."

"But I didn't drink alcohol! I told you." Mrs Stannard and Harcourt are looking at me pityingly now, like I'm a silly teenager who's got hysterical over nothing. Wildly, I look at Mills, hopeful that at least she believes me, but she's turning over to a fresh page in her notebook. Tears of frustration bubble in my eyes. I push my chair back and leave.

Outside, I take a deep gulp of cool air. As I fumble in my bag for my timetable, murmuring from the room reaches my ears. I pause, then press my ear to the door.

"What do you make of that, then?" It's Harcourt. "I know what I think. Alana's the type of girl who doesn't take boys turning her down well. She's worked herself up into a state and now believes New Year was all about her. Bit of a drama queen."

I freeze. *What?*

"I don't know Alana Ashman yet, but I can't believe Henry would do something like this," says Mrs Stannard. "Until last year I taught at St Julian's and I know him quite well. I'd say it's likeliest this is a misunderstanding. Henry might well have felt nervous around Alana and wanted a friend there. She's done modelling, you know."

"Ah," says Harcourt, as though this explains everything, and my jaw drops.

"You realize who Henry is, don't you?" asks Mrs Stannard.

"It's been flagged to us."

"I assume you're keeping what happened confidential. A few senior teachers at St Julian's know, but that's all."

"Of course." Harcourt pauses. "How has he been getting on?"

"Very well. You'd never know there'd been any kind of tragedy. He's co-captain of the rugby team, excellent grades. Best physics student I've had in years, actually. A nice boy."

"Rugby team, eh? A few of the girls we spoke to over the weekend said they, quote, 'try it on a bit'."

"They're teenage boys at a tiny single-sex school. Of course they try it on." Mrs Stannard sounds defensive. "I'm sure it's only harmless fun."

"I'm not so sure." Mills's voice is worried. "This is a pretty serious accusation. I know how understaffed we are, but it wouldn't look good if we brushed this off, especially these days—"

"Oh, we'll speak to Henry all right." Harcourt cuts her off. "But I'm sure it's nothing. Boys will be boys, eh?"

"Some of them bullied Thea Keats, didn't they?" asks Mills. "So I don't know if this is nothing. I've seen her file. The bullying sounded nasty – printing off drunken photos from her personal social media and spreading them around, setting up that fake Twitter account. . ."

"It stopped short of harassment," says Mrs Stannard. "And we never found out who was behind that. It's true that the boys played up in her lessons, but Thea's classroom control was lacking. To be frank, she was out of her depth. She had other issues, nothing to do with her job. You don't think there's a connection, do you?"

"Only the pool, but that doesn't mean anything," says Harcourt. "If there's never another death there it'll be too soon. Anyway."

There's the noise of someone getting to their feet. I hurry off. My face couldn't be any redder. This is beyond unfair! I didn't want to talk to the police. It was embarrassing, and scary, and made me feel stupid, but I did, because I owe it to Esme, and it was the *right thing to do*. But I've been written off as unreliable – for the most bullshit reason ever!

Will they even bother speaking to Henry? Mrs Stannard didn't help – she clearly still has a soft spot for him. "Nice boys" don't do things like this. Whereas girls like me are drama queens.

I'm so angry I'm actually shaking. How come boys automatically get excused and girls blamed? I want to break something, or scream at somebody. That drink was spiked. Somehow, Esme knew what Henry was planning. What if she paid the price for it?

Class, when I eventually get there, is the last thing I feel like. From the window I can see St Jules. I picture Harcourt and Mills driving over to question Henry. He'll know exactly who told on him. And then maybe he'll want to make me pay.

SEVEN

The end of the day crawls round. I can't wait to escape. As I hurry out Marley catches up with me.

"Hey, Alana! Sorry I ran off earlier. Doing a shit job of looking after you, aren't I? Look, do you fancy coming over later? I know Esme would want us to hang out. She did a great job helping me settle in when I started."

All I want is to get into bed and pretend none of this is happening, but I need a friend. Maybe Marley can tell me more about the boys, and who might have left the blue anemone. She must know Esme better than anyone. We exchange numbers, and I head for the bus stop. Then I spot Liam's car, parked further down the road. He's sitting at the wheel watching everyone stream out. I ignore my insides fluttering, go straight over, and tap on the glass. Liam winds down the window.

"Oh, hey. I didn't spot you come out." He sounds surprised, but also, I can't help but notice, pleased.

I clear my throat. "I accidentally stole your hoodie. You know, the green one."

"Sure. Bring it in sometime. No rush. So . . . how are you doing? Was your first day OK?"

How do I even start answering that question? "Not great. I didn't see you anywhere."

Brilliant, now he knows I was looking. Nice one, Alana. Liam rubs the side of his face, glancing away.

"You wouldn't. I, uh, go to St Jules."

For the first time I take in his white shirt, and the maroon-and-gold striped tie and blazer slung over the back seat. Why am I not surprised St Julian's makes sixth formers wear full uniform? "Oh. Right. I guess I won't see you around much then."

"Sometimes I grab food in town. Not The Hideout, it's way too crowded at lunchtime, but you can bring sandwiches into the library. The sofas on the second floor are nice, if you like quiet." He gives me a tiny smile. "There's also, randomly, a life-sized medical skeleton in the biology section called Hector. We hang out sometimes. He's surprisingly OK company."

"I'll remember that – oh, no!"

My bus is pulling away from the top of the drive. I

stare after it. Stupid! Why wasn't I paying more attention?

"Yours?" Liam asks. I turn away, fighting the urge to cry. Today has sucked. Everything here sucks.

"Better head off. I'll bring that hoodie in tomorrow."

"Hey!" Liam calls. "Don't go. I'll give you a ride."

"Really?"

"Yeah. That bus won't come again for ages. It's famously crap. And you've obviously had a hella bad day. Promise I won't stall this time."

"Aren't you waiting for someone?"

"Uh-huh. And now she's here." Liam leans over and opens the passenger door, avoiding meeting my eyes. My stomach does a funny little skip. It only occurs to me after I get in that in light of what the police said, accepting a lift from an almost-stranger isn't very smart. Is this what life is going to be like now? Being suspicious of every boy in town, just because a few rugby players are dangerous jerks? But I can't really see Liam being involved. If it wasn't for him, Esme would be dead. And I shouldn't judge him by his school.

"How did you know what to do the other night?" I ask as he swings the car round.

"CPR? Oh. You know. YouTube."

"YouTube?"

"Yeah. Seemed like something I should know, like how to jump-start a car and which way up to hold a baby."

"Head up, feet down normally works. Come on. You didn't really learn it on YouTube."

"If I tell, will you promise not to laugh?"

"Promise."

"I want to go to med school next year. So I asked Mom for a first aid course for my birthday."

He's in the year above me, then. "Why would I laugh at that?"

"Because it was my eighteenth, and that's a geeky present? I got this too. Just so you don't think I'm totally uncool."

He turns over his left arm, and I see the edge of a tattoo under his rolled-up sleeve before he puts his hand back on the wheel. Is Liam trying to impress me? "There's nothing uncool about saving someone's life."

Esme. We go quiet.

Liam breaks the silence first. "Um, hey, in the hospital, I feel like I might have come across as weird. If I did, sorry. The pool freaks me out is all. So, uh, your mom is a nurse?"

He seems genuinely interested so I go into detail about Mum's work. It helps distract me from how strange it feels to be in a car with a boy, alone. No one back home had learned to drive yet, not that they'd have been able to afford a car even if they had.

"Does your mom ever talk about nursing?" Liam asks. "Like, in schools? It's way short notice, but I'm doing an extracurricular assignment about medicine with some kids on Thursday. They're ten and it's part of their school careers week. I'm sure they'd love to meet a real nurse."

"She's usually too busy for things like that." I hesitate.

"But I have a free afternoon so I could come, if that would be helpful. I did work experience with her last year, and a week in another department too. That was a real eye opener – oh. You . . . you know where I live."

"You told me the other night."

"I did?"

"Uh-huh." Liam reverses into my driveway.

I feel myself blush, unclip my seat belt, and tell him to wait while I get the hoodie. Inside, I blow out a breath, pushing my hair off my hot forehead. I don't know what it is about this guy that's making me act this way – no, I do. He's down to earth. Thoughtful. Tall enough that I could actually wear heels around him. Like, proper heels, and still be looking up. Add in the American accent and how great he was the other night. . .

Stop. What am I thinking? Esme's in a coma. Some guy is *not* what I should be focusing on. Liam probably only wanted to check I was OK. But when, cringing a little inside, I hand him the hoodie, Liam gives me a wide smile. It's the first time I've seen him smile properly and I can't help thinking it makes him look really nice.

"If you're not busy on Thursday, sure, come along," he says, and my heart does a little leap. "It isn't paid, but you might get a coffee and a cookie. No promises, though."

"Well, if there are biscuits. . ."

"Great! See you Thursday." He pauses. "I heard the police spoke to you all, about drink spiking. We're not all toxic. Guys around here, I mean. Just so you know."

I'm not quite sure what he means. Is he a bit of an outsider? It's only as I watch him drive off that I realize I'm also smiling.

I go to Seb's room and knock on the door. He'd texted to say he'd caught the bus I missed. He's lying in bed with his eyes closed, Bruce curled next to him, but he sits up when I come in.

"Hey," I say softly. "How was it? You didn't reply to my messages."

"I didn't get the chance. There were people in my face the whole day."

"Full on?"

He nods. "I suppose that's better than people being actively nasty. At least in lessons it was quiet, and my head of year didn't talk to me like I was an alien. You?"

I sigh. "Kind of overshadowed by what happened to Esme. I'm glad it was OK for you, though."

"I saw the police car. Do they think there's a link with the teacher who died?"

I frown as I perch on his bed. "Thea Keats, from St Jules? No. Did you hear something?"

"Just rumours. Supposedly she was having a secret relationship with one of her students and killed herself before anyone found out."

"Oh. I heard they bullied her."

"Maybe both are true. Or neither."

Seb picks up his laptop. This kind of thing doesn't interest him. It interests me, though.

The rugby team and the Witches' Pool. Men and boys wielding power over women and girls. Whichever way you look, there's a connection.

Maybe Thea Keats's death wasn't as straightforward as everyone thinks.

I wonder if anyone else took the police up on their offer of a chat. There were plenty of whispered rumours this afternoon – that the police think Esme was attacked at one a.m., that the boys from the party have had to hand over their phones – but nothing big happened. The only other interesting thing that's come out is that most of the guys from Fairfield cleared out early to go to another party. Timestamped pictures are all over social media. Chances are whoever's responsible is from St Jules. No surprises there.

Why did Esme even go to the pool? It's so out of the way. Although . . . maybe it only felt so far because I didn't know where I was going. If I could check out the route in daylight. . .

The more I think about it, the more the idea takes root. Stillwater House itself is private, but the health club is open to the public, as are several footpaths down the wilder end of the estate. Someone mentioned that the Lockwoods offer a special gym pass for under-eighteens. No one needs to know how deadly boring I actually find gyms.

I go to my room to change, ducking under the low door frame. There, I see the glass of water on my bedside table, remember the spiked drink, and my insides go to mush. *Those boys gave me a date rape drug.* For ten minutes, I almost forgot.

A new thought bursts into my head: what if being new wasn't the only reason I was targeted? What if it was my modelling? Mrs Stannard made assumptions about that earlier. Maybe Henry did too. He could have stalked my social media after our meeting in the village shop. Perhaps that's how he discovered my liking for Britpop. One of my friends shared my favourite modelling picture. It wouldn't be impossible to look up my old agency and find more photos. One shoot was swimwear for a catalogue. Hardly sexy – but a boy might see it differently. . .

Ugh. I grab my phone and whack my online security up to maximum. Bumping into me in the shop probably wasn't even a coincidence – I'm pretty certain Henry doesn't live in my village. I don't want to think about him any more so instead I think about Esme. When Mum gets back I'm going to ask if I can visit the hospital. I know Esme's in a coma, but I really want to see her. I didn't realize until we moved here how much those long summer holidays meant to me. So many of my best childhood memories, so much of my childhood, is her. Together we rode bikes and sunbathed in the garden and, inspired by a trip to Hampton Court Palace, made up Tudor princess alter egos. Esme started writing a story about them which carried on long after summer ended. The last holidays she spent with us, three years back, we found a Mills & Boon novel on a park bench and laughed ourselves silly reading out the smutty bits.

Does she still write? I never asked. I blink back sudden tears and hunt for a pack of Post-it notes. Dad swears by these when he plans lessons. Writing down things that bothered her was something Esme did too – she used to email me all the time. I brainstorm everything I can think of, smack the Post-its on the wall and step back to look.

GHB. Think it was in my punch, and I was the target. Who spiked it? Henry? His friend? Third boy? How? When?

Esme ran off saying she needed to think (11.30)

Esme warned me about Henry (WhatsApp, sent 11.51)

Liam saw Esme before 12.00 "pretty wasted, not making sense" (last person to have seen her?)

Esme wasn't on the terrace for fireworks (12.00)

Esme unconscious in the Witches' Pool (1.00, police think). Why did she go there?

Where was Esme in the hour between the time she was last seen and the time she almost drowned?

Esme hit on the head (what with? why?)

Esme's necklace has vanished

Also: blue anemone. Joke?

I pause, then add: *Esme told me to be careful.*

Unless there's something I don't know, it seems a reasonable assumption that Esme was attacked because she realized what Henry was up to. There was plenty of time for her to have confronted him and his friends, who I'd guess are also on the team – everyone says they're a tight-knit group. The thing that triggered her was the weird Halloween/New Year's comment. At the time I thought it was an in-joke between Henry and his mate, but could she have understood too?

My wall looks like a police incident board. Playing detective is stupid, I know, but I need to do something with this rage and sadness. I owe it to Esme. Not just because she took my drink, but because of all those memories. She'd do the same for me.

If I visit the Witches' Pool again, maybe I'll discover something that makes the police take me seriously.

EIGHT

Marley lives in Attlingham, so I've two choices – bike, or bother Mum for a lift. I still can't get my head around how difficult doing even simple things is around here. How do people stick it? Mum's flat out in front of the TV, so I brave cycling. To begin with I'm convinced a car is going to appear from nowhere and catapult me into a ditch, but I don't pass even one, and the bike I got for Christmas is comfortable and smooth to ride. By the time I arrive I feel much more confident.

Marley's house is way bigger than I was expecting, a detached modern building with a sweeping driveway in a new development. She answers the door straight away and, after fetching us drinks, leads me to her bedroom. It's in the attic, meaning she has a floor to herself, as well as an en-suite and double bed. Above the headboard is a photo montage board. Funny selfies, parties, foreign holidays – this is the recent side of Esme I don't know well yet. It looks like she and Marley did everything together. There's a big light-up *M* on the bold turquoise walls that immediately make me wish my walls weren't boring magnolia. Despite the high gable roof, it feels cosy. My fingers, stiff with cold from the ride, slowly thaw.

Marley even has a walk-in wardrobe, which is mostly full of high heels. She shows me her favourite vintage pair, an eBay steal she wore to the party.

"They killed my feet so I ended up carrying them half the night, but they were so worth it," she says. "I adore shoes. Shame the school rules on heels are so stuffy."

"They probably don't want you tripping on the peeling lino," I say, and she laughs. "You've got a great house, Marley. I'm jealous."

"Not bad, is it?" She brushes my hair from my face. "God, you've got amazing skin, Alana. I'd love to make you over for my channel. You've modelled, right?"

Esme must have told her. Feeling awkward, I perch on the end of her bed. "Yeah, but not any more."

"How come?"

I look at my feet. "I wasn't any good." There – I've admitted it. "Walking in heels, posing for photos, confidence – I didn't have what they were looking for, apart from being tall and thin. I only gave it a go because Mum and Dad were keen. And the fashion industry isn't glam, it's ugly. My agent told me to drop a dress size to get more work! Don't get me wrong, nothing traumatic happened, but the whole thing made me feel stupid and humiliated and kind of fake. And I hate how it's something I always get judged by, even though I only did it for a few months."

"Wow," says Marley, after a pause. "That was quite a rant."

"Sorry. I get angry about a lot of stuff."

"Cool. I like it when people have opinions. Especially girls." She flashes a smile. "I love the rest of the gang, but they're so nice most of the time I have no idea what they really think about stuff."

I know what she means – sometimes it feels like girls aren't supposed to get angry or challenge what's around them. We're taught from day one that the way to get by is to be agreeable. Especially towards boys.

"FYI, though," Marley continues. "My channel's all body positivity and inclusivity, so it's not your classic 'how to do smoky eyes' kind of vlog. It's doing well. I've even got a sponsor. I chat about all kinds of other things too. Mostly feminism. And food."

The tension that balled up inside me when Marley brought up modelling unwinds. "Oh, wow. I had no idea. That sounds brilliant! Hey, do you read The F-Word? That's my favourite blog. I like reading what Scarlett Curtis says too."

"I so do! Alana, I think I love you." Marley holds up her hand for a high-five. We both grin. Then I remember Esme, and my face falls. Should I tell Marley about the drink? It feels like I can trust her, but maybe I should wait. Instead I ask, "Do you buy the date-rape-gone-wrong theory, then?"

Marley sighs. "I guess. There's not another explanation, is there? Esme's a good girl. Doesn't piss people off, doesn't have a vengeful ex or creepy stepdad or insert cliché of choice."

"Nothing strange happened over Christmas, or before then?"

She shakes her head. So unless I'm missing something, no one had reason to attack Esme. That supports my idea that whatever she realized that night was significant. "What happened after she ran off? You went with her."

"Nothing. She was feeling sick and said she wanted to sit quietly so I left her to it. That was the last I saw of her. Georgie Douglas heard her arguing with a boy some time before midnight, though. Said it sounded heated."

Before midnight is too early for the attack, but an argument is definitely interesting. I make a mental note to add it to my Post-it wall. "Who do you think might have attacked Esme? Xander? At lunch you said. . ."

Marley's expression darkens. "Xander thinks he can throw his weight around because his dad is a lord. If you Wikipedia 'entitlement' his picture's on it. There's no way he doesn't know something. Has he hit on you yet?"

"What? No! I've barely spoken to him."

"He will, so be warned. Don't know why I thought going to The Hideout today was a good idea; he's often there. Do yourself a favour and tell Xander where to stick it. He's a real shit with girls. Ask anyone."

I hesitate. Then I tell her about the blue anemone. Marley's eyes go wide.

"Crap. It was Xander's ancestor who drowned that pregnant woman who was supposed to be a witch. Xander actually dresses up as this dude every Halloween, the prick. Leaving you an anemone is totally his MO! Why try to creep you out, though?"

I can think of a good reason. "He's friendly with Henry, right?"

"In a competing for king of the pack way, yeah. What, you think Henry has something to do with this too?"

"Not exactly. It's just, I've heard bad things about the rugby boys, and. . ."

God, I'm a crap liar. I stop, waiting for Marley to notice. Sure enough, she leans forward.

"Babe, what exactly is bothering you? I know we've only just met, but Esme's my best friend and I want whoever did this to pay. If you know something. . ."

The need to share is really eating me up now. I give in and tell her everything. Marley stares at me, eyes bright. Then she looks away, blowing out a breath.

"Shit. *Shit*. The police really didn't believe you?"

"Nope. I still can't get my head around everything.

Henry and his friend were going to—" I swallow, a wobble going through my whole body. I can't say the word *rape.* If I do, I'm scared it will become real. "Do *you* believe me?"

The door to Marley's room swings open and Henry walks in. My eyes swell with horror.

"I don't have your stupid headphones," Marley snaps as he opens his mouth. "Piss off."

Henry spots me, and goes still. For a long moment, we stare each other out. Then he holds up his hands.

"I was only going to ask."

And he leaves. Marley gets up and kicks the door shut, swearing under her breath.

"Never knocks! I hope your brother's less of a bastard. Hey, are you OK?"

I find my voice. "He's your brother."

"Yeah. Didn't you know?"

No! I want to scream. *If I had, I'd never have said what I just did!* I can't believe how calmly Marley listened as I accused her brother. How the hell was I supposed to know they're related? Apart from the blue eyes they don't look alike. There must be a tiny age gap, even smaller than the eighteen months between me and Seb. And they go to different schools!

"Oh God." I cover my face with my hands. Between the gaps in my fingers I see Marley pull an *ouch* face.

"Well, this explains you being so upfront!" she says. "Don't be embarrassed, babe, please. I mean, I am shocked by what you said, naturally, but my brother... Well. My brother's a dickhead. I don't have anything to do with him if I can help it."

"Even so, he's—"

"A dickhead. Cuss him too, be my guest."

She sounds pretty firm. I lower my hands. "OK. Still, I wish I'd kept my mouth shut. How come he's at St Jules, and you're at Fairfield?"

"Hen won a partial scholarship. Rather him than me. Frills and fancies do my head in. It's made him into a real pain, always needing to be better than his buds, even though none of them care that our parents only pay half fees. Makes me glad I never bothered trying for any scholarships. The closest private girls' school's right over by the coast. Some of the St Jules guys have sisters there, and it's so. . ." She pulls a face. "The uniforms are deep purple. Not my colour. But relax, babe. I know Henry didn't attack Esme."

I'm so surprised I forget about feeling uncomfortable. "He has an alibi?"

"Alibi? Bit formal, but yeah, he was with Faith at one a.m., 'having an amazing make-out session' because they looooove each other! Her words, not mine. Well, sort of. It's the kind of thing Faith says. I'm not being a bitch, she's a total airhead. I don't know what Hen sees in her, to be honest."

"Henry's girlfriend was at the party? Then why was he chatting to me?"

"Cos you're fresh meat? He's a guy, his motives aren't exactly complicated. Him and Faith are on-off anyway. He dumped her a few months ago and she fell apart. Wouldn't give up until he took her back."

Henry and Faith must have a pretty weird relationship if she lets him flirt with another girl in front of her, then makes out with him later. She can't know what he was planning. There's no way anyone would be OK with that. "Right. Who's his friend?"

"The ugly guy who looks like he's escaped from prison? That's Ozzie. He's thick as, but he kills it in a scrum."

I slosh juice around my cup, thinking. I'm pretty sure now Ozzie was the boy who entered the cinema room. He was the one who made the weird comment that caused such a reaction in Esme. If she knew about the date rape drugs, and was about to report them. . .

Perhaps that's why they tried to murder her.

Everyone has been skirting round the M-word all day, even the police. It must be something they're considering. I look down at my hands. They're trembling, ever so slightly. Would the boys really be desperate enough to try to kill Esme? Staggering as it seems, the answer's probably yes. Even carrying GHB leads to a sentence, Harcourt said so. The rugby team are in the upper sixth. Some will already have turned eighteen. That makes them legally adults. They'd be named and shamed, kicked out of St Julian's, and at the very least have drug possession on their records for life. No university, no brilliant jobs. A dead-end future.

One insignificant girl's life? It might seem a price worth paying.

Maybe that's what the flower meant. Esme should have been the pool's latest victim. Only thanks to me and Liam, she wasn't.

It's a threat: back off.

Marley starts picking at her nail varnish, a deep crease between her eyebrows. I wonder if she's thinking what I am: Faith could easily be giving Henry a fake alibi. I'm going to have to watch myself, I realize. However much I like Marley, Henry's her brother.

I ask Marley who's on the rugby team. The sooner I know who to watch out for the better. Marley opens Henry's social media on her phone. The first photo that pops up is a group of boys in swimming trunks, posing in the sunshine with sunglasses and bottles of beer. It's the kind of laddish party picture I've seen billions of times but today the shiny white grins look shark-like. Predatory. The grins of rich boys who think they're untouchable.

Marley brings up another, this time of the boys in muddy rugby kits, standing side by side. Xander's in the centre, holding the diamond-shaped ball. He must be Henry's co-captain. Ozzie I spot at the back, Henry next to him. Then I notice the guy on the end, and give a start.

Liam. He's one of them.

"Oh." Even to me my voice sounds shaken. "I didn't realize Liam was on the team."

"Liam Taylor? He is and he isn't. He plays prop and shows up at parties, but he's not, like, buddy-buddy with the guys, according to Hen. Spends a lot of time lurking in libraries. I can't work out whether he's socially awkward or just massively studious. He's a bit weird – only moved here last year. I don't know him very well but if you ask me he has some kind of past."

A few hours ago I was looking forward to seeing Liam again. Should I still go out with him on Thursday? It might be dangerous.

Then again ... it could be the perfect opportunity to find out more about the rugby team. Even if Liam wasn't involved himself, he might know something. Away from his friends, maybe he'll talk. Now I think about it I'm not certain I did tell him where I lived. Do these guys know everything about me?

Marley and I chat a little more before I leave. At the door to her room she takes my arm, eyes serious.

"When you figure anything else out, Alana, please tell me. If Henry's wound up in this, I need to know."

Downstairs we bump into Marley's parents coming in from work. They're much older than mine and seem nice, but I'm distracted by wondering if Henry is nearby – which it turns out he is when he appears carrying my cycling gear, smiling as though he's being helpful. I all but snatch my helmet and fluorescent jacket. Somehow he manages to make our fingers brush. *Eww.* Even knowing he's touched my stuff makes my skin crawl.

"You're welcome," Henry says drily. He goes into the sitting room. I catch sight of Faith perched on the edge of the sofa, clutching a mug and staring ahead. Her hair is dishevelled, one of the buttons on her dress undone. It's pretty obvious what they've been doing. Why on earth did he try to drug me if he already has a girl who's into him?

The moment I'm cycling away, cool air on my face, I feel a hundred times better. Henry wasn't going to do anything in the house, not with his sister and girlfriend there – but he wanted me to know he could.

The next morning is dry so Seb and I decide to cycle the three miles to school. It's a smooth run, mostly flat, and I'm hoping the exercise will help wake me up. We've just set off when Seb calls that he's forgotten his phone. Rolling my eyes, I brake.

Nothing happens.

I brake again. A third time. Nothing. And I'm gathering speed. Panic shoots through me. I jerk the handlebars to one side and topple into the ditch.

My left side slams into the grass. Winded, I lie in a dizzy heap. Seb appears and scrambles down to help me up.

"Are you all right? What happened?"

"The brakes wouldn't work. I'm OK. Just bruised."

"That's weird. They were fine yesterday, right?"

I rub my elbow, wincing. There's mud all over my skirt, and my tights are laddered. Great. "Good thing you forgot your phone. Otherwise I probably wouldn't have found out until. . ." Until I reached the top of the hill that leads to school. The long hill, with a busy three-way junction at the bottom. I sit down heavily on the grass. Seb inspects my bike. I know what he's going to say even before he opens his mouth.

"Both sets of brakes wouldn't fail, Ally, not so suddenly. I think this has been done deliberately."

We run home with the bikes and then manage to catch the bus so we can avoid waking Mum for a lift. She was really ratty when she got home yesterday, snapping, "No!" when I asked about seeing Esme, and went straight to bed without her usual peppermint tea. I sink into the nearest seat, hoping my body will stop shaking. Seb watches me dig around in my rucksack for painkillers with a frown.

"I think we should tell Mum."

"What's Mum going to do? Put an ad in the paper asking whoever did it to own up?"

"Maybe she saw someone creeping around last night."

"She was spark out. My bike was only in the shed. Not hard to mess with. And if you're going to suggest I call Dad, don't. Leave it."

Seb gives me a look that says he thinks I'm being stupid. "We've only been here a week. You must have really pissed someone off!"

I glance down, not replying. Mum has enough on her plate without stressing about my safety. And better for Seb that he knows nothing. I don't want to make him a target too. Because that's what I am now. When I checked my bike basket, inside was another blue anemone.

NINE

Liam's dusty silver Peugeot is waiting when I walk through the gates after lunch on Thursday. I drag my steps, wishing I felt braver. A large bruise is smarting on my thigh from falling into the ditch. Maybe I'm being paranoid, but whenever I step outside school one of the rugby team seems to be there. When I got off the bus this morning I almost collided with Ozzie. There was no reason for him to be hanging around outside Fairfield. In the queue in The Hideout yesterday I swear a hand brushed my backside, and last night a car sat outside my house for almost an hour before driving off. It was too dark to see who was behind the wheel. I was half-expecting another blue anemone on the doorstep.

Are they trying to creep me out? Perhaps the whole team is in on this, not just Henry, Ozzie and whoever was outside the cinema room. Me versus seven big strong guys doesn't sound like great odds.

My stomach clenches. Maybe coming out today is stupid, even if Liam's innocent. Pumping him for information is great in theory, but what if he sees through me and his friends do something worse than sabotage my bike?

But every time I'm tempted to back out I remember how he helped save Esme, and that smile, and the doubts resurface.

"Hey." Liam's spotted me. He's ditched his school blazer for the leather jacket he had the other night. He looks good, even though it's pretty worn, with a hole over one elbow.

I hover by the door. "Where are we going? I would've messaged to ask, but I don't have your number."

"Sorry. I was going to give it to you but that seemed kinda, I dunno. Like I was assuming you'd want to text me." Liam tells me the name of the school, and, after messaging Seb, I get in the car. My hands shake as I fumble with the seat belt. We pull away, but only crawl a few metres before Liam brakes. He peers at me.

"Are you OK?"

"Yeah, fine."

"I didn't mean not giving you my number as an insult. Sorry if I said the wrong thing. Today is freaking me out. I've never spoken in public before. You don't have to come if you've changed your mind."

He sounds genuine. Now I feel torn. This is so difficult! I don't want to come across in the wrong way and I do like Liam, but it really doesn't feel safe to let my guard down until I've found out what he and his friends know about Esme. I repeat that I'm fine, and ask if we can listen to the radio. Liam takes the hint and stops trying to talk.

The town we arrive at thirty minutes later is nowhere near as well-to-do as Attlingham. The air is salty. We must be near the sea. The school is down a grimy-looking road opposite a line of cramped terraces and a children's play area with empty frames where swings used to be. Depressing though it is, I'm relieved to be out of the car.

Soon we're in a classroom that smells faintly of frying, moving plastic chairs to form a semicircle, which Liam's read is more engaging than having kids behind desks. The kids file in, looking bored, but they perk up when they clock Liam's American accent. Once he gets past the shaky beginning he has their total attention. He talks about studying medicine generally before passing over to me. My five minutes on nursing goes down well, but what they really enjoy is getting bandages out and being taught how to treat common injuries. Liam's even made booklets for them to take away. It's hard not to warm to him. The way he crouches down to get on the kids' level, treating even the basic questions as though they're meaningful, and how he's managing to draw in even shyer children. . . You can't fake that earnestness, or patience. He'd make a good doctor, I think.

Despite everything, the tension inside me eases a little.

By the time we leave, it's dark. We linger outside the car. Then Liam clears his throat.

"Should I take you home, then?"

I silently count to three. Then I make myself look at him, properly this time. "Maybe we could get a Coke?"

Liam's face lights up. A few minutes later, we walk into a café by the seafront. It's clearly going for the diner vibe, though it's kind of run-down, and a bit dark for my liking. Old-school rock and roll pumps out of overhead speakers.

"Are you good here?" Liam sounds anxious. "I'd take you someplace nicer, but I don't know this area."

"It's fine." The booths overlooking the beach are taken so I go to a table at the back as Liam queues. He keeps glancing at me. I pretend to be busy wiping salt off the table. When I do accidentally catch his eye, he gives me a hesitant smile that makes him look really cute.

When Liam finally joins me, he slides a tray on to the table. On it are two waffles drenched in chocolate sauce and whipped cream, as well as Cokes. "I don't know if you're hungry but I got this," he says. "Thanks for today. Did it go OK? I don't know any kids so I hope I got it right. What I really wanted was to kidnap Hector, you know, the skeleton from the library, but the librarian said no. I was worried having you there would make me extra nervous but it actually helped."

Judging by the way his leg is bouncing under the table, he's still nervous. Is that because he likes me, or because he's picked up on my jitters?

I turn my back on the window and pick up a fork, grateful for the distraction. I'm too on edge to dive right in so instead I ask how this place compares to diners in the States. Liam tells me about growing up in California, then relocating for his mum's high-powered tech job. I'm only half-listening, psyching myself up.

Then my phone starts buzzing: Dad.

Liam sees the screen. "Wanna pick up?"

"Nope," I say, and reject the call.

"Ah. What did he do?"

"It's complicated."

"I can do complicated."

A text pops up: *Just calling for a chat. I'll try again another day. Love you x.* I turn the phone screen-side down. The familiar rage that boils inside me whenever Dad acts as though he hasn't torn my world apart returns. Before I can stop myself the words tumble out.

"Dad cheated on Mum and got the other woman pregnant. He was seeing her months before he came clean. When I think how he lied, not just to Mum, but me and Seb. . . This woman's a teacher at my old school. So is Dad. Everyone knew. It was totally, utterly humiliating. And she's twenty-five! How's that for complicated?"

Liam winces. "He chose her over your mom?"

"He said he and Mum had basically agreed to split once

me and Seb were done with school." I put down my fork. I can't eat any more. "I knew they never spent time together, but I thought that was because of Mum's shifts. . ." Liam nods encouragingly. "I feel so *stupid*. Dad says nothing's changed, but that's total crap. He didn't even ask if I wanted to live with him. That hurts. We did so much – medieval fairs and museums and breakfast out most Sundays, just us, and he was talking about doing an archery lesson together. . . I thought he was better than that." Realizing that I am massively oversharing, I stop, cheeks flaring. "Sorry. Way TMI."

"I don't mind, honestly. I get it." Liam pauses, eyes flickering downwards. "My dad's not around either."

"Oh. I'm sorry. Did he walk out too?"

"Something like that. But we're talking about your dad. Are you blanking him completely?"

"No. Well, yeah, I guess. I just don't know what to say. We can't chat like stuff is normal, and I'm too angry to talk about what he did."

Liam watches me stab what remains of the waffle. Then he says, "There's a history society you could check out. It's a joint St Jules–Fairfield thing. They're putting on some kind of fair this term. Ask Ursula, she does it. I don't know about archery, but St Jules has a shooting range, and fencing strips. The public can use them at weekends. It's not the same as doing things with your dad, but it's something." A pause. "And I think you should talk to him. Don't wait to stop being angry. That might take years. Whatever happened . . . he's still your dad."

Maybe he's right. I can't block Dad for ever. Deep down I know that. I'm not ready to reach out yet, though. I offer Liam a half-smile of thanks. He's being so kind. I'd love to relax and just enjoy chatting. There's so much I want to ask. Not only about the fencing strips – I can't believe something that cool is practically on my doorstep! – but personal stuff, like how he found settling in here, and what else he's into apart from sport and the dance music he played while we were driving—

No. I can't allow myself to fancy this guy, not until I'm positive he had nothing to do with what happened. I push my plate away. "How well do you know Esme?"

Liam blinks, and I wish I hadn't been quite so abrupt. "Esme? We're friendly, I guess." He sounds guarded. "She lives next door to me. I usually give her a ride into school in the mornings."

"Oh. You never said. I didn't realize you knew her that well, I just assumed. . ."

"Like I said, we're friendly. I wish I'd looked out for her at the party. I could tell she was pretty out of it when I last saw her."

"What did you talk about?"

"I don't remember."

Evasive. Could Liam have been the guy Esme argued with? I need to speak to Georgie, the girl who overheard them. Surely she'd remember if one of the voices was American. "Who do you think might have brought those drugs to the party?"

"I don't know." He shifts in his seat. "Why are you asking me?"

"The police seem pretty interested in your mates. What about Henry? Ozzie? Xander? The other guys?"

I wait for him to deny it. But Liam says nothing for what feels like a long time. Then he looks at me, and involuntarily I pull back, not expecting his eyes to be so angry.

"Henry is not my friend."

"Why do you hang out together, then?"

"We're on the same team. We can't not hang out."

"You don't seem very shocked I'm asking about your teammates."

"What are you getting at, Alana?" Liam slams down his glass, and I flinch. "You think I knew? That I'm OK with girls being drugged and messed around with? If you believe I'm some kind of rapist, why are you here?"

"I never said you were. But it was Xander's party, and your friends are pushy with girls."

"This was a mistake." Liam gets up and walks off, leaving his barely touched drink. The bell on the café door jingles behind him. I grab my bag and run out after him.

"Liam! Don't be like this. I get that you're upset, but I needed answers."

"Yeah?" He rounds on me. "Whatever you've heard, you could've asked straight up, not pretended you wanted to hang out... I thought you liked me! Jeez, how stupid am I?"

I have no idea how this has so quickly spiralled out of

control. "No one's said anything to me about you. I'm only trying to find out what happened."

And I do like you. But somehow I can't say it. Liam opens the passenger door to his car. I get in, not making eye contact.

By the time we stop at the end of my drive, I want to pretend this afternoon never happened. My doubts about Liam have faded. That angry reaction was genuine. Surely he's innocent? Only now, of course, I've messed up any chance I had with him by asking all those questions! I unclick my seat belt, then stop. I can't leave things like this.

"I wasn't accusing you of anything. I needed to be sure you hadn't done it. You do see that, don't you?"

"OK."

"Honestly, Liam."

"I said OK."

"I did enjoy this afternoon. It was fun. And it was kind of you to listen to me talk. If Esme hadn't been attacked. . ."

Liam doesn't reply. Is he still angry? His expression isn't giving much away. Crap, I really have sabotaged this. I'm about to open the door when he shifts round.

"I get why you're on your guard," he says. "Walking out like that was not cool and I overreacted. Sorry. This whole thing has me rattled. It's . . . hard to know what to do, is all."

I'm not quite sure what he's getting at, but the apology clears the air a little. I try a smile. "So are we good?"

"If you're happy I didn't do anything, yeah."

We stay motionless, looking at each other. Liam fiddles with his seat belt, but he doesn't break eye contact. My heart starts to thump. I don't look away either.

He breaks the silence. "Can I, um..."

I nod. He leans in and kisses me. Quickly, as though afraid I'll change my mind. For a moment, I'm too taken aback to react. Then, as warmth spreads through my body, instinct takes over and I kiss him back. It feels good. Really good. So this is what all the fuss is about! Just as I'm getting into it, Liam moves back, looking flustered. I can't see properly in the dark, but I'm sure he's blushing, and from the hot feeling on my face I might be too.

"Sorry," he says. "I feel like that was kinda sudden."

"No," I say, a little breathless. "I liked it, honestly, I just ... don't have much experience, so..."

As soon as the words are out of my mouth I want to die. Liam laughs softly.

"Hey, it's OK. Don't be embarrassed. So long as you did like it, everything's cool."

"Definitely." Out of the corner of my eye I spot the hallway light go on.

"Guess I should let you go," Liam says. "Do you maybe want to grab lunch in the library tomorrow? Like, twelve thirty?"

"Sure. That'd be great."

"OK then." Liam gives me a quick peck on the lips. Despite the awkwardness, as I open the car door, I'm smiling.

*

Later Marley messages.

Marley: So how did the date/not date go? x

How do I reply to that? I settle for:

Me: Good. We had a misunderstanding but I think we cleared it up

Marley: That's good hunni :-)
So did he ask you out again?

Me: If lunch tomorrow is a date, yes

Marley: Well I hate to rain on your parade but before you get too into him there's something you should know

I push Bruce off my lap, sitting up straighter.

Marley: I found something out
Or rather my brother told me
I had no idea else I would have warned you

A pause. The text at the top of the screen informs me that Marley is typing.

Marley: Liam was expelled from his last school for dealing drugs

TEN

The next day passes quietly. There's no change in Esme's condition and the atmosphere at school and around town is still subdued. It's no better at home. Between work and supporting Esme's parents, Mum's barely been around. We've had what Mum calls "a proper chat" on the way back from seeing Laura and Doug during my free period, which was basically Mum checking if there was anything I needed to talk about. I know she does care, and Mum can't help her manner being so businesslike, but it came across as though I was an item to check off her to-do list.

And of course I bottled admitting that I've been threatened. I know I should tell her. I'd have gone to Dad in a heartbeat. Mum won't tell me to "toughen up", not about this, but I just can't picture anything coming out of me 'fessing up other than her instructing me to be careful. And she doesn't need this on top of a new job and a divorce.

So I tell myself I'm not scared, over and over, and seek distractions. I ask Ursula about the society Liam mentioned and she invites me to the next history fair planning meeting, which is taking place in The Hideout after school. There are about twelve of us – not mainstream, but not so small it's embarrassing either. The logistical stuff is sorted but catering isn't finalized, and there's very little headway on the entertainment. The only firm idea is to stage a play, and have students dressed as famous historical figures interacting with each other throughout the day.

"If you'd ever wondered what Elizabeth I might have said to Henry VIII, bam! The fair will be your lucky day," says Blake, a mixed-race guy with freckles who introduces himself as the "master of entertainment". I stop myself from pointing out that Elizabeth was Henry's daughter, and they interacted plenty before he died in 1547. Blake carries on outlining what he calls his "vision", accompanied by lots of theatrical hand gestures, and even at one point a drum roll. Normally this enthusiasm would make me warm to him, but he's wearing a maroon rugby kit.

"How do you feel about taking on one of the roles, Alana?" Ursula asks when Blake is finally done. "Elizabeth? We have a fantastic costume. The wig's horrendous, but maybe we could let that slide."

"If the dress fits, I'm so game! Elizabeth's a heroine of mine. If I had a time machine, I'd go straight to 1588 and listen to her speech about the Spanish Armada—" In the corner of my eye I catch Blake eye-rolling Ursula. Suddenly uncertain, I stop. "Um, won't someone else want to play her? This is my first week. I don't want to step on anyone's toes. . ."

"No one's volunteered so far. Like I said, horrendous wig." Ursula smiles, and Blake holds up his hands in an expression of surrender.

"I thought Kaitlin was going to do it, but fine," he says. "You mentioned other ideas to Ursula?"

A little shyly, I explain how events I've been to before come alive with jousting, archery, falconry and weapon parades. When the others hear that I know people who'd do this for us, to my delight, they perk up. Ursula waves away my concerns about the cost.

"There's plenty of budget. Blake, are you OK to tell Xander and get this idea approved?"

I frown. "What does Xander have to do with anything?"

"We hold the fair at Stillwater. Any big decisions need to be run past him."

Is there anything these boys don't control? Blake is watching me, eyebrows raised. My enthusiasm dies. Is he going to report back to his mates?

The meeting moves on to logistics. My eyes wander outside. The rugby team are hanging around the town square, lounging on the benches by the war memorial.

Bar The Hideout, everything is closed, and only a couple of people have passed by the entire half hour we've been here. Music pounds from a fancy car parked in one of the nearby lots. The guys are joking and pushing each other, obviously well aware of the group of girls admiring them from The Hideout's window seats.

Liam's there too, talking to Xander. Presumably once Blake's free they're off to practice, or pump weights in the Stillwater gym. He hasn't so much as glanced over, even though he must have spotted me. And no wonder. I stood him up at lunchtime. How can I eat sandwiches with someone who dealt drugs, when my drink was spiked? Did he get the GHB? Dealing seems totally at odds with the boy who earnestly explained medicine to those kids and encouraged me to open up about Dad – and the one who made me feel so good when our lips met. That's always going to be my first kiss and now it's spoiled. I can't believe he dared walk out on me when I was questioning him, all the time protesting his innocence when he has a past like this. So much for trusting him!

I need to move on from Liam. Far more important is working out who this third boy is. All of the guys on the team are potential suspects. Could it be Liam? Xander? Blake? There are two other boys whose names I don't know. One I can rule out – he isn't in any photos from the party and he's holding hands with a boy I recognize from Fairfield anyway.

"Earth to Alana!"

I jump. Ursula is waving her hand in my face. The others are heading out.

"You all right?" she asks. "I know that last bit was boring. At least there's a good view, eh?"

"That's not why I was looking," I say. Ursula laughs.

"Sure you weren't. But hey, I'm biased. See the ginger guy? That's my boyfriend, Calvin. We have the same guitar teacher. She introduced us. Said we ought to share the songwriting love." She laughs again. "I still wonder if she was setting us up."

My final suspect. Calvin's leaning on the bonnet of a car, speaking to Xander. I gaze at him for a long moment, though I don't know what I'm expecting to see.

"Thanks for bringing some new ideas," says Ursula. "The fair will come together in the end, it always has before, but so far agreeing on anything has been tough."

"I didn't realize it was such a big deal," I say. "I'm amazed a bunch of sixth formers are allowed to organize it."

"It's always been a school history society thing. Last year people from the community helped but we're trying to do it ourselves this time. Maybe too ambitious, who knows! Everyone from town comes, and further away too."

"Thanks for letting me play Elizabeth," I said. "Women in history is my thing. It's easy to assume all the big stuff was done by men, but there are powerful women all over, if you look hard enough. And not just queens. It's what got me interested in feminism more broadly."

Ursula nods, looking thoughtful. "No reason you can't

like both the timeless and the modern," she says. "My first love is classical guitar music, but that doesn't mean I don't enjoy a good headbang."

We both giggle.

"Hopefully Xander will OK your idea," says Ursula. "There's no reason he wouldn't, but sometimes he likes to be difficult, just because."

"Would it help if I spoke to him?"

"Leave it to Blake. Trust me, you're best keeping your distance from Xander." She hesitates, then lowers her voice. "I'm not saying he's a bad guy, he's one of Calvin's best mates, and he's nice enough to me, but my friend dated him and she said. . . Well, that's her story to tell. It might not be true, anyway, though enough girls have dumped him to make me think it is."

This echoes what Marley said about Xander. Maybe she'll tell me more. "Do you think he could have attacked Esme? According to the police, that happened around one a.m."

"No way. Xander was in the barn then. He seemed pissed off about something. Calvin took a selfie of us and you can see him in the background. It's timestamped and everything."

Annoying. Xander was looking pretty suspicious. "Is the pic online?"

She nods. "Speak to my mate Georgie. She's the one who overheard Esme arguing with a boy, though I can probably tell you as much about that as she can. They were on the terrace, maybe ten minutes before the fireworks.

Georgie only heard in passing, but it sounded pretty heated."

"She doesn't know who the boy was?"

"Nope. The only thing she remembers for sure was Esme shouting, 'And she's not the only one!'"

What could that be about? When Ursula leaves, I take out my notebook.

Alibis for 1 a.m., I write.

Henry – with Faith. Lie?

Xander – barn. Photographic evidence (check).

Unknown: Ozzie, Blake, Calvin.

After a moment's hesitation, I add, *Liam.*

I wake early the next day, so I head over to Stillwater straight away. It's chilly, and Seb's bike isn't as comfortable as my own, but I enjoy the ride. It feels like I'm up before the rest of the world, and the air tastes cool and fresh. The fields and hedgerows are white with frost.

The manor house looks even more impressive in daylight. How many rooms must it have – thirty? Forty? More? I can't help being envious of Xander living somewhere this full of stories and character, even if it is isolated. I bet he has a really interesting family history too.

The health club is round the back of the house in a modernized stable block, with a glass conservatory on one end that seems to be a café. I feel nervous as I chain my bike up. Coming here is risky, however much I tell myself no one will even know I'm investigating. I step into the reception. It's a mix between old and new, with soft lighting, chocolate-coloured beams stretching across the roof and a brick floor. A mounted screen slideshows the various rooms and equipment. Standing behind the desk is Xander.

Brilliant. I was hoping not to bump into him. Even though it's unlikely that he attacked Esme, he still could have been in on Henry's plan. Maybe he was looking forward to drawing lots with his mates, seeing who got to touch me first. . .

I give myself a shake. Thinking like this is not helpful.

Xander stops fiddling with his phone when he sees me. He's wearing shorts and what looks like the sweater from his rugby kit. I force out a smile.

"Hi. I wanted to sign up. I get cheap membership, right?"

"Eight a.m. on a Saturday? You're very dedicated."

"Just want to get into shape."

"You look in good shape already to me. Very good shape." He holds my gaze for a moment. "What are you training for?"

"Who says I'm training for anything?"

"Your kit does. Nice trainers."

I got given some high-end sportswear after a shoot. Trust him to spot the brand. "Hmm, this is all a bit Sherlock Holmes. I'm just here for the gym."

"Ah, no can do, then. Sorry. The membership deal is only for students in sports teams, or those training competitively."

"Oh. How much is a normal pass?" He tells me, and I try not to look dismayed. Without the discount, a pass is way beyond what I can afford. And I don't suppose I can simply wander round the garden.

Unless. . . I look him up and down. Then I straighten, flicking back my hair, and flash my best smile.

"Actually, I don't know if this qualifies, but I do have a competition coming up."

"Ah." He leans across the desk. "Tell me more."

Ignoring the voice in my head pointing out how totally unfeminist pretending to flirt with him is, I spin a lie about entering a modelling competition. As I thought, Xander's interested – especially when I unzip my tracksuit top and reveal the skintight sports vest underneath. He wants to know all about my shoots, though I pretend not to have photos on my phone when he asks to see.

"Impressive," he says. "I got the impression that the modelling was less of a big thing."

I look at Xander sharply. Has he stalked me online as well as Henry? "Why did you ask all those questions if you already knew?"

"Maybe I like the sound of your voice?" This time, the way he looks at me is a lot more blatant. It's only with a big effort that I manage not to look away. Then he switches to professional mode and sorts out my pass. Apparently modelling qualifies as training.

"Aren't you lucky you got generous old me this morning?" His chirpy tone leaves me under no illusions that he's bent the rules. "If it wasn't unkind, I'd suggest it was fate that our usual receptionist was struck down by food poisoning. I only ever cover shifts in emergencies."

I don't like the thinly veiled suggestion that I owe him. I cross my fingers he doesn't find out I've quit and call out the lie.

Xander insists on showing me the facilities and introducing me to the on-site personal trainer. He's polite and helpful, but every time I look at him I think, *You might be the third boy.* When he eventually leaves, I sigh with relief. Deciding to wait a few minutes before sneaking off, I step on to the cross trainer.

Soon maybe I'll have the answers I need. I just wish getting the pass hadn't meant giving Xander all my personal details – or flirting with him.

ELEVEN

The fire escape takes me out to the gardens. None of the three other people in the gym pay any attention when I leave, and I try to shake off the feeling that I'm doing something wrong. It takes a while to find the barn, even though it's signposted. The estate is even bigger than I thought. The fields down the far end look wild. Presumably they're off limits. Almost hidden by the long, overgrown grass is a decorative building with a domed roof and ridged stone. A folly, maybe.

The barn is locked, but outside I discover something interesting. As well as the main door and the French windows that lead to the patio, there's a fire exit, close to the cinema room. Henry and his friends could easily have left without being spotted. I ran out at about 12.40. Would they have had time to attack Esme?

I set off down the path. In the darkness I hadn't realized just how dense the wood is. No one at the barn could have seen someone in the trees, even with torchlight.

It takes ten minutes to reach the Witches' Pool. Unsurprisingly the area is cordoned off. Apart from singing birds, it's quiet, the water still and almost eerily tranquil. Maybe that's why the place is called Stillwater. It never struck me before, but that name is a little sinister.

Many of the branches around the pool have faded ribbons tied to them. A few scraps of paper still hang, but most have been destroyed by the wind and rain. Idly I turn one of the notes round. *Thea, always in our thoughts.* Several others have pictures of aeroplanes on, maybe drawn by a child. Whoever leaves these clearly visits a lot. I let the note go, feeling sad.

I stand looking at the Witches' Pool for a while. What was I expecting to find? There's nothing, not even a bench. And yet . . . that tells me something, doesn't it? Esme had no reason to come here.

With a start, I realize something else. I've been assuming that Esme headed out alone, but if the drug really was in my punch, by midnight she'd have been feeling the effects. Would she have been able to walk all this way by herself?

No, more likely is that someone led her here. And they didn't intend her to leave. If you were planning to kill someone . . . the Witches' Pool is the obvious place to do it.

I sketch a quick map in my notebook before heading back, deep in thought. Whoever brought Esme here must have been gone almost half an hour. Wouldn't an absence of that length be noticed? Perhaps it won't be difficult to narrow down a list of suspects after all.

"Good session?" Xander asks when I walk through reception on my way out.

"Yes, thanks," I say. "It's a nice gym."

"How was your walk round the grounds?"

I shoot him a look.

"If you really came to look at the pool you only had to ask," he says. "It isn't private. Plenty of footpaths down that end of the estate. Not that I didn't enjoy chatting."

He winks. Annoyingly, my cheeks flare. "I *did* want to use the gym," I insist. Xander only shrugs.

"I take it you've heard the legend of the pool, then, Alana?"

"What, about your ancestor murdering his lover?"

"Actually I meant the anemones. Pretty things. Do you like flowers?"

My breath catches in my throat. A smile is playing round the edges of Xander's mouth. Is he actually admitting to leaving the flower on my doorstep? Sabotaging my bike? Surely he wouldn't be so obvious?

Maybe that's the point, a voice in my head whispers. *He wants you to know he has the power to hurt you. Just like Henry.*

I wet my lips, hoping he can't see he's unsettled me.

"Flowers aren't my thing. And I'm not superstitious. Do you know if the police found anything by the pool?"

"I do, actually. I overheard them talking about it." Xander's smile returns. God, this guy really holds eye contact, it's disconcerting. "Would you like to know what?"

I nod, trying not to appear too interested. "Please."

"Come round later and maybe I'll tell you. I'm having a party in the swimming pool, just a small thing. My parents have people round and want me out of the house. They made negative noises when I mentioned alcohol, so its fun potential is sadly limited, but still. You're very welcome." He pauses. "But play nice with Liam. Was standing him up yesterday an attempt at playing it cool?"

So Xander knows about Thursday. When I don't answer, he sighs. "I'm a charitable person, so I'll assume something came up. Do you like him, then? You can confide in me. I'm the soul of discretion. He likes you, in case that wasn't obvious."

"You're hardly the soul of discretion if you're telling me this."

"I'm the soul of discretion ninety per cent of the time. Your choice, Miss Ashman." He pauses. "If you're very, very nice I might even show you the ancestral sword Lord Frederick Lockwood wielded during the civil war. Blake tells me you're into ancient weapons."

I narrow my eyes. "Are you making fun of my ideas for the fair?"

"Not at all. I'm almost tempted to organize a fencing display too, but that would require effort. And I'm so much better than everyone else around here that it would only be embarrassing."

Suddenly I feel less keen on checking the fencing strip out, even though it's something I've always wanted to try. I turn to leave, then stop.

"How well do you know Esme?"

Xander blinks, startled, and I feel a moment's satisfaction. "Well, this makes a nice change from being interrogated by Inspector Harcourt. I know Esme as well as I know the other earnest girls who take the charities committee oh-so-seriously: not at all."

Charities committee? I'm guessing this is some kind of club. Presumably Xander does it too. Perhaps the charities committee organized the bake sale Esme posted about on her social. "I wouldn't have thought fundraising for good causes was your style."

"Maybe I have hidden depths. Are you going to carry on interrogating me?"

He emphasizes the word *interrogate* and manages to make it sound suggestive. What a dick.

"All right," I say. "Where were you between twelve and one?"

"I was hosting."

"What does that mean?"

"Talking to my guests. Making sure the cocktails were satisfactory. Arranging canapés in a decorous manner."

"That's not a proper answer!"

"It's the answer I gave the police."

I bet that went down well. "Can't you be more specific?"

"It was a party. I was enjoying myself, not clock-watching. Maybe I walked a few people to their cars, I can't remember. That's my alibi, anyway. An alibi is what you were asking for, wasn't it, Inspector Alana?"

He actually thinks this is funny. I clench my jaw. As far as alibis go, it's not much of one. A lot will depend on the timestamp of the selfie Ursula mentioned.

I leave without saying goodbye. Xander's definitely playing some kind of game, but I'm not sure what.

"Let's go into town before chilling at mine," Marley says when I get into her car a few hours later. She's picking me up so I don't have to cycle or mess about with the crappy weekend buses. "I bet no one's shown you round properly yet. Not that there's much, unless you're into house porn or cutesy gift shops. There's a pub where Ed Sheeran supposedly took Taylor Swift. Not sure if him being Suffolk's most famous export is something to be proud of, but hey."

That makes me giggle. "My mum likes his music."

"So does mine, tragically. What d'you make of my lips? I'm trialling some gloss today."

"I never get on with gloss. Too sticky. Looks good on you, though."

"It does, doesn't it? So what've you been up to?"

I tell her about going to Stillwater. Marley pulls a face when I say how beautiful the house is.

"Rather you than me, babe. I hear it's cold, with crappy wifi as well as dodgy reception. The Lockwoods should sort that out. My brother says they're planning to convert part of it into a hotel and use the barn as a wedding venue. High-end hotels is what they did before Xander's grandfather died and left them everything – absolutely raked it in running places all over the world. Switzerland, Dubai, the Caribbean. Lucky Xander spent his childhood in one splashy location after another. Sleepy Suffolk is a real comedown. And doesn't he make sure everyone knows it."

That explains why some parts of the Stillwater Estate are open to the public and some aren't – modernizing the place is a work in progress. Marley seems to know a lot about Xander, considering she dislikes him so much. I wonder if he gets bored living here. While I love being surrounded by history, I'm also craving everything I used to take for granted, like cinemas and ordinary high street shops. There isn't a Starbucks for miles, and the supermarket is pretty limited.

Marley parks in her driveway. I'd expected the rest of the gang to join us, but when I ask, Marley says, "Thought we'd have some fun, just us." We walk to the town square, which despite the drizzle is bustling with a pop-up market selling everything from gorgeous-smelling fancy bread to second-hand books. As we wander up the hill towards Attlingham Castle, Marley tells me about everything that goes on throughout the year, like the Christmas fair and tennis tournament and flower show. I have to stop myself from stooping – Marley's almost a foot shorter than I am, even in heels, making me feel clumsy and awkward.

When the drizzle turns to rain, we get comfy on a low sofa by the window of one of the more traditional tearooms, watching people hurry past under umbrellas. There's not much legroom so I kick off my boots and tuck my feet underneath. Marley spots me hesitate over the prices, and insists on treating me to cake. It turns out we share a favourite, chocolate orange. Marley jokes it's another reason we get along, and even though it's not that funny, I giggle. Our tea arrives in a cute vintage teapot with mismatched cups.

Marley gets out her phone. "Let's film an update on the gloss. Ready? Hi, guys! It's three in the afternoon and I'm out with my friend Alana. Say hello, babe."

"Hi!" I toast the camera with my teacup.

"We're about to battle cake and tea. Will the gloss survive?" She pans down on the cake, making a *nom nom nom* sound. I giggle as she ends filming.

"You're actually going to upload that?"

"Sure! The fans love the traditional countryside town thing."

"I can't believe you genuinely have fans. That's so cool."

"It is, isn't it? But then I am cool. Thanks for noticing." Marley slides her fork into the rich, oozy frosting. "You didn't finish telling me about your morning."

Reluctantly, I bring up tonight's invitation. Marley's eyes blaze.

"Esme's unconscious, and Xander's having another party? In an effing *swimming pool*? I knew my brother was heading out later, but I thought they were bumming round the gym."

Of course Henry will be there. Great. I'm still deciding whether to go tonight. My first instinct was *no way*, but now I'm torn. Ursula WhatsApped to ask if I'd be there, so I won't be the only girl, and Xander's parents will be around. This time I'll be on my guard. If Xander really does know something, I'm going to make sure he tells me – one way or another.

As for Liam . . . maybe I should confront him, as avoiding each other seems to be impossible.

My phone bleeps: a notification. I glance at the screen – and recoil.

xanderlockwood is now following you.

What the hell? Didn't I up my privacy? It's not impossible to find me, if you have the right details, but. . . Crap.

Another ping.

xanderlockwood liked your picture

Even before I look, I just know the photo will be the modelling shot my friend uploaded. Sure enough, I'm sitting on a lounger side-on in a red cutaway costume and a sarong, face almost hidden by enormous shades and a sun hat.

Slowly, I lay down my phone. My chest is tight. It feels like I've been spied on. How dare he make me feel like this? Xander asked to see a photo earlier. I said no. So he found it himself. And then *liked* it. Just to let me know he'd got his own way.

I show Marley. Her lip curls.

"Has he left any comments?"

"Not yet. Jeez! What a creep!"

"Sure you don't fancy him?"

"No way. Yeah, he looks good, but he's clearly a massive player. Hardly boyfriend material."

"He's not. I should know."

"Whoa, wait!" My cup clinks against the saucer as I put it down. "You two dated?"

She shrugs. "Don't judge. It was only a couple of times. I dumped him."

Just like the other girls Ursula mentioned. "Why?"

"Because he's a dick?" Marley finishes her cake, not looking at me. It couldn't be more obvious there's more to this. I really hope he didn't do anything to hurt her.

After we finish eating and Marley films a short update – the lip gloss is disappointingly faded – we leave.

"I can pick you up from Stillwater later if your mum's working," she says. "Taxis are impossible to get on Saturdays. Stay over if you like."

"Really?"

"Yes, really, Lana." Marley rolls her eyes, but good-naturedly.

Lana. My cheeks heat – in a nice way. Marley must genuinely like me if she's inviting me to sleep over and hang out at the weekend. This isn't just loyalty to Esme any more. Feeling silly about how flattered I feel – I've so missed having a close female friend – I start to say that would be great. Then I remember.

Henry.

Marley blinks when I ask if he'll be home. Understanding comes on to her face.

"I can't believe a boy is getting between us already!" she quips. "Don't worry, babe. Hen normally crashes at Xander's after these things. Let me check and let you know, yeah?"

Relieved she's being cool about this, I smile. We go back to Marley's and hang out for a few hours before Marley drops me home. She shows me some of her body positivity videos, featuring girls I recognize from school. They're incredible. Marley has a brilliant, almost flippant way of talking through big concepts, and she's positively scornful when tearing down the nastier side of the beauty industry – pretty brave considering the companies she works with. Normally I'd be buzzing about all this, but my eyes keep straying to the pictures of Esme on Marley's pinboard. On a normal Saturday she'd be the one getting all fired up, not me. It feels uncomfortably like I'm taking her place.

I'm unlocking the front door when my phone shrills.

It's Mum. But Mum has just started her shift. Dread stirs within me.

Bracing myself, I pick up.

It's not the news I expected. Esme's awake.

TWELVE

Mum doesn't say much. Esme's too weak to talk and it's too early to tell if being in the water has done any lasting damage, but it's definitely promising. Mum even says I can visit her when she's a little stronger.

I hang up with a silly grin on my face. The world feels brighter. My friend is not going to die. She's going to be able to tell us what happened. Once she's better, we'll decorate cakes and visit the cat shelter and shoot arrows and all the other things we talked about on WhatsApp. I'll tell her all the things I've thought but never said: how I've always secretly wished I could be as calm and even-tempered and easy with people as she is. How being nice doesn't make her boring even though she used to worry it did, and how funny she is when she writes. How even in the years we didn't really talk I used to think about her.

And whatever happens, I'm not going to let us drift apart again.

It's almost eight by the time I arrive at Stillwater that evening, deliberately late so I can be sure Ursula and the other girls have arrived. Marley's at home video editing and has promised to come and pick me up if I need to escape. That makes me feel a little more confident. I walk through the health club reception and follow the smell of chlorine until I find the pool. A glamorous blonde woman who I guess is Xander's mum passes me. So he wasn't lying about his parents being around. As I stand at the door, it opens.

"I must be psychic," says Xander. "Somehow I just knew you'd arrived. Come on in."

More likely he saw me out of a window. I go to the changing room he shows me. As I strip off the clothes I put on over my costume, I wonder what the hell I'm doing. Earlier, I'd felt brave, almost powerful. I've told Marley that Esme's awake, but the boys won't know. For once, I'm a step ahead.

Now I'm here, and can hear the echo of male laughter, I don't feel brave or powerful. In fact, this doesn't seem very smart. Whoever tried to kill Esme is here. So are the boys from the cinema room. The sensible thing would be to stay home and wait for Esme to talk.

So why am I not being sensible? Because I'm angry, and want to show these guys I'm not the victim they tried to make me into? Because despite all this big talk, I'm still the new kid, and want to belong?

When I come out of the changing room, Xander's leaning against the wall, waiting. He's wearing a pair of trunks with a palm tree print that screams *look at me*, and, I have to admit, he looks pretty good in them.

"Evening," he says. "Nice costume. From the shoot, yes?"

He's found the rest of my swimsuit photos online, then.

"You'd know," I snap. "You're the creepy stalker."

"Come on. I was hardly not going to look. You did tell me all about your shoots."

Only because I wanted to get the gym pass! My cheeks burn as I adjust my halter neck straps. "Whatever."

"Someone's touchy. Do you ever think before you speak, or is rude and abrupt your default setting?"

I press my lips together. Xander sighs. "Fine, I won't compliment you, then. Happy? Nasty bruise, though. What happened?"

"I fell off my bike." I watch him closely, but Xander doesn't react. He opens the door to the pool and I follow him inside. It's predictably luxurious, with a sweeping glass ceiling and little lights twinkling at the top of the windows and mirrored in the clear turquoise water. The dim lighting gives it an intimate, relaxed atmosphere. No one so far is swimming. Ursula and another girl recline on sunloungers nearby, and everyone else is in the hot tub. I scan the room and spot Henry and Ozzie setting up speakers away from the water. Why am I not surprised that this is the kind of party where people sit around posing?

"I can't believe your parents are letting you have another party," I say as Xander and I walk round the side of the pool.

"They aren't. It's a small thing and I promised we'd behave. So no getting drunk and disorderly, please."

"I thought you weren't allowed alcohol tonight."

"Some beer may have found its way in."

Naturally. Since when do these boys give a toss about rules? I shake my head when he asks if he can get me anything. There's no way I'm accepting a drink I haven't poured myself.

"What did the police find, then?" I ask.

"Well, you're businesslike! We've barely said hello."

"You said you'd tell me."

"Did I? Ask me again in a few hours. Hello, losers. Space for two more?"

The group in the hot tub look up. Any annoyance I feel with Xander flips to hot embarrassment, because Liam's there, and his expression makes it very clear me appearing is both unexpected and unwelcome. Brilliant.

"Didn't I mention I invited Alana?" Xander says cheerfully. "Taylor, sort out whatever issues you have. I can't be dealing with brooding glances and sexual tension this evening."

I avoid eye contact. Liam mutters something. He doesn't move. There isn't much space in the hot tub, and while Xander might be happy to squeeze in with his mates, there's no way I am. Luckily, a girl climbs out. It's Henry's girlfriend, Faith.

"I'll get a drink with you, Alana," she says.

Grateful to be saved from standing around looking stupid, I follow her to a table where a range of alcoholic drinks are stacked. There's also an unopened bottle of Coke so I pour myself a glass.

I've seen Faith around school, mainly in the languages corridor or picking up big milky coffees from the canteen, but finally meeting her makes me anxious. I have no idea if she's angry about New Year's or not. I decide to be direct.

"Faith, I don't know if you noticed, but at New Year's I talked to Henry quite a lot. If I'd known he had a girlfriend I'd have backed off. So if I caused offence, I'm sorry."

I ignore the voice in my head pointing out that Henry was the one at fault. Faith fiddles with her hair. It's ashy blonde, even longer than mine.

"I saw what was going on," she says.

"Why didn't you say something?"

"I don't like to be clingy. Henry can talk to other girls, it's cool."

"I hope he's cool with you chatting to other guys, then."

Faith shrugs. That's a no. "I don't mind. It shows how much he cares about me."

I hide a grimace. Faith's clearly head over heels. There's

no way she'll believe Henry spiked my drink – or tell me if his alibi is a lie, either.

Faith asks how I'm finding school. After we've been chatting a while she leans closer and whispers, "You like Liam?"

Does everyone know about Thursday? Annoyingly, I go pink. Faith claps her hands together, laughing. I can't help thinking that for the first time, she looks alive.

"I knew it! You're both so shy. It's adorable."

Right now all I am is angry. While we've been speaking, the group in the hot tub has broken up. Liam's sitting at the side of the pool by himself. His trunks are plain navy ones, and he looks annoyingly good in them. I can see the tattoo on his forearm properly: some kind of bird with spread wings. It's kind of cool, I guess, though tattoos aren't really my thing.

It's also impossible not to notice that Liam keeps looking our way. I turn my back on him. "I don't know if I like Liam or not any more, actually, Faith."

"How come?"

"I heard a rumour I didn't like."

"Oh. Well, maybe you should ask him. Not all rumours are true. He's a sweetie, honestly."

Faith's smile falls, and her usual blank look returns. I'm not sure how to read that. Did she and Liam have something in the past, maybe?

Then a new voice says, "Hey."

I jump, almost spilling my Coke. I didn't notice Liam

coming over. Faith immediately gets up, saying she'll see us later, and heads over to where Henry's sitting in the hot tub. Liam clears his throat.

"So, uh. How's it going?"

I tip my cup from side to side, watching the dark liquid swish around. Then I drag my eyes to his.

"I heard a rumour about why you left your last school. About drugs."

Liam goes very still. Something that might be disappointment twists inside me. He sits on the lounger opposite mine, placing his beer on the floor. There's a haunted look on his face. In a moment he's going to start picking at the skin around his nails. "Is that why you didn't show yesterday?"

"Do you blame me? My drink was spiked. Excuse me for not wanting to hang out."

He flinches. "If I tell, will you promise not to spread it around? A couple of these guys know but that's it."

I shrug, then nod.

In a low voice, Liam says, "It's true. I didn't deal long, just a few months, and I didn't, like, do any really hard stuff myself. You won't get it, but I was fifteen and things were messed up at home. It didn't feel like anyone cared if I was there or not. And I was missing my old friends and life in LA. This country was a real culture shock. I guess looking back, it's a good thing I got caught. I was acting kinda self-destructive. Mom was so disappointed. Still is, really. We don't speak much. I live with my grandma now, Dad's mom. He grew up around here. Mom's in London."

"Is stuff better at St Jules?"

He hesitates. "I guess."

"You've definitely stopped dealing?"

"I had nothing to do with the GHB. I wouldn't do something that sick. I know what I used to do is wrong."

He sounds so definite. I think again of how he didn't hesitate with the CPR or getting Esme to hospital. None of that was staged. Despite being shocked, I can't help but feel sympathy. I know what it's like to have your home life fall apart – and how horrible it is to start somewhere new and have things you'd rather forget follow. Liam must feel like he'll never get away from those old, bad decisions, however hard he tries to be someone else. No wonder he was touchy.

"So. . ." Liam lets the word hang in the air. I look at him, taking a moment to work out how I feel about what he's just told me.

"So nothing," I say. "Thanks for being honest."

"That's all?"

"What were you expecting? Me to tell you off? Yeah, what you did was bad, but it was a while ago, and if you've changed. . . It's OK."

Liam doesn't look like he believes me. Then his expression changes. He smiles. "And there was me thinking my bad past was going to ruin everything. I got paranoid you knew when you started asking all those questions."

"I do want to find out what happened. That wasn't a lie."

"So . . . can we start over?"

It would be easy to smile and allow myself to like him again. Already I feel lighter. But I hold back. "I really need to be sure you didn't have anything to do with this. Sorry to sound so suspicious, but you get why, right? Where were you between twelve and one?"

"You're checking my alibi? I didn't know you were an undercover cop." Liam picks up his beer again. To my relief, he doesn't appear offended. "Big parties aren't my scene. All the small talk makes me feel awkward and I wasn't drinking so I kinda dipped in and out of the barn all evening – you know, fetching stuff, having a smoke. After the fireworks I was hanging out on the terrace."

"By yourself?"

"Yeah. I don't do dancing."

"How come you came to help me so quickly at the pool?"

Liam glances down at his feet. "Jeez, this is embarrassing. . . I noticed you when you first came in. I wanted to come over, say hello, but Henry was there. When I saw you go outside I, uh, followed."

This takes a moment to sink in. "You noticed me?"

"You're cute. I like tall girls."

My heart starts to thud. "What about unusually tall girls?"

"Especially unusually tall girls." He smiles again. "Not that you are unusually tall. At least, not from where this tall guy is looking."

Oh God. I look away, aware how pathetic it is that hearing him say this makes me so happy. "You followed me all the way to the pool? I'm not saying you're lying, but . . . it's a long way."

"I thought you might be going to a car. A couple of people parked that way. I forgot the path even went there. When I go down that end of the grounds I use the short cut."

"Wait, there's a short cut?" I lean forward. "Who knows about this?"

"Not tons of people. It cuts through the wood."

"Can you show me?"

"Now?"

I nod, trying to hide my excitement. Liam gives me a sceptical look. Then he gets up. The other boys wolf-whistle as we walk out to the changing rooms. I ignore them and pull my jeans and jumper over my costume, relieved it isn't wet. When I come out, Liam is standing there with his coat over a towel dressing gown, and trainers. Despite everything, I giggle.

"Stylish."

"No point getting fully changed. Come on."

THIRTEEN

Outside, one thing hits me straight away: it's staggeringly black. It's never truly dark in towns, even if the street lights aren't lit. Here, there's nothing. I can't make out trees I know are there. The only sound is the faintest beat of music.

"Here," Liam says, shining his phone torch. "That's where it starts."

I hug my coat close, peering forward. The trees look pretty dense. There's no way you'd realize there was a track unless you knew.

"You definitely want to go all the way to the pool?" Liam asks. I glance over my shoulder, picturing the comforting warmth and light we've left behind. Then I remind myself

Esme nearly died, and nod. Together we step into the woods. I'm hyper-aware of tiny sounds: our feet, crunching dead leaves, scuffling that might be foxes, the low hush of the wind. Soon the track opens up, though it's still narrow. An owl twit-twoos and I jump. My toe nudges something solid. The torch picks out a glass. Another lies about a metre away.

Gingerly, I pick up the closest, keeping my sleeve over my fingers. Inside is a red residue. Too light for wine – definitely a cocktail. Neither glass is dirty or scratched. These can't have been here long. They're identical to the kind used at the party. Someone – or two someones – used this path. Esme and the person who tried to kill her? Somebody else? Why did they drop the glasses?

At the pool, I check my watch: five minutes, half the time the path takes. Whoever did this might have only left the party for a quarter of an hour. Crap. Maybe it won't be easy to crack this after all.

I look around, but nothing's changed since this morning, so I rejoin Liam, who is hovering a few metres away. He's started picking at his nails. We walk back in silence. As we step into the open, Liam says, "Sorry about being quiet. That place . . . I don't like it."

This isn't the first time Liam's said that. "Because of Thea Keats?"

"Who?"

"The teacher who killed herself. You must have known her."

"Oh. Yeah. Sorry, I blanked a second. She didn't teach

me, actually. I just don't like it. So, uh, you want to go back inside? Or. . ."

He sidles me a glance. My heartbeat quickens. We've both stopped walking. Suddenly self-conscious, I tuck my hair behind my ears. "I guess so. It's cold."

"Sure. Let's go."

Neither of us moves. There's an awkward moment before Liam meets my eyes. *He wants to kiss me.* And I think I want to kiss him. He's answered my questions and he's been helpful and open. It feels OK to trust him now. Hoping I've read this right, I lean forward. Immediately his lips meet mine. It's so clear he's relieved I've made the first move that the tension melts away. The kiss deepens, and he winds his fingers into my hair. This is *so* much better than last time. Then a thought jumps into my head, and I pull back.

"The police didn't find Esme's phone, did they?"

"Huh?" Liam blinks, and I feel bad breaking off so suddenly. "I don't think so. It's probably at the bottom of the Witches' Pool. Why?"

"Nothing." But something at the back of my mind is niggling. If only I could put my finger on what. . .

Liam and I link hands and hurry back inside. Despite it being warm when I was pressed up against him, the cold really is biting. He waits for me to change, and takes my hand again as we walk back to the swimming pool. Immediately everyone notices, and there are "oohs" and nudges and another wolf whistle. I pull my hand away.

Xander comes over and smacks Liam on the shoulder. "Nice work, Taylor. Not many guys can pull in a flannel dressing gown. I think even I might fancy you a bit. . ."

"Bro, shut up." Liam rolls his eyes good-naturedly. Then Xander's phone pings, announcing that pizza has arrived, and everyone forgets about us.

I find myself sharing a pepperoni with Ursula and her friend Georgie, a fair-skinned, freckled redhead whose bikini pushes the boundaries of skimpy. She obviously has her eyes on one of the boys, though I can't tell which. I ask Georgie about the argument she overheard, but she isn't able to tell me more than Ursula did yesterday.

"I doubt it was one of this lot, hon," she says. "None of them are sad losers desperate for a shag. Why would they bother?"

I can think of plenty of reasons. Fun. Boredom. Power. We're interrupted by Ursula's boyfriend. He comes up and winds his arm round her waist.

"Hey, Cal," Ursula says. "Have you met Alana yet? Alana, this is Calvin. He just bought me these. Not even my birthday – lucky me!"

She taps the pretty silver earrings she's wearing. A musical note dangles in the centre of the hoop, a cute nod to their guitar teacher setting them up. The earrings are Pandora, easily sixty or seventy quid. That's some gift. Calvin gives me a fleeting look before locking eyes on Ursula.

"Dad's picking me up in ten minutes." His accent is a

local one and he speaks so quietly I struggle to make out the words. Unlike his friends, he doesn't project confidence, or a big personality, and for a rugby player he's pretty slight. "Do you want a lift?"

"Leaving early? You feeling OK, Cal?"

"Fine. Just not in the mood tonight. Not after, you know." Is it my imagination, or do his eyes flicker my way? He walks away to change. Ursula frowns after him.

"Huh. He seemed OK earlier when we were babysitting my little sister. I wonder what's wrong."

A guilty conscience, perhaps? "Maybe the attack on Esme has got to him."

"I doubt it. He barely knows her. There's no way Calvin has anything to do with this, anyway. He was with Blake when it happened."

Blake hears, and turns round. "Did I hear my name taken in vain?"

Does this guy think he's permanently onstage? I almost expect jazz hands each time he opens his mouth. Blake's wearing a loud kimono over his trunks, and I don't think he's being ironic. Judging by the pictures he posts online, eccentric is his thing. His dress sense veers close to children's entertainer territory. Still, at least he's not afraid to be an individual.

"We were talking about New Year's," I say.

"Course you were. I hear you fancy yourself as a detective. Interesting career choice. Shall I tell you my alibi? I'm guessing I'm on your suspects list."

A couple of the others laugh, and Blake toasts me with his near-empty beer bottle. The slur in his voice tells me it's not his first.

I grind my teeth but keep my voice light. "Go on, then."

Blake bursts out laughing. "I thought Xander was joking! Well, as you're so desperately curious, here's my answer." He strikes a pose, speaking as though he's in an Agatha Christie adaptation. "My friend Calvin and I were together at the time it happened, picking up *de l'alcool*. Can you believe that well-stocked bar barely had any beer? Round trip in my car, driving a teeny bit slowly owing to, ahem, reasons of mild inebriation, half an hour. So, *voilà*! *Le alibi*. Nowhere near the Witches' Pool, or indeed a water feature of any kind."

He bows, almost toppling over, and the others jeer. Someone pushes him into the water before I can ask anything else, and another boy jeers at him for having such basic taste in booze. An alcohol run doesn't sound like much of an *alibi*. In fact, it sounds *très shaky*. I don't remember seeing beer, it's true – most people were drinking fancy cocktails – but I don't buy that Blake would go out of his way to pick some up, even if it is the only alcoholic drink he likes. What were he and Calvin really doing?

When the pizzas are eaten, everyone takes to the water, lounging in the hot tub, or on lilos in the pool. The mood is lazy. Relaxed. In their trunks it's impossible not to notice how good these guys' bodies are. I'm irritated it distracts me so much. Am I like everyone else, worshipping the rugby team?

Even though it wasn't the reason I came, it feels good to have cleared the air with Liam. When he goes to get a drink, I spot Xander sitting in the hot tub, for once by himself. He's lying back with his eyes closed. I join him.

"You made a promise." I slide into the water.

Xander doesn't open his eyes as he says, "Did I, Alana? Remind me."

"You know exactly what I'm talking about."

"I don't remember promising anything. All I remember saying was *maybe* I'd tell you. Not the same thing."

"Don't you get bored messing with people all the time?"

"No, because it's fun." He opens his eyes and gives me a lazy smile. "How many days did it take for the anemone to die?"

My throat constricts. Then I find my voice. "You left the flowers. You sabotaged my bike."

Xander raises his eyebrows. "What? We're not talking about your bike. Are you drunk, Miss Ashman?"

"There was a flower in my bike basket, the same as the one left when my stuff was returned. You just said it was you."

"I left the anemone on your doorstep, yes, but that's all. If I'd sabotaged your bike I'd hardly admit it, would I?"

"Oh, whatever. Lie, then. How did you even know where I live? A normal person would have rung the doorbell."

"It was a bit of fun! Seems to have creeped you out more than I intended."

Yes, because my friend nearly died, and I know what your mates were going to do to me! I want to scream. I have no idea why Xander would admit to leaving one flower and not the other. To mess with me? I remember what I thought earlier, when Marley told me about his flashy childhood. *He's bored.*

"If you're not going to talk, I'm leaving."

"Oh, come on, Alana. Don't pretend you've been suffering all evening, hating every moment. Liam's not that bad a kisser, surely. If it wasn't for me you'd still be glowering at each other. You've had a great time."

"You're right, I have. Best night ever."

My sarcasm makes Xander laugh. "That's better! You win." He shifts to face me, arm leaning over the side of the hot tub. I become aware of how close we are and stop myself from instinctively moving back. "The police haven't found the weapon she was attacked with."

"How is that news?"

"Be patient. I don't know if you noticed, but there are lots of tools around the grounds at the moment. We have work going on. The police thought one of these was the weapon, but nothing matches the wound. It wasn't caused by anything from the barn, either. What does that tell you?"

I think for a second. "The weapon was something the attacker had on them. Something improvized."

"Exactly."

I frown. This evidence doesn't fit with my current theory of Esme being led to the pool. I wonder where the weapon is now. Hidden in the grounds, or perhaps the attacker took it away with them, assuming it wasn't something that would attract attention.

Why was Esme hit on the head, anyway? Did the attacker want to make extra sure she'd drown, even though she was out of it? Or did striking her give them some kind of kick?

"I could tell you something else too." Xander leans forward. He's too close now. This time I do move backwards.

"There's a 'but' coming, isn't there?"

"Brains as well as beauty. The 'but' is that I'm not going to tell you. Unless you fancy trying to persuade me. . ."

His hand brushes the inside of my leg, just above the knee. It's only a second, but it still sends a tingle through my body – and not entirely an unpleasant one. Flustered, I launch to my feet.

"No, I don't. You were telling me to get with Liam earlier, or have you forgotten that?"

Xander shrugs. Why did he even tell me about the weapon? Is it part of the game he's playing? "You've buddied up with Marley and her gang, haven't you? She'll be jealous when she hears you sat in a hot tub with me, half-naked. She'd love that to be her. Preferably more than half-naked."

"You wish! She can't stand you. You're just bitter about being dumped."

I'm hoping this will get under his skin, but Xander laughs.

"I think you'll find that I dumped her. Ask Marley how devastated she was and watch her squirm. Don't give me that look – it's true."

"So says the social media stalker! You think I'm going to believe that? I've heard all about how you treat girls—"

"What's going on?" It's Liam, fresh bottle of beer in hand. I realize my face is hot and angry.

"Your mate is sick."

Liam frowns at Xander. "Bro. What were you saying?"

"Nothing. I'll apologize if that makes it better. Sorry the truth hurts, Miss Ashman."

"The truth definitely will hurt when Esme talks," I snap before I can help myself.

"Like that's going to happen." Henry has come up behind Liam with Ozzie and Blake. He's kept his distance all evening. Now it feels like he's looking through me. His eyes are even more intense without his glasses. "Even if she wakes up, she'll be a vegetable. Not that she was exactly sharp before."

"At least if she came round the police might take their tape away," Xander says. "It really ruins the garden."

For a second, I'm sure I'm going to lose it. Have they any idea how cruel they sound, sneering at a girl in a coma?

This is the perfect time to turn the tables on them.

FOURTEEN

I glance round the four boys. Behind them, light glimmers in the turquoise of the pool. I take a deep breath. Then slowly and clearly, I say, "But Esme *has* come round. Didn't you know?"

Xander gives a start. So do Liam and Blake. Ozzie glances at Henry, eyes big. I look at Henry but he's watching me coolly, impossible to read.

"Thank you for telling us." Xander's tone is suddenly formal. "How is she? Is she speaking?"

I'm so tempted to say, *I don't think I'll tell you.* "She's doing well. I guess the police are going to want to speak to everyone again now."

Henry makes a dismissive noise. "Then I'll tell them the same as I did before: I was with my girlfriend, well away from the Witches' Pool."

"Did you tell them what happened in the cinema room too?"

It comes out before I can help myself. Have I gone too far? Henry's voice is cold as he says, "You got the wrong idea about that."

"Did I?"

"I was being friendly. Nothing more. It was a bitch move to whine to the police. Lucky they didn't believe you. A lot of guys wouldn't take being accused of something like that very well, you know."

Is that a threat? I become aware that I'm just one girl versus four of them, and this is their patch. Ursula, Faith and Georgie seem to have disappeared. The exit is right over the other side of the room, my way blocked. And I'm only wearing a swimsuit. My stomach does a scary flip. "How do you know they didn't believe me?"

"They said so. More or less. Anyway, you aren't my type. Giraffes with no tits don't do it for me."

My cheeks go hot. Instinctively, I cross my arms over my chest. Ozzie laughs, as though making me feel small is somehow clever, and Henry looks smug. Then Liam steps up to him.

"Stop it," he says.

"Loosen up, Taylor. I'm joking."

"It isn't funny. Apologize."

"Piss off. Why should I? She landed me in it. And she doesn't have any tits. No wonder she's upped her privacy. Those slutty photos of her posing are so hilariously unsexy. No class."

"Apologize!"

"What're you going to do, hit me?"

Liam's fist shoots out. Henry staggers back into Ozzie. And then the pool is filled with the shrill wail of the fire alarm.

For a second, no one reacts. Then Xander leaps up.

"Grab the robes and get out. Quickly."

"What, outside?" Ozzie asks.

"Yes! Someone's dicking about, probably, but ... just get out."

Confused and a little scared, we do as Xander says. The fight that seemed about to kick off is forgotten. We pile on to the lawn. It's absolutely freezing, especially as most of us are wet. I spot a furious-looking Henry pressing a wad of tissues to his bleeding nose. Everyone is looking at me, as though this is my fault. I turn my back, hugging myself tightly.

After what feels like ages, the fire alarm stops. Xander comes in from the hallway as we hurry inside.

"Party's over," he snaps. "My dad's in an apoplectic rage. Whichever one of you losers pulled that stunt, if I find out, I'll kill you."

I follow the other girls into the changing area – they hadn't left after all, just popped into the steam room. Georgie says something about there being a small fire here last year during one of Xander's parties. Suddenly his reaction makes more sense. When I check my phone, there's a message from Marley.

> Marley: On a scale of 1–10, how cold did those suckers get? ;) Waiting on the lane by the wood x

I suck in a breath.

"I bet Xander was angry." Marley has a big grin on her face as, slightly out of breath from running, I open the passenger door to her car. "With any luck, his dad will be furious. He's super strict. Sorry, babe, I wasn't planning on having fun with the fire alarm, but it was impossible to resist."

"You've got guts! Aren't you scared of getting caught on CCTV?"

"Nope. Xander's dad won't check, he'll assume one of Xander's mates was messing around."

"But what if—"

"You sound so shocked! Chill out. Even if I do get caught, so what? Serves him right for partying when Esme is in hospital! Not to mention the creepy stunt with your photos."

"You're not annoyed I went?"

"No, silly! Tell me what you found out. Revenge feels so good!"

She starts to laugh as we pull away, and after a moment, I laugh too.

*

In Marley's en-suite, I change into my pyjamas, feeling mixed up. Despite their alibis, I'm more sure than ever that these guys hurt Esme. I haven't got my head around what happened at the end yet – it was all so quick. What Henry said was horrible but I didn't expect Liam to punch him. I wish we'd got the chance to speak, but Liam vanished after the fire alarm went off.

And so much for flooring the boys by revealing Esme was awake! I bite my lip. What was I hoping for? A confession? Someone to slip up? Maybe I played that card wrong. I learned nothing, and now they know. Worse, I feel grubby, like I used Esme somehow.

"You OK, Lana?" Marley calls.

"Nearly ready," I call back.

"I hope Xander's getting a parental bollocking right now." Marley is sitting at the vanity table in a leopard-print nightshirt when I come out. "Final rating on the lip gloss 5/10, by the way."

I think back to the electricity that bolted through me when Xander's hand brushed my leg. He must find reeling girls in so easy. If things were normal I'd be super-flattered a guy like him was even looking my way. . .

But things aren't normal. And Xander might be a rapist.

"Marley," I say, "why did things end between you and Xander?"

She swivels round. "What?"

"He says he dumped you. I don't believe him, obviously, but I. . ."

Marley puts down her make-up remover. One eye is naked, the other heavy with liner. "He's lying."

"Why?"

She wets her lips. Suddenly, she looks a lot younger. Vulnerable. "Can you keep a secret?"

"Of course."

She draws a deep breath. "When we were going out, Xander asked me to send him pictures. You know. Naked pictures. And . . . I did. It was stupid, but I wanted him to like me. Guess even body positivity vloggers feel insecure about how we look sometimes." She flashes a bitter smile. "He said all the right things – I was beautiful, fun, yadda yadda, and, God, he was an amazing kisser. . . But he was pushy when we were together. Like, really pushy."

"He didn't force you to do anything, did he?"

"Nah." Marley tosses her head, some of her old attitude returning. "I've done self-defence classes. If he'd tried anything he'd have found himself on the ground pretty quickly."

I'm not sure about that. Xander's taller than me, and, I couldn't help noticing tonight, pretty toned. I can't imagine a petite girl like Marley getting the upper hand.

"Anyway, I came to my senses and dumped him. Unfortunately, the bastard got revenge." She pauses. "He sent my pictures to his mates, then posted them anonymously online. Boys from Fairfield saw too." Her voice wobbles. "I know I act tough, but it was awful, Lana, the absolute worst. They didn't show my face, so you wouldn't realize it was me unless you were told, but the guys knew. The names I was called, the laughter... They've been deleted now; a teacher caught them looking and the whole team got suspended because they wouldn't grass Xander up, but I'm worried the pictures are floating about online somewhere. If this got out on my vlog I'd be toast! My brand is smart, switched-on feminist. Everything I upload is clean. A lot of my fans are young. My sponsor would do a runner, the other companies I work with would too... I don't go on about it, but my channel's making money. I'm proud of it. I might be able to be an influencer full-time when school's out. I can't have all my hard work ruined by a stupid mistake!"

My heart goes out to her. "Oh, Marley, I'm so sorry! I know exactly how you feel. The boys have been all over the photos from my shoots, calling them slutty... I hate how that word always gets used to take a girl down! This isn't your fault. What an utter shit Xander is! Do you think he's done this to anyone else?"

"I'm scared he has. Why else would so many girls dump him suddenly? I was tempted to report him, but I'd be the loser. Whenever Xander gets into trouble, Daddy's millions bail him straight out."

She swallows. I give her a fierce hug, silently raging at the way Xander's treated my friend, and how, all over the world, guys like him walk over girls and get away with it. It's the same story over and over. Esme, silenced because she knew too much. Thea Keats, walking into the water because she was humiliated. The unknown woman murdered by Xander's ancestor to preserve his good name. Countless other women drowned in the pool at the hands of men who felt threatened.

Which is why you need to be careful, a voice whispers in my head.

We turn out the lights and clamber into bed. I lie listening to Marley's breathing. I've never shared a bed before and I quite like the comfort of knowing another person is close by. The covers shift. A hand finds mine and squeezes it.

"Thanks for not judging me," Marley whispers.

I squeeze her hand back. "Of course I don't judge you. And thank you for making me so welcome. Tomorrow I'll ask Mum about visiting Esme. We can go together. Even if she can't talk I know she'll want to see us. And then, when she's better, however long that takes, we can catch up on lost time. The three of us."

"Sounds good." Marley's voice is sleepy. "I'm glad you're my friend."

Happiness bubbles inside me. *Friend.*

The next morning, there's news.

Esme is dead.

FIFTEEN

School on Monday feels like a funeral. No one seems to know what to say, or do. We shuffle between lessons but nobody can concentrate, and the teachers don't make us.

Nobody can believe it. One moment, Esme was coming round. The next, a sudden relapse. These things do happen, I know that from Mum, but I really thought she was going to be OK.

Esme. The girl who baked the best carrot cakes and named her kitten after Wonder Woman and wrote the Tudor princess story I loved. Gone. It feels wrong, so utterly unfair. Esme wasn't perfect – as a kid she could be over-serious, and scared of conflict, and it used to make me angry when she wouldn't speak up for herself because I ended up opening my mouth instead and getting into trouble. It sounds like that was changing, though. Volunteering at the shelter, and her work with the charities committee – Esme was finding her voice. I wanted to get to know the new angry, passionate Esme, who had things to fight for and change.

I'm still having trouble grasping that she's dead. Is it abnormal that I haven't cried yet? The only feeling inside me is a numb heaviness. In some ways I knew Esme well, in others not at all. I've no idea how I should be reacting. I haven't even lost a grandparent before.

In the canteen at break it's deathly quiet. I look round at the sombre faces.

Someone I know is a murderer.

Suddenly, everything I've done seems silly and childish, a kid playing detective. How could I believe that I could make a difference?

I should give Marley and Esme's other friends time alone. My grief and theirs are completely different, and I don't want to intrude.

My phone pings.

> Liam: Hey. You're on break, right? I'm in the library if you want a quick chat.

The local library is just over the road from Fairfield. Grateful for a distraction, I pop over and climb the stairs to the second floor. Liam's collecting a coffee from the self-service machine. He asks if I want anything and I shake my head, curling up on the closest sofa. He moves to sit next to me, then pauses and instead sits opposite. We're alone, the only sounds the ticking of the wall clock and distant shrieks from the lower school playground. Liam's right, it is a good place to hide.

"I should introduce you to Hector." Liam breaks the silence. He gestures to a bay window, where a skeleton dangles from a stand. It seems a lifetime ago that Liam joked about hanging out together. How has it only been a week?

"Hi, Hector," I say flatly. "Wish we were meeting under better circumstances."

Liam shifts. "So how are you doing?" he asks.

I hug my knees closer. "It hasn't really sunk in. My mum's devastated. She's seeing if she can take time off to help Esme's parents."

"I've seen them. Only from my bedroom window, but they looked like zombies."

Each time I think about Laura and Doug, my chest goes tight. "We went over yesterday. They're in pieces. I didn't know what to say. Esme is – was – an only child, too."

"Driving into school alone doesn't feel right. We had this silly thing where we'd toss a coin to see who got to choose the radio station. Esme always went for a cheesy old-school one, and sang along to annoy me. . . It's not fair. She had so much she wanted to do."

"I wish I'd had the chance to get to know her again," I say sadly.

"Do you want a hug?"

A hug isn't going to change anything, but I nod. He joins me on the sofa. The hug feels weird, and he smells faintly of cigarettes, but there's something comforting about how solid he is, and that he cares about how I feel. Mum has been so consumed by Esme's parents that Seb and I have come a very distant second. I'm not sure whether I resent that or not.

"Who would kill her?" I whisper. "Why? I could buy a date rape attempt going wrong, some scared, sick, drunk boy panicking. But that's not what happened. She wasn't their target."

"Because you were."

How on earth does he know? Then I remember. I mentioned drink spiking to him the other night. Have the other boys worked out I know about that? It would be a surprise if they hadn't. I wonder what names I've been called. Bitch, for sure. Probably slut too. That word always comes out when boys want to put a girl down.

"I can't prove anything," I say. "Esme knew, though. And I think that's why they attacked her."

"You believe that?"

"Who else could it have been?"

Liam glances down at his scuffed-out brogues. Something about the way he holds me suddenly feels different. I pull back so I can see him properly.

"Liam, if you know something, please tell me."

"I don't. Sorry. I wish I did."

"But you believe me?"

He nods. There's a flicker of something in his eyes. Pain? Worry? Anger, even?

"Are you going to carry on hanging around with them?" I ask.

"I don't hang out with Henry and Ozzie apart from at parties, Alana. Why do you think I spend so much time up here? I don't like or agree with much the guys say. It's not cool. I've called them out before, but no one cares what I think. If I make trouble they'll drop me from the team, and I'll go back to being an outsider loser. Rugby's the only reason I have friends. Well, apart from Xander. We're pretty tight. But I'm never sure the others actually like me."

Then they're crappy friends. My all-too-familiar anger returns. If more boys challenged their mates on the way they think they can treat girls, we'd have fewer problems with this shit. I almost say so, but I don't want to have an argument, not now. And how brave am I really? Would I risk losing hard-won friends in his position?

"Let me ask you an honest question, Liam. If it came to it . . . do you think your mates could kill someone?"

He doesn't say anything for a while. Then, finally, he nods.

"Do you think they did?"

Liam doesn't answer.

When I return to school all the sixth formers are surging into the hall again. The police are here.

The head teacher doesn't waste any words. "If any

of you know anything, however small or embarrassing, please come forward." She then introduces DI Underwood from the Murder Investigation Team, who'll be handling the case going forwards. Hearing the word *murder* sends murmuring round the hall. Suddenly, everything is much more serious – and scarier. Underwood's younger than Harcourt, with a businesslike manner, sharp face and slick suit. He announces that he wants to speak to a number of students again and reads out a list.

"Alana Ashman. Marlena Durrant. Faith Kemp. Georgina Douglas."

My first thought is, *That's me*. My second is that Liam didn't mention the police visiting St Jules. They've come here first. What's going on?

I soon find out, because I'm up first. Underwood takes ages flicking through the notes his constable hands him. Is he trying to rattle me?

"Alana. Tell us your movements between midnight and twelve thirty, please."

I open my mouth to ask why – Esme was attacked at one a.m. – then decide to cooperate. Underwood nods.

"Tell us about discovering the body."

So that's what Esme is now, the body. It sounds so clinical. I do as he says, then ask, "Why are you speaking to us again?"

"Because we now know Esme entered the water by twelve thirty."

I stare at him, brain whirring.

Twelve thirty means the alibis I've found for one a.m. are irrelevant.

Twelve thirty was when I was in the cinema room with Henry.

Henry, who now definitely couldn't have drowned Esme, and has an alibi I know is true – because I gave it to him.

My skin goosepimples as I realize that it was around twelve thirty when Ozzie entered the room. Even if he used the path in the woods, there's absolutely no way he could have attacked Esme, then run back to the barn, before or after I saw him. He didn't do this either.

I'm not sure whether I want to scream or cry.

The constable slides a phone across the table to me.

"We'd like you to look at this video," says Underwood. The constable clicks play. The footage is from the barn, people assembling at one end, laughing. A familiar voice whoops that it's a brand-new year. The constable taps stop.

"This video comes from Ursula Griffiths's phone," says Underwood. "It's quite long. She encourages everyone to speak about their New Year's resolutions. Apparently it's tradition." Of course – Henry mentioned speeches when we left the barn. I'd forgotten. "The video runs from 12.15 to 12.32. It's enabled us to eliminate suspects now we have a more precise timeline."

So everyone in this video is innocent. "Oh." It seems such an empty response, but I can't think of anything better. Underwood glances at his notes. I sense the interview is nearly over. Not expecting to be told, I ask how they know Esme was attacked earlier than they first thought. But Underwood answers.

"Two reasons. One, we've discounted the evidence pointing towards her entering the water later." He doesn't elaborate on what this is and I know there's no point asking. "Two, since the investigation became a murder inquiry, we've looked into forensics in more depth. With drowning, a person's chances of survival are much higher in cold water. Low temperatures reduce the brain's need for oxygen. That means it can keep going longer, focusing blood to the most essential organs. Esme could have been in water that temperature for up to an hour and made a full recovery. That's why the CPR you gave her was successful."

That sounds pretty thorough. I feel deflated. When Underwood asks if I have any further questions, I shake my head.

Instead of heading to class I lock myself in a toilet cubicle. My intention is to WhatsApp Ursula about the video, but I forget that when I see a new message from Liam.

Liam: Cops just showed.

So there's a whole team of detectives on the case. Finally they're taking it seriously. No more "boys will be boys".

There's a video from NYE, I type. Whoever isn't in it is a suspect. Do you know who they're interviewing?

He replies almost instantly. Xander. Henry. Ozzie. Blake. A pause. Me.

Crap. You'll be OK. You didn't do anything.
Just tell the truth and don't worry.

Liam doesn't reply. Has he been called into an interview? I read the list again. Calvin's name is missing. Presumably he was with Ursula when she was filming. I'll check with her but if he was, he's innocent. And now I know for sure Henry and Ozzie are too...

That doesn't leave too many options.

Eventually I drag myself to class. I'm desperate to find Marley, see what the police said to her, but Mrs Stannard collars me for a "confidential chat" to check I'm OK. By the time I escape, Marley and the others are gone. Checking my phone – still nothing from Liam – I race to The Hideout. Outside, I stop dead. My mouth goes dry.

Henry and Ozzie are barring the door. They're wearing military uniforms which look ridiculous until I remember that St Jules has an army cadet unit. According to Marley it's Ozzie's thing; apparently he wants to train for army cavalry when he's done with school.

Henry steps into my path. "Could I speak to you, please?"

Henry is the last person I want to see, but curiosity gets the better of me. Ozzie heads off with a "Laters, matey." I follow Henry to the war memorial. He sits, nodding at the other end of the bench. There's something imperious about the way he does it, like I'm his servant. I fish my water bottle from my bag and take a glug, staying standing.

"What?" I ask.

"I wanted to say sorry for Saturday. I hope you're not too upset."

Ugh, even when he's apologizing this guy is a creep. "Believe it or not, today I don't care about being called a giraffe with no tits." As soon as the words are out I realize they're a mistake. Now he knows I remember, and that what he said got to me. "Are you going to apologize for spiking my drink too?"

He ignores that. "We got off on the wrong foot. You've seen the police, right? You know I didn't go near Esme. I hope we can get on better now."

I stare at him. He's smiling. Unbelievable. How stupid does Henry think I am?

"After what you tried to do to me? No way! Yeah, I can't prove it, but I *know.* And if Esme hadn't drunk that punch, perhaps she'd have been able to fight back, or swim to safety. You didn't kill her but you're hardly blameless."

"Are you seriously lecturing me? You really think you're something! Newsflash – you're not. But have it your way." He gets up. "Here's a friendly warning. Keep away from Liam. His druggie past isn't his only secret. He wasn't in the video. Maybe he was the one holding Esme's head underwater. . ."

I fling my water at him. It splashes across his trousers, right over the crotch. He cries out, leaping up. I march away, banging into The Hideout and grabbing a tray from the pile by the chiller cabinet and slamming it down on the counter. My feeling of satisfaction wears off almost immediately. Henry was winding me up, but he had a point. With him and Ozzie out, there aren't too many suspects left.

I join Marley and her gang at our usual table, eyes on the door in case Henry comes in. No one talks much.

When I ask Marley how she got on with the police, she says, "Fine. All they wanted to know was why I wasn't in the video. I told them I hate speeches so went outside to cool off and they were OK with it."

As we're clearing the table at the end of lunch, I spot Faith perched at the breakfast bar by the front window, prodding a few floppy spirals of pasta. She always seems to be by herself if she isn't trailing after Henry. I know how *that* feels. I find myself going over.

"You OK?" I ask softly.

Faith jumps, dropping her fork. For a second, she looks terrified. Then she sees it's me and relaxes. "Sorry. I was miles away. Did you ask me something?"

"Just if you were OK. You spoke to the police, right?"

She nods. "They were kind. The detective said he knew I didn't do anything. I wish I could have been helpful, but I was in the bathroom when Ursula made that video."

"They called Georgie's name too. Any idea why? She's your friend."

"Georgie? She'd laugh if she heard you say that," says Faith, with sudden bitterness. "We used to be close, me, her and Ursula. Not any more. I don't know where she was. Probably getting with some boy. She usually is. I should go. Thanks for being nice." She gets up, and as she grabs her things, I notice her hands shaking.

I must be feeling funny because at home I challenge Seb to a computer game, which normally I never do because I'm so bad at them. We've passed an hour shooting evil robots when Mum comes in, a deep line furrowed between her eyebrows.

"Mum?" I ask. "Did something happen?"

She heaves a sigh. "Yes."

"Is it to do with Esme?"

"It's confidential, love."

"We won't tell anyone."

Mum is silent. Then she meets my eyes.

"In the early hours of Sunday morning, someone unauthorized went into Esme's room. CCTV suggests it was a boy. And we think he's the reason she died."

Mum refuses to say more, but she doesn't need to. I've seen crime dramas where killers sneak into intensive care and hold pillows over patients or meddle with wires to oxygen machines or pull out plugs. It's terrifyingly easy to walk into hospitals if you know where to go.

I go upstairs, head spinning. It's one of the rugby team. It has to be. I told them Esme had come round. No one else knew. Whoever it was decided not to leave anything to chance and finish her off – no doubt in heavy disguise.

Oh my God. If they're that ruthless, what might they be planning to do to me? I wrap my arms around myself, suddenly struggling with breathing. I'm out of my depth. *Seriously* out of my depth. The deeper I dig, the more of a target I make myself. I've brushed off the anemones, my bike accident, but how can I ignore this? I *have* to stop.

In my room the Post-it wall greets me. And my fear flips to anger. *All wrong*, I think, and tear everything down. If she'd drowned by half twelve, this was a lot slicker than I thought. Less than an hour after she ran off spooked, she was in the water.

How *can* I stand by and do nothing when Esme's dead? *Someone* needs to fight for her and the truth.

There's no way I can go round the hospital asking questions. I'll have to leave that to the detectives. Mum said they've been all over hospital CCTV, and questioned staff. My best bet is to concentrate on New Year's, the attack, the drugs. The same person – or people – must be responsible.

What exactly was it Ozzie said? *I think New Year's is about to knock Halloween into second place for my favourite celebration.* Why mention Halloween? It's so specific. I grab my phone and find Xander's name in my followers list. Big surprise, most of his photos are of himself posing in the gym in expensive sportswear, or showing off his flash car, or with his arm around pretty girls. There are a ton from Halloween. This party looks rowdier than New Year's. One shot shows a pyramid of empty bottles, someone in a skeleton costume crashed out behind them. In another, a gang of boys I'm pretty certain aren't from St Jules or Fairfield have stripped down to their boxers and covered themselves in fluorescent paint. A third shows a girl curled into a foetal position on the floor, zombie schoolgirl costume vomit-flecked.

I can't believe you uploaded this you prick, comments a Year 13 who I'm assuming is the girl's friend. *TAKE IT DOWN.*

Convince me, Xander replies, with a winking emoji. What a tool. You can't see the girl's face, but it's really mean to keep it up. Naturally he's only uploaded flattering ones of himself. I have to admit the tailcoat and cravat suit him. The costume's more Jane Austen than seventeenth century, though – way too late for his murderous ancestor. Maybe Marley got that wrong.

I carry on scrolling, but I'm no wiser. The party looks huge, with lots of unfamiliar people. What was I expecting to find? A flashing sign reading CLUE? Halloween has to be important. Or else why would Ozzie—

Then I realize. The answer's obvious.

New Year's was not the first time these boys have tried drugging girls. They've done it before. At Halloween.

And they got away with it.

SIXTEEN

I feel utterly sick the rest of the evening. Even after I turn out the lights, I can't relax. It all fits. Henry and Ozzie seemed so confident in the cinema room. Complacent, even. When I think about the other girl they've done this to I want to cry. She's probably someone I've met. Does she feel as small and alone and vulnerable as I did?

Even worse, she might not be the only one. What if they've been doing this for months?

I stare into the blackness, picturing the way Henry smiled when I arrived at the party and how friendly and genuine I thought he was. Was I not a real person to him, just a thing to enjoy? Is that how he sees girls? I've read about this stuff online, raged about it, but I never thought it would happen to me. Was I naive?

I wish I knew who Halloween Girl is. Is she too scared to tell anyone in case she isn't believed, or branded a slut? Does she even remember? She might not, if she was drugged too.

A new thought slides into my head.

What if Halloween Girl is Esme?

Immediately I dismiss it. There's no way Esme would have gone partying if something that terrible had happened.

But . . . maybe she blamed herself. Thought she'd got completely drunk and made a stupid mistake. Then when Ozzie opened his mouth it all came flooding back. . .

I need to know. I don't have a choice any more. This isn't just about fuelling my rage and grief into finding out who killed my friend, it's about exposing these monsters before they rape again. Scary as that word is, I'm going to start using it, because rape is what it is. And I'm terrified they will. The casual hand that skimmed my bum in the lunch queue, the photos of Marley that Xander shared, the boys' toxic confidence in the face of a police investigation. . .

Worse, even when – if – someone presses charges, they'll probably breeze away scot-free. I've read enough blogs to know people almost never go to jail for sexual assault. It's their victims who get life sentences.

I was lucky. Another girl in a few weeks or months might not be.

*

Over the next few days I make plans. Despite digging through social media, all I've learned is where the Halloween party was: the old wing of Stillwater House, which is now scaffolded for renovation. Marley would know more, but I don't want to put her in a difficult position. Horrible or not, Henry's still her brother. No, I need to be careful and subtle – basically, the things I'm not. If they find out I'm on to them, they'll do worse than sabotage my bike.

A better idea is to ask Liam. He's dropped me home every day this week, Seb too. He said it was because the weather's too crap for cycling, but he always waits for us to step inside the house before driving off. It's been nice to chat, even though his driving still terrifies me. We're meeting up properly on Saturday. Neither of us is calling it a date, though we both know it is. It feels wrong to feel so thrilled when Esme is dead.

Liam comes to pick me up after lunch. Mum insists on meeting him before we go anywhere, but, to my relief, seems to like him, especially when she discovers that Liam's the one who put Seb on to his latest fascination, an app where you can track all the airborne planes in the world. It appeals to Seb's love of data. Every so often he comes into my room to inform me that there's an EasyJet flight to Stockholm above us, or Ryanair heading into Stansted.

"So was that better or worse than being interrogated by the police?" I ask as I sink into the passenger seat of Liam's car, closing the door on the pelting rain.

"Way better," says Liam. "Your mom doesn't think I killed someone."

"They're giving you a hard time?"

"The shit from my last school doesn't exactly count in my favour." A pause. "I've spoken to the cops twice this week. So have Blake and Xander. Nothing new's happened, they're just piling on pressure so we slip up. That's what Xander thinks, anyway. They're really suspicious of him."

Of course – out of the people missing from Ursula's video, Liam, Xander and Blake are the only boys without alibis. Blake's story about going to get alcohol with Calvin has been proved to be a lie, as Calvin was in the video. Liam has no evidence that he was outside by himself. I'm not sure where Xander's claiming he was now but he certainly wasn't in the barn until later, when he shows up in the background of the selfie. I've checked that; the timestamp is 12.53. Xander looks really annoyed. Something else bothers me about it, but I can't for the life of me work out what.

"Do the police think Xander did it, then?" I ask.

"Not exactly. But they keep going on about his phone. The one he gave them to look at is about two years old."

A rich kid like Xander probably upgrades his phone every year. No wonder the police suspect he's holding something back. "Are you scared?"

"No, because I didn't do it." Liam turns his key in the ignition. "Let's go someplace we can forget all this. I don't mind driving a while. This town gets claustrophobic."

"OK. Thanks for being kind to my brother, by the way. He loves that app."

Liam's smile doesn't quite reach his eyes. "No problem. Watching airplanes is kinda therapeutic. So, um, assuming you've not decided I'm a total geek, where did you want to go? I was going to say the castle, seeing as you like history, but the weather's kinda ruined that. There are famous Tudor tombs in the local church I guess we could look at, if you'd like."

He sounds less than thrilled, and I giggle. "Thanks, but I've seen those already. Let's find a café. Not The Hideout, somewhere quiet. I want to ask you something."

"That sounds hella ominous."

"It's about Halloween. I think something happened, and I don't know what to do about it."

Liam looks at me as he pulls out. I flush, aware that this probably isn't the kind of thing you chat about on a date. A few minutes later we're parking outside the health club at Stillwater.

"There's a café here," Liam explains. "It's kinda upmarket to match the health club. Lots of green juices and healthy food, but they do cake too. Hearing rain on the glass roof is pretty cool. Plus there's plenty of legroom."

"Are your friends around?"

Liam finally cottons on to my discomfort. "Oh. Sorry. No, I don't think so, unless they're in the gym. Xander won't be. His parents don't let him in the café. Spends too much time chatting to customers." He pauses. "Would you rather go someplace else?"

Hell, yes, but I'm too impatient to find out what Liam knows to make a fuss. Before we can get out, a car parks alongside us. The driver is Blake. He looks as surprised to see us as we are him.

Liam winds down his window. "Hey, bro. Weren't you at a wedding today?"

For once, Blake looks like he doesn't know what to say. His outfit – a Hawaiian shirt and clashing waistcoat – doesn't scream wedding, though it's hard to tell with him. "What are you doing here?"

Liam nods at me, and says we're going to the café.

"I guess you had the same idea." I hide my dismay. I can't speak to Liam properly if Blake's around. He's probably meeting his girlfriend. Marley told me he was dating someone from the next town. But Blake shakes his head. "The sugary delights are all yours, my friends. *Bon appétit.*"

He messages someone quickly before pulling away. I trade a look with Liam.

"What's that about?"

"No idea. I'm sure he said the wedding was today. He kept complaining how boring it was gonna be."

"The gentleman doth protest too much, methinks." Liam looks blank, and I sigh. "I'm misquoting Hamlet. Blake would get it. Remind me, what's his new alibi?"

"Something to do with losing his phone and going to his car to see if he'd dropped it. I know what you're thinking – it sounds shady. But Blake's OK. He loses it around alcohol, but he wouldn't hurt anyone."

"Loses it?"

Liam reddens. "I shouldn't have said that. All I meant is when he drinks he gets, you know, volatile. Thinks people are making fun of him, that kind of thing. Blake acts like a big personality, but he's kinda insecure. Before we all got cars he used to miss out on lots of social stuff because his commute to school takes for ever. And St Jules is, like, really white. It all gets to him sometimes. You know it's no fun feeling like an outsider."

He speaks the last sentence in a terrible mimic of my accent, which on another day would have me giggling. I completely get Liam's point. Blake doesn't have it as easy as the other guys. Even so . . . volatile could lead to violent. No wonder the police are putting pressure on Blake. He's acting suspicious as hell.

Deciding not to push Liam further, I open the door and we dash across the gravel, holding our coats over our heads to avoid getting drenched. Inside the conservatory, the slightly muggy warmth is welcome, and we find a comfy wicker sofa in a quiet corner hidden by plants. The café feels chic and stylish, with a decorative tiled floor and glass-topped tables. Thanks to the weather it's slightly dark, but Liam's right. It is cool to clutch a steaming mug while the rain pounds above us.

The only other people here are a group of middle-aged women with towel robes and wet hair, and they're too busy chatting over their cakes and green juices to overhear us. I wait for the waitress to bring our cake – pretty Victoria sponge dusted with icing sugar – before telling Liam what I think happened at Halloween, and that Halloween Girl could be Esme. He sips his coffee slowly, letting me talk.

"I'm guessing you drove Esme home," I say. "Do you think she could have been drugged?"

Liam places his cup on the glass table in front of us. He rakes a hand through his hair. His eyes look troubled.

"She was definitely upset. Like, more than the tearful drunk kinda way. I did ask if something had happened."

"And she said no?"

He nods. Of course Esme said no. I doubt she even told Marley.

"If these guys did slip off with a girl, where do you think they'd have gone? Upstairs?"

"I guess. Downstairs would have been way too risky. The first floor was supposed to be out of bounds, though. Parts of the main house aren't safe. That's why the builders are in the old wing now."

Like Henry would let a few rotting floorboards stop him getting what he wanted. I glance up. It's only drizzling. "Can you show me?"

"What, the old wing? Sure, but we can't go in. Like I said, building work. Xander's mom and dad want to convert that part into a hotel." He pauses. "Are you for real?"

I nod. I'm being a really bad date, but, as much as I want Liam to like me, I want to find out what happened more. We finish our cake and drinks. Outside, the air has the earthy post-rain smell I love. Faint excitement flutters inside me as we approach the scaffolded part of the house.

"So." Liam waves his hand at a heavy-looking wooden door. "I want to say this was a servants' entrance, but history isn't my strong point. Those windows there" – he points to the left – "belong to the rooms the party was in."

I try twisting the handle. Rather to my surprise, it isn't locked. Through it I can see a dusty hallway full of crates and tools.

"Doesn't look like much has been done yet." I pause. "I could take a quick look…"

"Alana, seriously, no." Liam takes my arm. "We can't walk into someone else's house, even if he is my friend. There won't be anything to find anyway. Halloween was months ago."

I shake Liam off. I'm about to step inside when a new voice says, "If you wanted a tour you only needed to ask."

I whirl round. The door clangs shut. Xander has appeared next to Liam, wearing an expensive-looking tracksuit.

"What are you doing here?" I snap. He raises his eyebrows.

"Isn't the answer obvious? I thought you were supposed to be smart."

I press my lips together, annoyed at myself for blurting out something so stupid. Even though I haven't done anything wrong, I feel like a thief caught with their hand in the till. "You said he wasn't here."

Liam shuffles his feet. "I didn't think he was."

"Oh, is this a date?" says Xander. "Sorry, I didn't realize. Funny venue, the back of my house. I'll get lost. I only came to say hello. You have no idea how boring working here is sometimes."

"I feel so sorry for you. Smiling when people walk into the gym reception must be exhausting."

"That depends who they are. Some people are easier to smile at than others."

And he smiles at me. I stare at him, speechless. I can't believe he's doing this in front of Liam! "You'd better get back, then. I'd hate to think someone's missing out on a smile."

"I'm not on reception today. There's a physio session in the pool. My parents seemed to think me helping would be educational. And maybe it would, if I was allowed to do anything other than listen to people talking about their injuries." He pauses. "I do give good massages, though. Just FYI."

"I thought you were going to get lost?"

"I am. You should too. Seeing as you are, technically, trespassing."

My heartbeat quickens. It's not a threat, exactly. But the teasing note in his voice is gone. "I only wanted to look inside. Is there much to see?"

"All the best stuff is in the part of the house we use – old letters, portraits, painted ceilings, a priest hole, even a bed Charles I supposedly slept in. The old wing... If you're into mould and rotting floorboards, you'd be in heaven. Otherwise, there's nothing. Except possibly a broken neck if you fall through the floor." He pauses, daring me to say more. When I refuse to take the bait, he sighs. "I'll leave you to your date. Don't do anything I wouldn't."

"Jerk," I mutter, watching Xander stroll off. I'm pretty sure that was a joke. And yet. . .

I wonder if he knows why I'm really interested. Was coming here a mistake?

Liam clears his throat. I'd almost forgotten he was there. "Sorry. I don't know why he was being such a jerk. Do you want to go home?"

"No. Do you?"

"I just thought—"

I realize I'm on the brink of ruining this date. I take his hand and suggest we go for a walk, but I'm only half-listening as Liam tells me about his med school applications, and how he's hoping to study back in California. Instead, my head is full of Halloween, and how it links to Esme's murder. Is it worth trying to sneak into the old wing another time? Speaking to some of the girls? If I felt really brave, I'd nose about in Henry's room sometime, but I don't suppose he'd be stupid enough to keep GHB anywhere, and it would only cause conflict with Marley.

When the light fades, we return to the car. As Liam turns his key in the ignition, the door to the health club opens. Henry and Ozzie saunter out, sports bags slung across their shoulders. They're too busy laughing at something on Henry's phone to spot us, but this gives me zero comfort. If they've been in the gym they'll have seen Xander. Chances are he's told them about me poking around. So much for being careful.

Back at my house, Liam parks up out of view of the windows.

"We can do this again, if you like," he says. Relieved me being distracted hasn't put him off, I smile and say that would be great. He smiles back.

"Awesome," he says. "I was worried I was being annoying, talking so much."

"You need to worry less. I meant to ask, what's the story with the tattoo?"

"Oh." He glances at his forearm, hesitating. "You know the nature reserve by the castle? I used to go as a kid whenever we visited Grandma. It kind of became a special place. There are these wild birds there. We used to enjoy watching them. The way they flew always reminded me of airplanes, so . . . I'm not explaining well."

"You're explaining fine," I said. "I like that it means something personal. So . . . what do you want to do next time?"

"Well, I looked online and there's an archery club forty minutes' drive from here. Or Xander told me there's an old-school bowling alley and arcade not too far away. Those games are always fun. Though maybe that's too nerdy?"

His enthusiasm reminds me of how he was during the session with those kids. When he opens up, he's really sweet. I giggle. "Liam, you know the kind of things I'm into. Nerd does not bother me. Even if your brand of nerd is techier than mine."

"OK. Noted. Ask Seb if he wants to come to the arcade, if you like. He likes games, right?"

"Do you mean that?"

"Sure. I like Seb." He rubs his chin, suddenly awkward. "I never thought someone like you would be interested in me."

A pause develops as I search for something to say. Drawing a blank, I fill the awkwardness with a kiss. And just like before, it feels great, better, even, because I'm comfortable with him now. I can't believe I've slipped into something this good so easily.

If only he didn't have such dangerous friends.

The light feeling inside me fades.

Late that night the doorbell rings. I freeze, listening to gravel crunch as someone runs down the drive. A few seconds later a car engine roars.

I know what I'm going to find even before I peep through the letter box: another blue anemone. I open the door and pick it up, inhaling the sickly sweetness I'm starting to hate.

This is a warning: *back off.*

So something did happen in the old wing. I'm right. But do I have the guts to carry on investigating?

I toss the flower on to the driveway and lock the door.

SEVENTEEN

The next few weeks are tense and emotional. The national press seize on the story of Esme's murder. It's a media dream, right down to the Witches' Pool. One of the tabloids is especially scathing, slamming the guys as bored rich kids who play dangerous sex games and do drugs, the dazzled local girls powerless to resist their charms. Reporters buzz around town, shouting questions when they see anyone who looks like a sixth former. The teachers warn us to say nothing. I've never seen Attlingham so alive. It feels like we're on one end of a microscope, with the rest of the country on the other.

The police investigation stalls. It doesn't appear their

inquiries at the hospital have thrown up any leads. They've questioned the rugby boys several times. The MIT had to back off because the parents have kicked up a fuss, with Xander's dad threatening to take legal action for harassment, but Liam's convinced it isn't over. I feel sorry for him. Xander and Blake are still seventeen, so the police can't question them without a parent present, but Liam's on his own.

We're all afraid, though we don't talk about it, and collective grief is heavy in the air. Girls who used to walk up to St Jules to get lifts with the boys start waiting for the bus. Parents leave work early to pick up their daughters. One girl transfers to another school. Each time I pass the cutesy illustrated sign welcoming me to Attlingham, claustrophobia tightens round me.

Even at home I don't feel completely safe. There haven't been more anemones, but somehow that makes me even more on edge, as though I'm simply waiting for the next threat. I double-check my bike every time I use it, and keep my keys in my hand as a weapon when I walk anywhere quiet, but it doesn't feel enough. After me bugging her, Mum has installed a doorbell camera, but that's not going to offer much protection if whoever's doing this really wants to hurt me...

Mrs Stannard asks Marley if she minds clearing out Esme's locker. It doesn't feel the kind of thing she should do alone so I join her. This isn't going straight home to study, which is what I promised Mum – thanks to moving mid-year, I'm playing what feels like endless catch-up in most of my subjects – but she'll understand. Back home I used to care about grades, but since Esme died, schoolwork feels pretty meaningless.

Marley and I get to work, making piles of things to be binned, recycled, or returned to Esme's parents.

"It's so sad, seeing her life reduced to these things." I sigh. "I can't see her parents wanting much of this. And yet the one thing they're desperate to have they can't find."

"What's that?"

"Esme's special necklace. You know, the fake antique one she was wearing at the party."

"Didn't the police find it by the pool?"

"Nope. Must have sunk into the mud."

I flick through a couple of notebooks, remembering the hours Esme spent writing about our made-up characters, and the thrill I got each time she finished a new chapter. She doesn't seem to have shared her stories with her Fairfield friends. It was still a big part of her, though. Her mum told me so last weekend.

"She was always scribbling away." Laura had sounded teary. I shifted on the sofa, feeling awkward. I'd visited often since Esme died, but I didn't like the haunted way Laura gazed at me today. Was she wishing I'd been in that pool, that she was the one comforting Mum? Watching her best friend's daughter sipping tea where Esme must once have sat, very much alive, must be impossibly tough.

I had escaped by asking if I could see Esme's room. When I got there I almost wished I'd stayed downstairs. Nothing had been touched since New Year's, or at least that's how it looked from the make-up spread across the dressing table and the dresses slung over the back of the chair. It felt like the room of a girl due home at any moment.

I drifted round looking at the bookshelves and the collection of china cats on the windowsill, but when I got to the desk I stopped. In a box at the side were a pile of notebooks. Notebooks I recognized.

The Tudor princess story.

I sucked in a breath. As I reached to pick one up there was a creak outside. Laura stood in the door frame, ghostlike and silent.

Quickly I put the notebook back. "Sorry. I didn't mean to snoop. It's just, I remember these, and—"

"I know. She told me." Laura came in. She took the box and held it out. Realizing what she meant, I shook my head.

"No. I can't—"

"Alana. I want you to take it. These are your memories, not mine. Please."

I couldn't really refuse, so the box came home with me. I'd flicked through a couple, but actually reading our story wasn't something I felt ready for yet. Not all of the notebooks were old, either – I could tell from the handwriting that several had been written in recently. *Another day*, I thought, and placed the box on top of my wardrobe.

"Lana?" Marley asks. I give myself a shake and turn my

attention back to the pile in front of me. The notebook on top is barely used. The front page is dated 14 December, titled *meeting.* Judging from the doodled hearts in the margin it must have been a boring one. On the opposite page are several games of hangman, one player with the small, round handwriting I recognize as Esme's, the other's jagged and slanting. The game at the bottom catches my eye.

The hangman says, *WHAT'S YOUR NUMBER*

Underneath, Esme's written, *That's not a proper hangman!*

Says who? And the other person has scribbled their number.

I stare at it. This is a boy, surely. Fourteenth of December was only a couple of weeks before she died.

Marley said Esme never had a boyfriend.

Maybe she was wrong.

I slip it into my bag.

At home I study the page more closely. This hangman could be totally irrelevant. I'm already pretty certain why Esme was killed. So what if some guy fancied her?

It is odd she didn't mention him to Marley, though.

Before I can overthink it, I tap the number into my phone and dial.

One ring.

Two.

Three.

After eight, it goes to voicemail. A boy's voice apologizes for not being able to take my call.

It's Xander.

Downstairs, I lean in the doorway to the sitting room. Seb is watching a wildlife documentary, sitting straight-backed and concentrating fully. To one side is his laptop, open on Wikipedia. I don't know how he can process so much information at once. My mind feels like a washing machine, churning round and round.

I shouldn't be shocked Xander was playing hangman with Esme. They did the charities committee together, which it turns out is a joint Fairfield–St Julian's club, much like the history society. Marley says Xander only bothers with it for the ego trip. Last year he had the idea of auctioning his mates off at a fundraiser for the local hospice. Surprise, surprise, Xander raised more than anyone else.

No, what shocks me is that Esme would see anything in him after what he did to her best friend, maybe other girls too. I thought she had better instincts. There's no way I can mention this to Marley. She'll explode. Esme's funeral is next Saturday. Thanks to the investigation, it feels like we've been waiting for ever. I don't want to ruin Marley's memories. Is this why Xander dodged handing in his proper phone? The police never found Esme's, so unless someone told them, or Xander admitted it, they wouldn't know there was a connection between them at all. So this is what he's hiding. I wonder why.

On the TV screen, a panther skulks through the trees. Trees. I frown. Trees. Wood. A wood. The woods at

Stillwater. Me, walking alongside it trying to call Esme. A faint answering ringtone. . .

Coming from the woods that lead to the Witches' Pool.

"Have you heard the saying about the needle and the haystack?" Seb was less than impressed when I asked if he could help search for Esme's phone. Now we're here he looks even less impressed.

"Yes, but this is a phone and a wood."

"A large wood."

"We might get lucky." I sweep my eyes along the dirt track Liam showed me. "I know it's around here because of where I was when it rang. According to Google, GPS tracking doesn't work properly in wooded areas. The MIT might not have searched this far up, especially if they assumed she used the path."

"I don't understand why you don't let the police do this. You do know this is their job?"

"I'll hand the phone over if we find it."

"After you look at the messages?"

I never lie to my brother so I don't deny it. We get to work. Whenever you see police dramas on TV they have special poles for searches. We've come with household equivalents: a broom and a rake. Seb brushes the dead leaves aside slowly and methodically, and I do the same.

Half an hour later, my optimism is fading. All we've found is litter. Seb's starting to grumble, but I'm reluctant to give up.

"It's pale blue," I say. "Should be easy to spot. Perhaps it's further in?"

"Is it likely she'd drop it? Wouldn't it have been in her bag?"

That's a good point. Esme's bag was found by the pool. Would she even have known about this short cut? Liam said not many people did.

"Perhaps I'm wrong," I mutter as I clamber further into the thicket, past where I discovered the cocktail glasses. I'm starting to get nervous about being seen. Xander isn't around – there's a match this afternoon – but a man barking down a phone passed by when we were chaining our bikes up. I'm pretty certain he's Xander's dad. Explaining what we're doing could be tricky.

"Found it," Seb says. I wheel round.

"Really?"

"Just joking."

"Not funny."

"Ally, it's not here. The phone could be anywhere. Sound travels weirdly sometimes. . ."

Baby blue flashes from beneath the leaves. I cry out and squat down.

"I've found it!"

"That joke was only funny once," says Seb, but he goes quiet when he sees what I have.

At home I wait impatiently for the phone to charge. Luckily it doesn't seem broken. I am not snooping, I tell myself, though I know that isn't true.

The tinny Samsung jingle sounds. Esme's lock screen pops up. *Crap.* I don't know her passcode.

Seb peers over my shoulder. "We can probably guess it," he says. "Most people choose something memorable."

I try Esme's birthday, then the year we were born. No luck. What else could it be? Seb holds out his hand. I pass the phone over and watch him tap away.

"Seb, I don't see how we're going to crack this. There's so much about Esme we don't know."

"And plenty we do." His eyebrows are knotted in concentration. "I'm trying various combinations, starting with obvious birthdays, like her parents', and then significant dates, like anniversaries."

I open my mouth to ask how on earth he remembers any of this, then close it. Seb's memory is a million times better than mine. It's easy to forget he once knew Esme well too. "I'll make you a cup of tea."

By the time I return, Seb's cracked it.

"You're brilliant," I grin. He shrugs.

"I am moderately brilliant, yes. It was Laura's birthday in reverse, 0730. So not that obscure." Seb pauses. "Are you sure this is a good idea?"

"No, but I'm doing it anyway."

"For someone so smart you make some really stupid decisions. I know what you're doing, Ally. At least, I think I do. Esme's killers need to be brought to justice, yes. But why do you have to be the one to do it?"

I glance down, thinking over the emotions I've felt since

coming to Suffolk. Fear. Revulsion. Sadness. Grief. Above all, anger. The quiet rage I never seem to be able to get away from, the rage that started when Dad broke the trust I'd taken for granted. "Someone has to."

"Yes, like the police." When I don't respond, Seb shuffles closer. "Ally... I'm worried about you. This laser focus on solving Esme's death, your crime wall... You're not acting like yourself."

"I'm fine, Seb."

"Are you?"

My grip on Esme's phone tightens. A clamp-like feeling is spreading across my chest. Suddenly there's not enough air, and I'm hot all over. Panic rises in my gut. I don't have time to fall apart! Maybe I'm not OK. Maybe I'm even being self-destructive. But whatever I've gone through can be dealt with later. Once I've stopped these monsters.

"I have to carry on," I whisper. "This isn't just about Esme. It needs to stop."

Seb sighs. "Please don't get hurt, Ally."

A lump forms in my throat. I don't move for quite some time after Seb leaves. Then I brush my eyes dry and tap the WhatsApp icon on Esme's phone. Straight away I see a conversation with Xander.

But the last message isn't what I was expecting.

Need to talk important come witch pool now

Esme sent it at 00.16 on the night she died.

EIGHTEEN

Slowly, my brain processes what this message means.

Esme was alive at sixteen minutes past midnight.

Esme wanted Xander to come to the pool. Why? Was she with the killer? Or did he arrive later?

Let's assume Xander saw the message immediately. In theory, he could have reached the pool in five minutes . . . which puts him at the scene of the drowning exactly as it was happening.

Suspicious as hell. And yet I'm confused. Why would Esme go there, then message him? It doesn't fit.

Hoping to find an answer, I scroll to the start of Esme and Xander's conversation. The early messages are fun and friendly, and make me feel a little sick. They chat a lot about the charities committee, with Esme sharing links to animal welfare groups she wants to fundraise for. Maybe I'm wrong about Xander doing it as an ego trip. A couple of days in, the chat turns flirty.

Xander: Good morning, Miss Morgan
So are you posting millions of pictures of a random kitten or am I to assume it's yours?

Esme: Diana is my early Christmas present!
Utterly gorgeous, I'm in love 🖤

Xander: I'm more of a dog person
She's cute though
Takes after you 😉

Esme: I look like a cat?
That's a very weird compliment 😛

Xander: Now you're fishing
If you want a better compliment come out with me tomorrow
I'm sure I can think of one
Hello?
You've gone very quiet...

Esme: Still here
Sorry, shocked

Xander: Well I did ask for your number...

Esme: I thought we were just chatting

Xander: Is there a no incoming?

Esme: Not exactly
I do want to say yes
I mean I'm flattered
But it wouldn't be very loyal to Marley
And I heard the rumour about you and that teacher

Xander: FFS
I'll call you

The conversation picks up later. Whatever Xander said, he must have been persuasive. It's pretty clear the date happened. I'm guessing they agreed to keep it secret to avoid upsetting Marley. Then, after Christmas, things change:

Esme: Hey. How are you? No hard feelings about what I said?

Xander: It's fine

Esme: You're not annoyed?

Xander: No

Esme: See you NYE then
I'll introduce you to the friend I mentioned
I think she'll like you

That's *me*. If Esme thought I'd be interested in Xander, she couldn't be more wrong! She must have ended things. Is that why Xander pretended he didn't really know her? I wonder how he felt about being dumped, again. His replies are kind of noncommittal.

I reread everything and pause on "the rumour about you and that teacher". I'd forgotten the whispering about Thea Keats being involved with a sixth former. Wasn't she living in a cottage on the Stillwater Estate? Xander must have bumped into her outside school all the time.

Eww, just eww. Even if my dad wasn't a teacher this would gross me out. Thea was young and pretty. Could there be something in this after all – and, more importantly, a connection between her death and Esme's?

All along I've been so sure that Esme was killed because she knew about the date rape drugs, but if Xander is the killer, his motive could be a lot more personal. Perhaps he wasn't happy about Esme ending things. If he really had something going with Thea the same could have happened with her.

Ugh, I don't know. Loads of people have said Thea's death was definitely a suicide. I've no real reason to suspect it wasn't. Yet I can't shake off the feeling that maybe I've been looking at Esme's murder all wrong.

There's nothing else that strikes me as strange. Looking through quickly gets upsetting, especially the photos. These are the last days of Esme's life. And she had no idea.

I'm about to put the phone down when I remember I haven't looked at her call log. Not to my surprise, pretty much everything is either to or from her parents and Marley. Then something jumps out at me. Six calls to an unknown landline, lasting less than thirty seconds. All in early November.

Immediately after Halloween.

This can't be a coincidence. I stare at the eleven digits. Then I copy them into my own phone, and tap call.

A pre-recorded message comes down the line. "This is the Suffolk Rape Crisis Helpline. . ."

I glaze over as the voice on the other end says something about opening hours and where to find advice.

So I'm right. The boys did rape someone at Halloween.

Was it Esme?

It's after eleven by the time I climb into bed and switch off my bedside lamp. I feel numb. Esme. Rape. Halloween. The words churn round. I don't want it to have been her, but how can it not have been? Liam said Esme was upset when he drove her home from the party. She was reluctant to go out at New Year's. Why else would she phone the helpline? I picture Esme working up the courage to reach out, then bottling it each time the advisor picked up, and my stomach twists.

And yet . . . if it was Esme, why did Ozzie mention Halloween right in front of her? Everyone says he isn't very bright, but surely he wouldn't be that stupid? And Henry barely reacted. Does that mean Esme *isn't* Halloween Girl? Then who is? How come Esme knew what happened?

A ringtone shrills through the darkness. Mine. I jolt upright. No one calls this late with good news. The screen shows an unknown caller. For a second I think it's the Rape Crisis Helpline ringing me back, but it's a mobile number. Could something have happened to Dad?

I pick up. "Hello?"

Over the other end of the line, I can hear the beat of music. Then Xander's voice says, "Evening, Alana."

NINETEEN

I almost drop the phone. "Why are you calling me?"

"You called me. I'm being polite and ringing back."

I'm about to say *how did you know that was me*, but he must have lifted my number from the health club database. In a flash, I realize not hiding my caller ID earlier was really stupid.

I let out a long breath, then draw another, telling myself to keep my voice even, and not let on he's spooked me. "At almost midnight? I might have been asleep."

"I've been busy." Hearing Xander's voice in my ear is disconcertingly intimate in the darkness. He sounds a lot posher over the phone. I fumble for the switch to my lamp. "So why did you ring me?"

"Nothing important."

There's a pause. A wild thought crosses my mind: he's disappointed. Then Xander says, "Well, right now, I fancy company. Watching YouTube videos by myself is no way to spend a Saturday night."

"Call someone else. I don't want to speak to you."

"Hang up, then."

I should do just that. So why don't I? My heart starts to beat faster. I remember his hand brushing my leg in the hot tub, and the heat that rushed through me. He hasn't said anything about me and Seb being at Stillwater earlier. We must have got away unseen.

Why is Xander at home, anyway? The rest of the team are out celebrating their win, or at least they were half an hour ago when Liam last messaged. Xander doesn't strike me as someone who'd leave a party early.

"Look at your WhatsApp," he says. "I've sent you something."

I lower my phone and stare at the blurred image, not sure if I want to tap download or not. I know the pictures boys send to girls, and the kind they expect in return. He played this game with Marley. There's no way I'm walking into the same trap.

"Is this something gross?"

"It's totally innocent, I promise."

I click on the image. It turns out to be a selfie of Xander, hair ruffled and wearing what I assume is a pyjama top, next to the most ludicrously fluffy dog imaginable.

"What the hell is that?" I demand before I can stop myself.

"My mother's pedigree Samoyed, Bella, and she's very sensitive, so I'll pretend you didn't call her a 'that'. We're hanging out."

I don't know how he expects me to react. Is he actually trying to use his mum's admittedly adorable dog to pull? Why is he going after me? I've made it pretty clear I'm not interested.

"Your turn," says Xander.

"What do you mean?"

"You have a cat, don't you? Take a selfie with it."

How does he know about Bruce? "No," I say, coming to my senses. "Whatever you're trying on, I'm not interested. You know I'm dating Liam. If you're really desperate to know what my cat looks like, google 'black moggy'. I'm hanging up."

"I knew I should have sent a photo of the ancestral sword rather than the dog," Xander sighs. "How about you interrogate me again instead? Promise I'll be honest."

He's got me now, and he knows it. My finger hovers on the red disconnect button, then falls. Xander would be a hell of a lot less cocky if he knew I have Esme's phone. I'd love to wipe that smug smile right off his face, but I'm not about to make another dangerous mistake.

No, I need to play smarter. "Why didn't you want me to go in the old wing the other day?"

"That again? Yawn. Ask something else."

"You don't get to choose the questions. Answer."

"It's falling apart." Xander sounds bored. Exaggeratedly bored. "There is quite genuinely nothing there. Next."

"Were you in on the plan to rape me?"

The music in the background stops. "Is that a serious question? If so, I'm insulted."

"Why? Looking good doesn't mean you wouldn't do something like that."

"You think I look good? I thought so."

"Don't change the subject! I know there were three boys. You're friendly with Henry and Ozzie. Why shouldn't it have been you?"

There's a pause. Is he shocked? Upset? Working out how to play this? "I really am insulted now, thank you very much. The answer is because it wasn't. We don't all think with the same brain, you know."

"Is that why you're home by yourself? I thought you were Mr Popular."

Xander goes silent again. I'm about to ask if he's still there when he says, "My parents had a dinner party and wanted me to help host. Can't have the honourable Featherstones pouring their own Châteauneuf-du-Pape, oh no."

Have I hit a nerve? He sounds kind of bitter. "Could've said no."

"I prefer not to piss my parents off. Especially at the moment." Xander's tone is defensive now. "They're getting fed up with being dragged to the police station. I'm surprised you've not demanded to know if I drugged and killed Esme too. Seems like your style."

"Your parents seriously asked that?" I'm so startled I forget who I'm talking to. "Mine would never believe for a second I'd do anything that bad, even Mum, and she's pretty critical."

"Yes, well, your mother isn't my dad. When you come from a family like mine, expectations are sky high. And I'm not angelic Cambridge-bound Barney Featherstone, whose achievements I've been hearing about all bloody evening." A pause. "So how is your mum critical of you?"

"Is this some kind of trick question?"

"Why do people always think I'm messing about? I asked because I was interested, actually. But interrogate me instead if that's what you prefer. I'm sure you've a long list of questions about all the things I've supposedly done. Bring up the rumour about Miss Keats too while you're at it. I haven't heard that one in a while. Answer, no, I bloody wasn't banging her, and I've had enough of people thinking I was. As for—"

"Why do girls dump you, Xander?"

There's a pause. Then he hangs up. I'm convinced he's going to ring back with some smart answer but he doesn't. Rather thrown, I lower my phone. I was pretty abrupt with that last question, more so than I intended, but I'm not sure that's what really got under his skin. Maybe being questioned by the police has knocked his confidence more than he lets on.

I still don't understand why Xander called me tonight. He wheels out the flirty chat and baits me with things like the sword he knows I'd love to see, but I can't believe he really likes me. Not as anything more than fresh meat, anyway.

He's obviously had a crap evening. I'm pretty sure the interrogation thing was an excuse to keep me talking. Is it possible Xander rang because he was *lonely*?

Who knows? And who cares? I'm not about to start feeling sorry for the creep. Tomorrow, the police will have Esme's phone. If he's a killer and a rapist, they'll find out pretty quickly.

On Monday the news flies round: Xander Lockwood is at the police station being questioned. By lunchtime the message Esme sent is common knowledge. I listen to excitable chatter, feeling numb. Handing the phone in was awful. The detective I spoke to didn't buy my story of "happening to find it" and made me feel like a speck of dirt for looking through everything first. I told them about the glasses I found too. No doubt the MIT will be searching the woods for further clues today.

Liam and I are meeting for a Coke in The Hideout after school today. The last time we were here we agreed to be "official". I still can't get over how nice-weird it is to call him my boyfriend. To my surprise, he's standing by his car in one of the town square parking spaces talking to Henry rather than waiting inside. Instinctively I duck behind an old phone box, close enough to overhear their conversation.

"I can't believe he did such a stupid thing." Liam sounds wound up.

"I can." Henry has his hands in his pockets, smiling. "Xander thinks he's smart and he isn't. Shame a new brain is the one thing Mummy and Daddy can't buy him."

"Don't be a jerk. Not everyone gets straight As."

"What I can't believe is he dated Esme Morgan! Must have been desperate. No wonder he kept it secret. She was a five out of ten tops. Maybe six with really heavy make-up. Ooh, are you gearing up to hit me again?"

For a moment I think Liam's going to do just that. Instead he looks away. Henry's smile widens.

"Well, you were right that giving the police his old phone was stupid," he says. "Like he'd be seen dead with that piece of crap! Where did they find Esme's, anyway? I thought they'd stopped poking around at Stillwater."

"They didn't find it. Xander thinks someone went snooping."

"I bet he's furious! Wish I'd been there. Has he actually been arrested?"

"His dad hired a hot-shot lawyer so I guess it's serious."

"Doesn't look great, does it? People commit murders for worse reasons than being dumped. Anyway, his problem. Speaking of phones," – Henry pushes his glasses up the bridge of his nose, manner becoming businesslike – "are you sure yours is clean?"

"Yeah, it's fine. I told you."

"Hmmm. Well, even if you're lying, I won't be the one getting it in the neck."

Liam mutters something. Henry's expression sharpens.

"What did you say?"

"Nothing."

"It sounded like, 'Yeah, because you never get your hands dirty.'"

Liam scuffs his foot on the ground, staying silent. Henry shoots him a look of contempt.

"Look, Taylor, I got you what you wanted. And you got me what I wanted. We're friends really. Remember that." He pauses. "How's it going with your crazy girlfriend? Got past first base yet?"

Liam sticks two fingers up at him. Henry's actually grinning as he saunters off.

"I saw you with Henry," I say as I kiss Liam hello. "What did he say to annoy you?"

"Nothing. Just something about the next match."

Liam swiftly changes the subject to what we'll do next week at half-term, and I tune out. My boyfriend just lied to me. He's afraid of Henry, that's for sure. Why? And what the hell was that about them getting each other what they wanted?

After our Cokes Liam drops me home. Before we say goodbye I ask again how Esme seemed when he drove her home from the Halloween party. His answer is the same: drunk and tearful. When I push it, Liam rolls his eyes.

"Alana! Nothing bad happened to Esme on Halloween OK? So stop asking."

"Sorry. I'm just sure there's something I've missed. Marley says the same as you, but—"

"But nothing!" he snaps, and I flinch. There's a silence. Then Liam draws a deep breath.

"Sorry, OK? I didn't mean to lose my cool. I had a bad day."

No, you're rattled because of Henry. I have to bite my lip to stop myself from calling him out. All it will do is cause friction – despite acknowledging that his friends can be jerks, Liam clearly values being part of the team more than I first realized. He says rugby's the only time he can switch off, and that when he's with the guys he forgets himself.

I press my hand to my forehead, suddenly exhausted. "See you."

Liam catches my arm. "Have you decided where to go on Thursday? It's your turn to choose."

Liam and I have fallen into a sort-of routine of spending our half-days together. Last week we wound up at a practically deserted robotics showcase an hour away at the University of Essex. Technically, it was a crap date – Liam kept apologizing, saying he'd heard it was better – but the whole thing was so surreal it somehow became fun, especially afterwards when we found a surprisingly good campus noodle bar for dinner. That whole afternoon, Attlingham felt very distant indeed.

But it won't this Thursday. How can it, if Liam won't

be fully open with me? Do I know him as well as I think? And can I overlook who his friends are, if we're going to work out?

It's depressing and hurtful. And I thought what we had was so good.

I mumble goodbye and go inside. I can't concentrate on homework or finishing my witch trials book, so I mooch around online instead, but there's nothing new on my favourite blogs and all Marley talks about when I message is a sponsor she's hoping will endorse her channel. They're a huge celebrity-backed online retailer. It's exciting, and I'm pleased for her, but a couple of weeks ago she'd have been sharing this news with Esme. Marley doesn't talk much about her feelings, but I can tell she's not as OK as she seems. I hate the feeling that I've effectively replaced Esme.

Sadness creeps over me. Will my memories of Esme have a shadow hanging over them for ever? She wasn't a sad or tragic person and I hate that death has turned her into one. If only I could figure out her connection to Halloween!

Think, Alana. *This is Esme. She hasn't become a totally different person the last three years. Something terrible happened. What would the Esme you knew do?*

What she always did when something bothered her, my mind whispers, and I sit up sharply. Of course. She'd write it down. And I have a stack of her notebooks just metres away.

I pull the box from my wardrobe and tip everything on to my bed, sorting the old from the new and quickly flicking through. Esme will have had other notebooks – God, I lost count of the hours I spent with her wandering around Paperchase – but there are quite a lot here, which makes me think—

And then I find it. A page of bullet points, with a number I recognize as the Rape Crisis Helpline's at the top. It's a prompt sheet, to help Esme make the phone call.

- *Girl at school raped (no names, stay anonymous)*
- *Halloween Party*
- *3 boys*
- *Girl doesn't know who boys were*
- *Thinks she was drunk, I'm scared she was drugged*
- *Girl doesn't want to report it*
- *What should I do? How can I help? Should I tell police?*

And, at the bottom, crossed out:

- *I know this cos I was there. I was drunk and locked myself in an en-suite to throw up and when they came into the bedroom I was too scared to stop them in case they did it to me too. Does this make me a bad person?*

TWENTY

So Esme was a witness. I read her notes again, piecing together all the clues that now make sense.

I feel torn. On one hand, I'm angry at Esme for doing nothing. Rape is evil. Girls need to look out for each other. I get that she was scared, and drunk, and vulnerable, but even if she'd made a noise the boys might have stopped and run before she could see them. . .

But then maybe they wouldn't. Perhaps they'd have decided two girls were twice the fun.

I sigh, and let go of some of my anger. None of us know how brave we are until we have to be. Would I have done the same? And why the hell am I blaming Esme? She's not the bad guy here.

No, the only people I blame are these sick boys.

And I know what to do next.

It's Friday afternoon and I'm at Stillwater with the history society. With less than a month to go we need to firm up arrangements for the fair. If there's no rain it should be really good – I've booked jousters, falconry and archers, all people I've seen perform at fairs before, and we've loads of space in the gardens and two adjacent fields. There have been a few grumbles about me using my connections rather than people from previous fairs, but Ursula – and, to be fair, Blake – have shut them down.

I'm a little sad because Mum and Seb can't make it. The fair clashes with Seb's favourite weekend of the year, that of a big cat event in Birmingham. He's been going since he was ten and always returns loaded with toys and games for Bruce to ignore. Travelling isn't something Seb is normally keen on so Mum makes it into a big deal, going up the night before and staying over. I enjoy it too, especially the first evening, where we pick up tacos from a tiny Mexican place and eat them by the river. This year, it feels especially important to keep the tradition going. I would have missed the fair, but Seb surprised me by insisting I stay.

"You should do your thing, not mine," he said last night while we were washing up. "I'll be fine with Mum. We might meet up with Florence."

"Who's Florence?"

"A girl in my class. Her family breed British Blues. That's where Esme got her kitten from. And she likes gaming."

It sounded like my brother had actually made a friend – something that never happened in our old school. Unable to help myself, I hugged him, my wet hands making soapy prints on his jumper.

Someone calls my name. I snap out of the memory and go over to where Blake is talking those of us in costumes through our roles. He's decided I'm to have a couple of ladies-in-waiting and has roped in Faith and Marley. Marley will also be doing everyone's make-up and filming snatches of the day. I still don't trust Blake, but when he can be bothered he is pretty good at organizing stuff.

Behind us, Ursula walks round with Xander plotting where to position stalls, food stands and entertainment. He looks downcast, and for once doesn't seem to have much to say. Liam told me that the lawyers got Xander off the hook for now, but he's still the MIT's number one person of interest. He's mine too. The thing that bugs me is that message. Esme asked *him* to the pool. Not the other way round. Whichever way I look, it doesn't fit.

My mind is only half on channelling Elizabeth I. When Blake decides to rehearse a mock-sword fight between the guys playing knights, I creep away. They'll be ages. No one will miss me. I hurry to the old wing. No one's around. I slip through the door Liam showed me.

The hallway is gloomy, and the thick dust makes me sneeze. Hoping any rotting floorboards will be obvious, I step past the crates to the stairs.

This is a long shot, I know that. Halloween was over three months ago. But Liam did say he thought nothing had been touched since. I climb the stairs, testing each step before moving on to the next. Everything feels stable so far. Starting to feel more confident, I reach the top. It's even fustier up here, the narrow windows letting in little of the overcast daylight, and far less grand than I imagined.

It's very quickly clear that there's only one usable bedroom. The floorboards outside wobble so I step inside, closing the door. Inside it's murky, floor-length diamond-print curtains letting in the tiniest crack of light. Parts of the wallpaper peel, and the four-poster bed is a right mess, duvet heaped on the mattress and pillows on the floor.

A tingle goes up my spine.

As I tiptoe forward something behind me creaks. I freeze, barely breathing.

Seconds pass.

Nothing.

Safe, I think, and my shoulders sag.

I scoot round, opening the wardrobe and squatting to peek under the dressing table, all the time trying not to sneeze. Beneath the bed are three dusty bottles of beer and a couple of red feathers, the kind that might come from a feather boa.

A Halloween costume – probably the girl's. I bet I could

find a match on social media. And if the bottles belong to the boys. . . My chest swells. That means DNA. Identities. On hard surfaces like glass, prints last a long time. The police told me that when I handed Esme's phone in – they had to take my fingerprints so they could eliminate them. Presumably they swabbed the cocktail glasses in the woods too. I wonder if they found anything.

Trying not to get too excited, I photograph the bottles on my phone, then, pulling my sleeve over my hand, drop them along with the feathers into my backpack. At the back of the room is the en-suite. I picture Esme clutching the dated avocado-coloured toilet bowl, sweating, disoriented and terrified, trying to block out the sounds from the bedroom. Did she stumble out when the boys left, returning to the party as though they'd simply popped out for a cigarette? Did she find the girl sobbing on the bed, and try to comfort her? I hope Esme wasn't the only person Halloween Girl told and that she has other friends to support her.

Ugh. Time to get the hell out. I move towards the door – then stop, staring at the bed. There's something underneath the duvet. Something human sized. Is that *hair* draped over the pillow?

My throat constricts. The duvet isn't moving. But that's definitely the top of a head. Dark brown hair, like mine.

I count to five, then whip the duvet back. And I scream. Facing me is a scarecrow dressed in a Fairfield uniform, the wig on its head tied back like mine often is. Its crude, smiling face leers at me. Blue petals are strewn everywhere.

I scramble, almost falling over myself. My back bumps up against something. I whirl round, but it's only the wardrobe.

No one's here. *But they knew I was coming.* I rush to the door. Then I hear a thud from the corridor.

Seconds tick as I remain motionless, breath rasping and blood pounding in my ears. Again, there's silence. This is an old house, I tell myself. The noise could have come from anywhere. Even outside. If I don't get moving, I'll be missed. I step forward – and the ground gives way, plunging me into blackness.

When I come to I'm lying on something hard. Every muscle feels stretched like elastic. Blurry faces swim around me. One leans close. A voice says, "Alana? Talk to me. What hurts?"

"Everything," I croak.

"I'm going to ask you to move your limbs, one at a time. If anything hurts badly, stop."

Liam. There are other voices, I can't place whose. Liam asks me to move my left arm, then my hand. They feel stiff, but not too painful. I do my right, then my legs.

"Nothing seems broken." Liam reaches in his pocket. His key ring – a slim metal thing I'd assumed was a pen – turns out to be a torch. He shines it first in one eye, then the other. Then he asks, "How many fingers am I holding up?"

I squint. "Um, four?"

"How many now?"

"Three?"

"We need to get you to hospital." He takes my hand. Someone else helps me into a sitting position. I can't see clearly, and for the first time, it occurs to me to feel frightened. "What happened?"

"Don't you remember?"

Even thinking is a strain. "No."

"You're in the old wing at Stillwater. You fell through the floorboards. I think you're concussed. Do you think you can stand?"

With Liam's help, I make it to my feet. Then my legs buckle and everything wobbles. What happens next is fuzzy – there are snatches of darkness, then sky, and suddenly I'm in a car, though it definitely isn't Liam's, because whoever's behind the wheel can actually change gears smoothly, and he's next to me in the back seat. It's only when I'm sitting on the hard A & E chairs that I ask what happened again.

"I don't know." Liam has his arms around me. "The others heard a crash and found you unconscious in the rubble."

"Oh." I frown. "How come you were around? You weren't part of the rehearsal."

"I was in the gym. Blake came and got me. Why did you go upstairs?"

"I don't know. Something to do with avocados."

"Avocados? You're *definitely* concussed."

"There was an avocado—"

Toilet. Everything comes flooding back. The scarecrow. Esme as witness. Feathers. Bottles. Evidence. Wildly, I look around. "Where's my backpack? You did bring it, didn't you?"

"I didn't think to."

"I need it!"

"Alana, calm down. We'll find your bag, OK? It's probably still in the house. I'll message Xander. He can fetch it."

"That's no good! He'll go through it, or the others will, and everything will be gone. They knew I was coming! On the bed, there was a scarecrow, made to look like me, petals – they want to scare me into thinking I'm next!"

"I don't understand how it happened," I say at home as Mum hands me a glass of water. "When I went into the room, the floorboards were OK. When I left, they weren't."

"From what Liam said, you shouldn't have even been there." Mum's tight voice tells me she's struggling to keep calm. "What possessed you to do something so reckless? Honestly, Alana! I know you've been through a lot, and you're grieving, but I thought you were holding everything together. Didn't you think?"

I avoid meeting her eyes. "Has anyone brought my bag home yet?"

"The blonde boy who loves himself dropped it off," says Seb.

Xander. Brilliant. Seb brings my bag over. One glance inside confirms what I feared: the bottles and feathers are gone. Tears cluster in the corners of my eyes. Mum watches, frowning. When she speaks, her voice is gentler.

"Liam tells me you were saying all sorts of weird things in the hospital. What's going on, Alana? Are you scared about what happened to Esme, or is it something else? This isn't like you. Are you OK?"

In the corner of my eye, I catch Seb looking at me significantly. He hasn't told Mum about my bike accident or searching for Esme's phone, exactly as promised. My heart swells with love for my brother and his loyalty.

"I can't think now," I mumble. "I want to sleep."

"Sure?"

The word lingers in the air. I imagine telling Mum everything – including that I've involved Seb. Oh God. She'll be scathing. Furious, even. I've made what she'll see as wrong call after wrong call. I'll try to get her to understand, but fail, because that's how it always is with Mum. Totally different wavelengths.

Could Mum getting involved actually make things worse? If she doesn't dismiss me – and, let's face it, she might, because the scarecrow sounds totally unbelievable, and no doubt it'll be gone by now – all she'll do is go straight to the police, even though I have zero evidence.

And maybe then it won't only be me the boys target next

time. Up until now that hadn't occurred to me. I can't risk putting my family in danger, I just can't. Especially Seb. He's never fitted in anywhere before and I'd rather fall through the floorboards again than take that from him. For a second I wonder about confiding in Liam or Marley. I'd only put them in a difficult, even dangerous, position.

My concussed head can't take this any more. But I'm sure now. It's better – and safer – I do this alone.

The next morning I feel hella bad, as Liam would put it, but my brain's a lot sharper. I'm sure of one thing: while I was in that bedroom, someone sabotaged the floorboards. Didn't I think I heard footsteps? The boys must have been expecting me to go there ever since I asked Liam to show me the old wing. Xander saw us. He must have told the others. The petals in the bed were wilted, so the scarecrow was left a while ago.

There's no point trying to figure out exactly who did this. All the rugby team were at Stillwater, in either the gym or the rehearsal. None of them will grass their mates up if I ask who sneaked off. I could have died. Perhaps for the first time, what I'm dealing with feels frighteningly real. I'm trying to track down three rapists and a murderer.

And he's prepared to kill again.

Mum isn't convinced I'm well enough to attend Esme's funeral but doesn't stop me going. The church is already rammed when we arrive. It looks like the entire Fairfield sixth form is here, as well as quite a few St Jules boys. That means Esme's killer is too. Anger swells in my chest. Everywhere I can see flowers. And right at the front is a bouquet of blue anemones. It's a struggle not to hurl them across the church.

Pinned on a board by the door are photographs of Esme's life. I make myself stop and look, even though it's almost unbearable. Esme was so different with her natural hair colour. She hated the bad dye job Marley did. And now she's going to be buried with it.

"Alana!" To my surprise, Calvin comes over. "How are you feeling?"

Have I ever spoken to Calvin without Ursula being there? I'm not sure I have. If anything, I thought he disliked me. He always seems nervous whenever we do talk. That would be suspicious if he hadn't been in Ursula's video. "OK, I guess."

"Good." He gives me a half-smile. "You seemed so out of it in the car. Liam was really worried. So was I, if I'm honest. I would've stayed in A & E, but Liam said he had it covered."

My confusion clears. So it was Calvin who drove me and Liam to hospital. To my relief, he heads off with a "Take it easy, OK?" It's good to know at least one of the rugby team is a nice guy.

I feel mortified when Xander's parents come to ask how I am. Neither make a fuss – this is a funeral, after all – but his dad mutters something about not letting Xander have friends over if they can't behave. Even though that's more a criticism of Xander than me, I feel like the stupidest person ever. What if they press Mum to pay for the damage I caused?

Music starts to play. Everyone turns to watch as the coffin is carried in. It's snowdrop-white, engraved with delicate flowers and cats. I feel something stick in my throat. Sixteen. My age. All those things Esme will never get a chance to do. Not just boring stuff like exams and jobs, but things she'd have been looking forward to. Writing stories. Campaigning properly for animal welfare. Falling in love.

All around, people are sniffing. As the service progresses, the sniffs turn to sobs. By the time Laura and Doug get up, I'm crying too. Both look years older and struggle to speak. Neither of them mentions how Esme died. Instead, she is *taken too soon*, *her life cruelly ended*. Perhaps *murdered* is too chilling a word.

Afterwards Marley comes to the front. She unfolds a piece of paper, and spends a moment composing herself. Then, voice strong, she says, "I remember when I first met her. She was quiet and meek, and never challenged anybody. How that changed." She flashes a sad smile. "Anyone who knew Esme will know how vocal she was, whether it was over animal abuse or whether cakes with vegetables in are really cakes at all. She was a sweet, good-hearted person and a true friend. I wholeheartedly believe she'd have gone on to have a bright future, whether she was writing, or shaking things up with one of the charities she cared about. I'll miss her so much."

After the service, people mill around chatting before heading on to the wake. The flowers remain where they are, clogging the air with sickly sweetness. Something suddenly occurs to me and I frown. Those anemones. Whoever's behind this has to get hold of them from somewhere – and that somewhere is probably the florist in Attlingham. Is it possible whoever runs the shop remembers who ordered them?

It's worth checking. If I'm smart, I can do it safely enough.

"Your speech was good," I say when Marley comes over.

"Thanks, Lana. Are you doing anything for the rest of the day, or are you feeling too dodgy? The rest of us were thinking of going shopping."

I stare at her. "You're not serious. Shopping?"

"We've got to do something." Marley sounds defensive. "I'm desperately sad, you know I am, but Esme would've hated all the speeches and tears. We'll stop in on the wake, but I'd rather visit places we had fun and remember her that way. You know – celebrate her life, instead of dwelling on her death."

I shake my head, and Marley goes to join the rest of her gang. If Esme had been hit by a car, or killed in an accident, celebrating her life might make sense. Murder is different. There's no forgetting murder, no moving on, not until it's solved. Laura and Doug lost their only child. I know people grieve in different ways, but can't Marley and the others see that? Or am I just angrier than other people?

The wake is in Attlingham Village Hall and is just as unbearable as I expected. When the crowds start to thin, Liam, Seb and I go for a walk around the nature reserve by the castle and Attlingham Mere. It's been dry for a few days so it doesn't matter that we're wearing the wrong shoes. Out in the fresh air, I start to feel more human. When we first arrived in Suffolk – God, that feels like a lifetime ago – I didn't know that a mere was a large, shallow lake. The Witches' Pool, swimming at Stillwater, the almost constant rain, now this – it feels like water's following me wherever I go. Overlooking us from the hill is St Julian's. The rugby goals glint in the sun. I remember something Liam said once: this town gets claustrophobic. I'm starting to understand what he meant.

None of us talk much apart from Seb, who not for the first time is fretting about whether Esme's parents are looking after her kitten properly. As time passes, I start to wonder if there's something else wrong with Liam. He seems closed off. "Does anyone like funerals?" he growls when I ask if he's OK, and I decide to leave it. When I suggest we go home and see what's on Netflix, I'm expecting Liam to refuse, but he nods.

Probably doesn't want to go back to his grandma's, I think, leaning back in the passenger seat as we turn on to the winding, narrow lane that leads to my village. Liam's grandma, who I met briefly earlier, has a busy social life heading up various local committees, so he spends a lot of time by himself. I'm a little hurt he's never invited me over. He's seen my house in its messy, disorganized glory, so if he's scared I'll judge, he's wrong. It seems pretty odd to have never been inside my boyfriend's house a month after we started dating. Sometimes I wonder—

Then my body lurches forward, belt snapping tight over my chest as the car veers off the road.

TWENTY-ONE

A horn blazes. Something crunches. Light dazzles me. I must close my eyes because when I open them again, we're stationary. It takes a second for me to realize the car hasn't actually crashed, we're just at the side of the road, tight against a hedge. Beside me Liam clutches the steering wheel, his breathing ragged. Neither he nor Seb appears to be hurt. Seb leans between our seats, eyes big.

"How did you not see that car's headlights?" he exclaims. "It was clearly coming round the corner—"

"Obviously not to me!" Liam shouts. He slams his hand against the steering wheel, then undoes his seat belt and jumps out. Seb and I trade a scared look as he walks round the car, swearing loudly.

"We didn't hit anything, did we?" I whisper.

"No, but it was close."

I try to open my door, but the hedge is in the way. Liam gets back into the driver's seat, face pale.

"I don't think the car's seriously damaged, but it's gonna need a garage," he says. "Mom will kill me! I already wrote off one car. I'm just so angry I didn't. . . Why do I screw everything up? Even a fucking simple thing like this?"

He hits the steering wheel again. This time his hand smacks the horn, and we all jump. The sound seems to snap Liam out of his anger. He looks at me properly, a worried crease between his eyebrows.

"I am really, really sorry. I wasn't concentrating. It's totally my fault. Are you guys OK?"

I put my hand on his arm. "We're fine. Are you OK?"

Liam turns his key in the ignition, not answering. It takes ages for him to reverse back into the road. His hands are shaking badly. I notice his nails are the worst they've ever been. I really don't think he should be driving at all, but it's only two minutes to my house and Liam takes it slowly.

Inside, I make us hot drinks. Granules spill over the side of the cup as I spoon the coffee in. For the first time I realize I'm shaking too. When I carry the cups in, Liam's sitting right on the edge of the sofa, ignoring Bruce who is rubbing against his legs.

"I should go."

"At least calm down first." I hold out a cup. "You made a mistake. It was easily done, especially today. . ."

I ignore Seb mouthing, "No, it wasn't," relieved that he has the tact not to say it out loud. Liam takes the coffee but doesn't say anything. The atmosphere is so strained that I turn Netflix on and pick a film at random. We stare at the screen, though I'm pretty certain none of us are really watching.

Fifteen minutes in, Liam gets up.

"I think I can drive home now."

I pause the film. "You don't have to go."

"I want to. Sorry. I can't do this today." He starts to walk out, then stops. "Is that your dad?"

He's looking at a photo of me, Dad and Seb taken in Malta – the last family holiday we'll ever have. I hung it a couple of days ago, convinced Mum would remove it, but she doesn't seem to have noticed.

I nod. Liam looks at the picture for an embarrassingly long time, then walks out. I follow him to the door.

"Liam, what's really wrong? Is it Esme, the car or something else? You're scaring me a little."

Liam mutters sorry and leaves. I watch him turn on to the road, almost scraping our wall. Then I go back into the sitting room.

"Seb, can you not mention this to Mum, please? She'll never let me go anywhere with Liam again if she finds out he's written a car off."

"If you want." Seb unmutes the TV. "The accident was totally avoidable though."

And that's what's worrying me.

Please tell me when you get home, I message Liam. Hours pass without a reply, though two blue ticks tell me he's seen it. I can't concentrate on the film, and the pizza I shove in the oven tastes like cardboard. Putting his friends aside, up until now Liam's mostly been someone I've been able to rely upon: kind, good at listening, never pushy. Sure, he has his insecurities, issues, even, but I figured I shouldn't ask about those and that he'd open up when he was ready. Maybe that was the wrong approach.

Or maybe I'm out of my depth.

Mum arrives home at around eight, clearly exhausted. Shortly after she goes upstairs to change, the bell shrills.

On the doorstep is Marley.

"Hey, Lana." She sounds slightly breathless. "I won't come in, our parents want us to eat with them and we're way late, but I bought you this. Hope you like it."

She thrusts out a carrier bag and blows a kiss as she hurries back to the car waiting for her. A little dazed, I close the door. Inside the bag is a small box wrapped in tissue paper, and a tiny card.

Enjoy, bestie, Marley's written. *I've got one too. Today made me think about how important friendship is. Love you xoxoxo*

My breath catches in my chest. *Bestie.* Does she really mean that? We've not known each other *that* long. Inside the box is a delicate rose-gold bracelet with a star for the clasp.

Feeling suddenly choked up, I put it on. It matches my favourite earrings. I can't believe Marley remembered.

"Pretty." Mum comes up behind me. "Is that from Marley? I saw her out of the window."

I nod. Mum goes to the door of the kitchen, then pauses. "Who was the boy in the car with her?"

"Her brother, I guess. They share a car. Does it matter?"

"No," says Mum, after a pause.

The bracelet sits heavy around my wrist all evening, even though it's feather-light. I don't know what's wrong with me. I should be happy. I've wanted a special friend for so long, and Marley's fun and smart and a feminist. So why do I feel so strange? Is it because Marley's shifting me into Esme's place without really seeming to care that she's gone? She'd say it isn't like that, and I shouldn't judge others for being less emotional than me, but it's difficult not to. Especially today.

I spend a while looking at the costumes from Halloween on social media. There are loads of red feather boas. But trying to work out who Halloween Girl is feels so wrong that I soon stop. She probably wants to forget what happened. This is her secret, not mine.

I drift on to looking at photos of Esme. Neither she nor Xander ever uploaded anything together. The only picture with both of them is one Xander shared from New Year's of him posing with a drink. Esme is in the background, chatting to me. It's pretty bad taste of Xander to keep it up, even if he does look good in that sweater. Then I pause, because I'm pretty sure in the later selfie of Ursula and Calvin that Xander was wearing a navy T-shirt.

Sure enough, I'm right. So he changed his top

mid-evening. Big deal. But it is a little odd – unless he keeps spare clothes in the barn, Xander would have had to walk all the way to the manor house to do so.

Liam finally replies when I'm getting ready for bed.

I'm home

Are you OK? I send back.

No

I stare at the two letters for a moment, then hit dial. To my relief, he picks up. I recognize the music in the background as a slow ballad Mum likes, a number one from when she was my age. Nothing like the dance music Liam normally plays in the car.

"What's really wrong?" I ask.

"Nothing. I'm OK."

"You just said you weren't."

Silence comes down the line. I wish I could picture his room, but I've never seen it.

"Liam, you can talk to me, you know."

Another silence. My words feel clumsy. If only I knew the right thing to say.

"It's OK if you feel sad. I know you and Esme were friends."

"It's not just that."

I remember the look in his eyes when he saw the photo in my house. "Is it your dad?"

Just as I think I'm going to have to guess again, Liam says, "Yeah."

"When was the last time you saw him?"

"Almost seven years ago."

"I'm sorry. That's . . . well, a long time."

"It is and it isn't. You forget stuff. But other things you remember perfectly."

He sounds so sad. If only we weren't having this conversation on the phone and I could give him a hug.

"What did you used to do together?"

"Everything. He was away a lot because of his job, but we were close. I'd wait up for his calls, even when he was in totally different time zones. Most days he'd speak to me more than Mom. Guess I should've figured they weren't getting along sooner. I wanted to be just like him. Even stupid things, like being good at art, even though I suck. I'd spend hours trying to draw like he could. Each time he came home from a trip he'd look at what I'd drawn and. . ."

Gently, I ask, "Why did he walk out? Did things break down with your mum?"

"Do you know a pathetic thing I used to do?" Liam doesn't seem to have heard me. "I saved the landline as 'Dad' on my cell. Then I'd ring myself up, just so I could see his name on the screen."

"Even if he's not around, I'm sure he loves you really. One day he'll call you for real."

"I don't think so, Alana."

Is he crying? His voice definitely sounds muffled. "Would it help if I came over?"

He goes quiet again, for so long that I think he's gone. Then he says, "Are you sure you want to go out with me?"

"What?" This is so unexpected I actually gasp. "Is this about you crashing the car? I don't care about that, and if you're going to ask if you're being annoying again, you're not—"

"You could do better."

Where has this come from? Liam said something similar weeks ago, but I thought we'd got past that. Sure, he can be awkward, but I always thought that was because he felt like an outsider. I get that; it's one of the things that draws us together. Before I can reply, Liam says he has to go. When I call back, he doesn't pick up.

Liam still isn't answering the next morning, so I cycle over to his grandma's. No one answers when I ring the doorbell. The only place I can think Liam would have gone this early is the gym at Stillwater. Unfortunately, I've headed in the wrong direction to drop by. Instead, I decide to cut across to Attlingham and see Marley. Perhaps she can help me figure this out.

Marley herself answers the door, and it's clear from her expression that I'm not who she expected to see. I open my mouth to apologize for getting her out of bed, but the words die in my mouth. She's wearing a necklace I recognize instantly.

Esme's.

TWENTY-TWO

"You didn't message," says Marley. One of her hands moves to pull the collar of her dressing gown higher.

"Is now a bad time?"

She hesitates, then steps back. "Let me shower. Five minutes."

I lean my bike against the wall, take my helmet off and come inside, a little weirded out. I only caught sight of the necklace for a moment, but I swear it was Esme's. Could Marley have been given it as a keepsake? It seems unlikely, given how desperate Esme's parents were to find it.

I wander into the sitting room and immediately regret it. Henry's reclined on the couch, wearing only his boxers and watching *Love Island*, which I can't believe is his thing. On the coffee table are several empty bowls and mugs. Two plates, two bowls, two mugs – Henry must have eaten breakfast with Marley. He glances up, eyes narrowed. I back out, then jump as the front door opens.

"Morning, Alana." It's Henry and Marley's parents, carrying shopping bags. I must look pretty disturbed, but neither of them mentions it, Mrs Durrant keeping up a bright stream of chatter as I help her sort out the groceries in the kitchen. Mr Durrant goes into the garden to fill up the bird feeder.

I pick up a bag of penne. On the cupboard door is a photo of a younger Henry and Marley standing on a tropical beach.

"St Lucia." Mrs Durrant sees me looking. "Our first holiday as a family. It always makes me smile."

"Henry and Marley don't look anything like each other."

"He looks like their dad, she looks like their mum." She laughs as I fail to hide a disbelieving look. "I don't mean us! Their birth parents."

"Oh! I didn't know they were adopted."

"Well, you've not been here long, have you?" Mrs Durrant turns her back as she fills the kettle. "Tea with no sugar, is that right? Would you mind asking Henry if he wants anything?"

"Coffee, please, Mum." Henry appears in the doorway, carrying the dirty crockery from the sitting room. "I can make it if you like."

Mrs Durrant smiles, saying there's no need. Henry shrugs and stacks the dishwasher instead. I narrowly manage to avoid pulling a face. Is this for my benefit, or is he genuinely helpful at home? Then I frown as I remember something from ages ago: Mrs Stannard, asking the police if they knew who Henry was. She mentioned a tragedy. Did something awful happen to their birth parents? That might be why Marley's never mentioned being adopted.

Marley appears a few minutes later, looking fresh in an oversized cream jumper and leggings. Her neck, I notice, is bare. Mrs Durrant excuses herself, and goes outside to talk to her husband. Henry's already returned to the TV. I wait for the back door to close before I ask, "Was that Esme's necklace you were wearing earlier?"

"Course not, silly!" says Marley. "Esme and I had the same one. Here, look." Marley brings up a selfie on her phone from maybe a few years ago of her and Esme blowing kisses to the camera. Sure enough, they are wearing identical necklaces. She grins as I sheepishly hand back her phone.

"If I seemed weird earlier, it's cos you caught me as I was getting in the shower and underneath the dressing gown I was naked! I did yell at Henry to get the door, but catch him shifting his lazy butt."

That all makes sense. I am getting way too paranoid. As we go up to her room, I say, "Your mum told me you were adopted."

"You didn't know? I thought it was obvious. Our

parents are pretty ancient!" She laughs, then asks what's up. I explain about Liam.

"Weird," she says, sipping the coffee Mrs Durrant made for her. "I've got no gems of wisdom, sorry, babe. He was probably just freaked out about the car."

Or the funeral. Two good reasons for being odd. Even so, I can't shake off my worry. "I wonder if he's OK."

"Course he is. Your Mr Taylor's got it all, the way I see it – including a fit girlfriend who I'm hoping is going to let me make her over this morning." Marley flashes a smile. "You got time? We've been talking about filming something for ages. Send Liam a pic when we're done. That'll cheer him up. Even better, go round and surprise him. You might get lucky."

She winks. I pull a face. Marley knows Liam and I aren't doing anything more than kissing. I'm never sure how much experience she has with boys. She seems pretty clued up for someone who as far as I know only ever had a few dates with Xander.

I'm not in the mood, but I let Marley wipe away my mascara and sit in a chair by the window while she decides what look to give me. Once we get started, it's fun – Marley's school gossip and flippant anecdotes about online trolls is exactly what I needed. The look she pulls off is amazing, way better than the stylists on my shoots.

"I wish I was going somewhere more interesting than home," I say when she turns the camera off. "I didn't know I could look this good."

"Says the model." Marley pulls a comical face. "You need to learn to love yourself, Lana. No one gives a shit that you're tall and flat-chested, you know. It's all in your head."

That's almost too close to Henry's giraffe with no tits comment, but I manage a laugh. Marley giggles too. The mood's much better now, perhaps because the slam of the front door half an hour ago means Henry's gone out. "When do you think the video will be up?"

"Probably not until I come back." It's half-term week, and tomorrow Marley's going to Scotland with another friend. "Hopefully it'll get a buzz going. My last vid went down brilliantly, I'll show you."

She gets the video up on her phone and starts scrolling down – then freezes. I look over her shoulder. One comment in a stream of thumbs up and heart-eye emojis jumps out. A girl – at least, I assume it's a girl, as her screen name is xJenniferxLiux – comments, *Hey M, remember me from the Bramford days? I wanted to say I love your channel. Hope you're doing well xxx*

The screen abruptly goes blank.

"Wrong video." Marley tosses her phone on to the bed. She gets up, pacing up and down. Then she goes into the en-suite and closes the door.

A bit alarmed – the message seemed innocent enough – I wait a minute, then call, "Marley? What's wrong?"

Marley doesn't answer immediately. Then there's a flushing sound and she comes out. "What are your plans for half-term, babe?"

It's like the last five minutes hasn't happened. "Marley, are you all right?"

"Yeah. Just felt sick suddenly. So. Half-term."

Reluctantly, I answer. "I haven't got much planned. Just the rugby match. I wish I could dodge it, but I promised Liam."

"Poor you being forced to watch fit boys running around in tiny shorts." Marley grins, looking more like herself, and I let it go. "Shame I'm not around to glam you up. Give your boyf added motivation to play well. So, fancy watching a film, or do you need to shoot off?"

By the time I leave Marley's, I'm feeling a lot more relaxed. Rather than go straight home, I head into Attlingham.

The florist's is in a creaky old building down one of the quieter streets. When I arrive, the elderly woman inside is turning the sign to "closed" half an hour early. With a huff, she allows me into the shop.

"How can I help?"

I mentally cross my fingers that she's more helpful than she looks. "This will sound strange, but someone's been sending me flowers. Blue anemones, to be specific. I think they've been ordering them from here and I was wondering if you would be able to tell me who it is. A description, if you don't know the name."

The florist's cross expression doesn't shift. "Doesn't ring any bells."

"Are you sure? I think it's a boy my age, maybe more

than one. That must stick in your mind? He'll have been here more than once. Last time a few days ago?"

She looks me up and down, eyes lingering on my fully made-up face. Then she shrugs, glancing at her watch. "Can't recall any boys. My daughter might. She'll be back from holiday next week."

Next week is a fat lot of good. I try not to show my frustration. "Can I write your daughter a note, leave my number maybe? It's really important. Actually, can I leave a message for the boy too, in case he comes back?"

"If this is some kind of secret admirer thing, I'm not getting involved—"

"It's not." The florist scowls, and I wish I hadn't interrupted. Lowering my voice, I say, "I'm sorry if I was rude, but this guy, or guys, is using the flowers to harass me. All I'm asking is for you to tell him the flowers aren't welcome. And that I'm not scared."

She gives me a long look but does take my name and scrawls a note, muttering something about women usually taking flowers as a compliment. I thank her and leave, resolving to return next week. Whether the florist will bother to pass my message on, who knows. I've probably wasted fifteen minutes. But doing something is better than nothing.

The match is on Friday, at St Julian's playing fields. Marley mentioned glamming up, so I decide to play along and end up in a lacy dress I bought because it matched my cherry-coloured lipstick. It's way too short – story of my shopping life – but it's the closest colour match I have to the maroon of the St Julian's kit, which Ursula and Georgie told me was the unofficial supporter dress code. With boots it doesn't look too outrageous. Or at least that's what I tell myself until I arrive on the pitch and realize with increasing horror that I've got this hopelessly wrong. All the girls are wearing jeans, even Georgie, who's well known for challenging the sixth form clothing policies. She falls about laughing when she sees me.

"Jesus, Alana! Are you trying to give Liam an ultra unsubtle hint? I think I can see your pants! Seriously, hon, this isn't *TOWIE*. When we said maroon, we were talking accessories. Not whatever *that* is."

"Oh, ha, ha," I snap. My legs are already goosepimpling and I want to disappear. What a total idiot I feel! Thank God no one can see the rest of what I'm wearing under this coat. "I thought girlfriends dressed up for these things?!"

"Not in freezing February we don't! Good job Blake doesn't like brunettes, else I might be feeling threatened right now."

She starts giggling again. I shove my hands into my pockets, cheeks burning. So much for fitting in! It's glaringly obvious now that when Marley mentioned glamming up, she was talking make-up. Great.

Georgie wanders off and I say hello to Ursula, who pretends she hasn't noticed my outfit. "Since when was Georgie into Blake?" I ask. "He's dating that girl from the next town, right?"

"Nope, they're over," says Ursula. "And about time! He and Georgie have been sneaking around for weeks. Calvin and I are fed up of covering for them. I refused to lie to the police, though."

"What do you mean?"

She rolls her eyes. "New Year's! Georgie and Blake were in his car making out most of the evening. They were scared of his girlfriend finding out, so Blake got Calvin to agree to that stupid story about them driving out to get booze. Cal shouldn't have backed him up, he's way too easily influenced. Georgie and Blake had to come clean after I handed over the video. I'm not sure the police are convinced Blake really was with Georgie. They keep asking if she's lying for him. Still, his problem."

Ursula carries on telling me what a jealous nightmare Blake's ex-girlfriend is, but I'm not listening. Blake has an alibi. He must have arranged to meet Georgie that time Liam and I bumped into him at Stillwater. Unless Georgie is lying, he didn't kill Esme. He isn't the third boy either. And it can't be Calvin.

The match kicks off. I should be watching Liam, but my eyes keep finding Xander. It's him. It has to be. The third boy. He had motive and opportunity. He's the number one suspect for taking the beer bottles out of my bag. He hid his relationship with Esme. The police believe he did it. They just can't prove anything.

By the time the match is over – a storming win to St Julian's – my whole body is stiff from cold. The boys run over, whooping and laughing, sickeningly full of themselves. It's a real effort to smile when Liam scoops me off my feet and spins me round, obviously on a high. I lean back before he can kiss me in front of everyone.

"Congratulations." I try to sound genuine. "You did really well. Or I assume you did from all the cheering. I still have no idea how this game works."

"I'll explain sometime." He puts me down. Seeing his eyes move downwards, I say quickly, "I know, I got it wrong."

"I wouldn't say that. But I'm your boyfriend, so. . ."

He grins. Relieved he seems to be happy, I smile back. Perhaps today we can get things back to normal. I've seen him a couple of times since the car accident, but he wasn't himself, and just shrugged when I asked if he wanted to talk. Whatever he's dealing with, I wish he'd share, and let me help.

"Listen up!" Henry's voice rises above the chatter. "We absolutely smashed it today, and that calls for a celebration. Let's go and get wasted. Who's in?"

A huge cheer erupts from the crowd. Liam looks at me. "Are you coming?"

No freaking way. Before I can open my mouth, Liam says in a rush, "I know you don't like my friends. I get why. But I'd really like you to come, even if it's only, like, for an hour. I'll make sure no one bothers you. Maybe afterwards we can go someplace else and I can make up for things being weird."

The hopeful, almost shy, expression on his face makes it difficult to say no. It reminds me of the careers talk, and how cute I thought it was that he cared about getting it right.

"Does it mean that much to you?"

He nods. "Please?"

That's it. Now I can't refuse. So I agree to go for an hour or two, and try not to feel like I'm making a mistake when Liam's face lights up.

The converted Victorian farmhouse we end up at belongs to Calvin's high-flying lawyer parents and is set down a bumpy dirt track in the middle of nowhere, fields all around, not that I can make them out in the fading light. The clouds are thick, dark and low. The atmosphere feels heavy, as though a storm is closing in. Something about the branches on the naked trees makes me picture hangman's nooses dangling from them. Oppressive. That's how this place feels. I shiver and hug my coat close as I follow the others inside.

Calvin's parents are away so the music gets turned up and the fridge loaded with the booze we stopped at the supermarket to buy. The boys waste no time popping the beers open. I realize this is going to be the kind of party where people get very drunk very quickly.

Two hours later, the bin is overflowing with empty bottles and the kitchen floor is sticky with spilled drink. Calvin's fetched his guitars, and he and Ursula are giving us an impromptu concert, their friends whistling and singing along. Clutching a juice, I sway along to the beat, hoping I look like I'm enjoying myself. My eyes are on the clock. I feel uncomfortable and anxious. Liam lent me a T-shirt from his sports bag so at least my top half is covered, but I've had constant jokes about the length of my skirt.

I haven't seen Liam for ages. I track him down to the patio, where he's sitting on the steps to the garden with two team reserves. He's smoking, something I've never seen him do before, and there are empty beer bottles next to him.

"Hey, Alana." He gives me a big smile, holding out his hand and pulling me on to his lap. I shift round so I can see him.

"You told me you'd quit."

"I have. Sort of. I only smoke sometimes when I drink." He leans forward to kiss me but I pull back. Alarm bells are ringing in my head.

"You said you weren't going to drink. You need to drive."

"I didn't say I wasn't drinking. I said I wouldn't get so out of it I couldn't drive later. But it's still early."

"Not that early." I try to keep the dismay out of my voice. "It's been two hours. Closer to two and a half." I get off his lap. "Liam, you can't drive like this."

"Sure I can." But he's way over the limit. He promises not to drink anything else, but the other boys jeer and start shouting for him to get another beer, and I have a horrible feeling he's going to cave.

I can't believe he's let me down! Cheeks burning, I go inside, snapping that I'm going to the loo when Liam tries to follow. Feeling like I might cry, but just about holding myself together, I go into the kitchen. Maybe I can find someone who wants to leave soon. But while I've been outside, the party has moved on. Before, it was loud and boozy. Now, couples are sucking each other's faces off, someone's passed out on the sofa, and I can hear retching. None of the girls I trust seem to be about. There's no way anyone's leaving anytime soon.

And whoever chose the music has popped some Britpop on the playlist. Sudden fear swells inside me. My love of Britpop was what Henry used to get close to me at New Year's. Is this a message? I wheel round, half-expecting to see him smirking at me. He isn't – but that doesn't mean he and the others aren't watching. . .

As I pass the door to the downstairs loo, it swings open. Crouched by the toilet is Faith.

"Water," she calls. "Please?"

I fetch some and watch her glug it down.

"Are you all right? Do you want to lie down? Or . . . well, I guess I could get someone to find Henry, if you want him."

Faith bursts out laughing. "Why would I want Henry? He doesn't care! Don't act like you do, either. I know what the girls say about me, that I'm stupid, and slutty, and . . . I don't know, stupid."

"No one says that."

"You all think it, though. Admit it. You think I'm a pathetic joke with no friends."

She collapses into tears. I try to get her to stand, but she screams at me to leave her alone. Desperate now to find somewhere quiet, I go upstairs. On the landing I bump into Ozzie.

"Hey! Why so sad?" He makes a grab and catches my waist, pulling our bodies against each other. I writhe away and dive into a nearby bathroom, locking myself in. Ozzie hammers on the door, slurring that if I come out he'll make sure I have a good time. There's something wrong about the pitch of his voice. Has he taken drugs? Just as I'm panicking he'll knock the door down, he gives up and leaves. I sink on to the floor.

Trying not to freak out, I run through my options. Calling Mum at the hospital isn't really something I can do. Marley's away. Everyone else I know is here. I have no idea where I am, so ringing a taxi is out – plus they're impossible to get hold of quickly at weekends. Feeling dizzy, I stare across the room. I'm stuck. Is it even safe to go downstairs? I've never seen these guys really drunk before. If they're high too. . .

Someone knocks, calling my name. I jump, phone clattering across the tiles. When I inch the door open, I see Xander leaning against the wall opposite.

"Is everything all right?" he asks. "You've been gone a long time."

So he has been watching me. My heart starts to race.

Unlike everyone else, he doesn't sound at all drunk. That should be comforting, but it isn't.

"Fine," I mutter.

"I wouldn't go down there if I were you. This party stopped being fun a while ago. I'm leaving before things get messy. Do you need a lift? I promise I won't get distracted by your lack of a skirt . . . unless you want me to, of course."

Home. I picture myself safe in bed, closing my eyes on this nightmare evening.

It's so, so tempting.

Or it would be, if it didn't involve being alone with Xander.

He, Henry and Ozzie probably raped someone. They would have raped me. I'm almost convinced he drowned Esme. I can't take any chances. So I ignore the stupid comment about my dress and shake my head. As I pass, Xander catches my arm.

"Alana. Don't be stupid. Let me take you home."

I shake him off and hurry downstairs. My skin feels like it's burning. From the sitting room I can hear laughter, and the sound of breaking glass. I hesitate a second. Then I grab my coat from the hooks by the front door.

I don't stop running until I'm out on the lane. There, I stop, bending over with my hands on my thighs as I gulp air. Thank God I'm out of there! I hold up my phone. When it finally picks up my location, Google Maps tells me I'm five miles from home. That's walkable, I tell myself, ignoring the sinking feeling in my stomach. It's starting to snow. Already there's a patchy white carpet across the road.

Thankful my boots are flats, I set off. I try not to use my phone torch, but when I stumble in a pothole and almost fall in the ditch I'm forced to turn it on. My battery's running low already. How much longer do I have before it dies?

Fear turns my stomach over. This was a terrible idea! I'm alone in the middle of nowhere, it's pitch-black, sub-zero and I might as well have bare legs for the warmth these tights are giving me. What if I slip and break my leg? Get picked up by some predator? Lose my way, and catch hypothermia? My chest is tight now, my breathing ragged, but I'm more scared of going back to that house. *You can do this, Alana. One foot in front of the other. In an hour and a half you'll be home. . .*

Within minutes, the falling snow thickens. I can't feel the tips of my fingers, even with my hands clenched in my pockets. Then I hear a purr in the distance. Headlights appear at the bottom of the lane.

My first thought is, *I can get a lift*. My second is, *crap*, because if he really was leaving, the car is probably Xander's. On one side of me there's an open, empty field. On the other is a thick hedge.

Hiding isn't an option.

I force myself to carry on walking. Blood pounds in my ears as the engine gets louder, louder, louder. The road floods with blinding light. My hands fly upwards to shield my eyes. A low, flashy bright yellow sports car draws alongside me. The driver's window whirs down.

"So you'd rather walk home in the snow than get in a car with me," says Xander. "Amazing."

I stumble forward as though I haven't heard. He crawls alongside me in first gear. After a few seconds I snap, wheeling round to face him.

"I don't want a lift! Leave me alone."

"Well, excuse me for attempting to be chivalrous! Aren't you freezing? I could get you home in ten minutes."

"No!"

"There are mints in the glove compartment. Possibly sweets. Or if you fancy something hotter and more substantial we can slum it at the chip shop—"

"I said no!" I'm shouting now. Xander stares at me. Then he puts his foot down, and the car pulls past me. But instead of disappearing, he swings into a layby a few metres ahead. And he steps out.

TWENTY-THREE

Xander closes the gap between us, coming to a stop about a metre in front of me. My eyes dart left, then right. Should I jump over the ditch and bolt across the fields? If I got a head start ... no. Didn't I see only a few hours ago how agile this guy is? He'd catch up easily.

Maybe he's already killed one girl who knew too much.

No one knows I'm here. No one knows he's here.

Killing another would be easy.

"What exactly is your problem?" Xander's voice is hard.

I stare at him, still mentally running through my options. "My *problem*?"

"Yes. You clearly have one. I'd like to know what it is.

Was it the joke I made about your skirt? If so, this is a total overreaction—"

Something inside me snaps. Before I know it I'm shouting, fear exploding into anger. "My problem is what you've done! I know about Halloween, and New Year's. For all I know, you're a murderer as well as a rapist!"

Immediately I know I've made a mistake. But Xander merely tilts his head.

"You have proof I'm a rapist, do you?"

The way he says it is so cold. I swallow, hugging myself, poised to bolt if he makes a grab at me. But I hold his gaze.

"I did before you got rid of it. You picked up my bag and went through it while I was in A & E. Admit it."

"That could have been anyone. All I did with your bag was take it to your house."

"Like you did on New Year's, with the anemone?"

"Oh, seriously! That was just a bit of fun. Poor taste, maybe, but nothing more."

"Cutting my bike's brakes? The scarecrow in the old wing? Were they 'a bit of fun' too?"

"I don't know what you're talking about. That wasn't me." He presses his lips together. "FYI, not that you care, but my parents went nuclear over your little accident in the old wing. Guess what? You being stupid is my fault! I've spent half-term doing the shittiest jobs Dad could find as punishment. He withdrew me from the fencing tournament I've been training for, and only let me play today because our reserve wing player is crap. And I've a curfew. Things at home weren't great anyway, and now they're worse. So thanks, Alana."

Does he actually think I'm going to feel sorry for him? I don't believe for a moment that he isn't behind the other flowers, or the scarecrow. I hug myself harder, not saying anything. Xander narrows his eyes. For a second I think he's going to lose it. Instead he digs his hands into his pockets, drawing himself up straight. He's about an inch taller than me. Maybe closer to two.

"So. You think I'm a rapist. When did this supposedly happen? Enlighten me."

I have no choice but to be bold now. "A girl was raped at Halloween by three boys. Esme witnessed it. Henry and Ozzie were going to do the same to me at New Year's and a third boy was in on it. The only person that could be is you."

He flinches and turns away. For a long moment he's quiet. Then he says, "It may have escaped your notice, Inspector Alana, but I don't actually like Henry. He doesn't like me. And I don't think drugging and banging girls without their consent is cool. Why the hell do you think I would?"

"Maybe you're annoyed you keep getting dumped. Maybe you don't get as much action as you feel you ought to. Maybe you mess with girls for kicks, just because you can."

Xander's mouth twitches. "This is Marley, isn't it? What lies has she been spreading about me?"

"I know she broke up with you and you're bitter about it."

"For the last time, *I* dumped Marley! She was possessive and I didn't like it. I only asked her out in the first place because she kept following me around."

"I bet you're going to deny pressuring her for photos too."

"What photos?"

"You know what photos!"

"No, I don't!"

I grind my teeth, glancing away. "What about Esme? Did you ask her out to pay Marley back? And why did you lie about it?"

"I asked Esme out because we got chatting and she seemed fun. Nothing to do with Marley. And I lied because I'd look suspicious if the police knew the full story. Boyfriends always get a hard time. No one knew we'd dated, her phone was missing, and I thought I'd get away with it. Satisfied? And I never pestered anyone for photos."

"Does the whole team getting suspended for laughing over nudes ring any bells?"

"That? One of the subs was messing about with some girl and thought the photos would impress us. Nothing to do with me. He's lucky I didn't grass him up. So Marley says it was me, does she? That explains a lot." A pause. "Maybe she's lying and I'm telling the truth. Has that occurred to you?"

I slap him. Or at least, I almost slap him. Xander grabs

my wrist before I can land the blow. I snatch it away, horrified by how close I am to losing control.

"Do you actually think I'd believe an entitled bighead like you? I can't believe you're trying to lie your way out of this! I've seen what you're like with girls. You've been trying it on with me for weeks, even ringing me—"

"You rang me first."

"Oh, whatever!" I shout, close to tears now. "You want me to believe you had nothing to do with this? Tell me what really happened the night Esme died. The Witches' Pool. Did you go there when she texted?"

Xander goes very still. I wait, eyes not leaving his.

Eventually, he speaks. "I saw Esme's message straight away. It seemed strange, especially as we'd called it quits, but I picked up some drinks and went to the pool. Esme wasn't there. I called her name, waited a little. She didn't show."

"You didn't see her body in the water?"

He shakes his head. I frown. Esme had already been attacked by this point. Something doesn't stack up.

"Halfway back I heard a sneeze," Xander continues. "Someone was hiding in the bushes. When I went to see who, they sprang forward and knocked the drinks I was holding all over me." In a flash I remember the cocktail glasses I trod on in the wood. "Then they ran off and managed to lose me."

That I don't believe. Xander knows those woods better than anyone. "Did you see who it was?"

Does he hesitate? "No. Too dark." A pause. "The police

found the glasses I was carrying, in case you think I'm lying. My fingerprints are all over them."

I only have Xander's word for that. Even if the prints are his, that doesn't prove his story – the glasses could have been planted later on. I open my mouth to ask what he did next. Then I realize I know.

"Your clothes. They had drink all over them. You went to change."

"Which is why I have no alibi. Correct."

Ursula said Xander seemed pissed off later in the barn. Now I know why. The photos prove he did change. To my horror, this part of his story does ring true.

"I'm not this toxic person you think I am," he says. "Maybe I'm not always very nice, and I accept that I'm an irritatingly privileged posh boy who pushes his luck, but I didn't kill Esme. And I'm not a rapist."

Xander waits. I scuff my heels against the road, not looking at him.

"You really don't believe me," he says. I keep my eyes fixed on my feet. There's another pause, an even longer one. Then I hear him sigh. "Fine. Think what you like. But will you at least let me drive you home? Or am I going to have to wait two hours with you for a taxi? I assume you're not still planning to walk."

I don't think I could even if I wanted to. I can't feel my fingers or toes. And I'm scared my phone torch will die soon. Unwillingly, I follow him to the car. I hesitate by the passenger door.

"Ring someone and talk to them during the journey if it makes you feel safer." Xander's voice is chilly again. But this time I think it's because he's hurt. "I'm not going to try anything. You can't stand me, I've got the message. Despite what you think, I know when to back off."

I get in.

He drives me home in silence. We don't make eye contact. At my house, he waits until I'm inside to pull away, and something about that makes me want to cry.

I don't know what's going on, or who to trust. I creep into bed and fall into a dreamless sleep.

When I wake up, there are about a billion messages from Liam. I delete them all, then type: *I don't want to talk to you*, and turn my phone off. He appears round mine mid-afternoon, wearing yesterday's clothes and looking rough. It's harder to tell someone to get lost in the flesh, so we sit in the car, and he apologizes.

"I wasn't intending on getting drunk. It just kind of happened. I lost track of time."

I give him a look. Liam clearly realizes how lame that sounds, because he glances down at the dashboard.

"OK, I wanted to drink, and I guess once we were there I thought you'd enjoy yourself. Sorry. I shouldn't have asked you to come. I knew that really."

"Then why did you?"

He mumbles something. I blink, not sure I've heard right.

"You wanted to *show me off*?"

He reddens.

I stare at him. Slowly, I say, "Asking me to go somewhere with guys you know I feel uncomfortable around was about you looking good?"

"You make it sound so bad. Alana, you're gorgeous. Of course I want people to see us together. Any guy would. You're a freaking model—"

"No, I'm not! I did a handful of shoots. I wish people would stop going on about them! Is that what I am to you? Some kind of trophy girlfriend?"

"I never said that—"

"I was relying on you, and you let me down. I felt so unsafe I tried to walk home in the snow. You didn't even message to ask if I'd got back OK!"

"I knew you were home. Xander rang me. He was furious, he said... Look, I screwed up, OK? This is what I do, screw things up. Not just denting the car, big things, things that matter. I knew sooner or later I'd screw us up too."

I have no idea what he's talking about and I'm too angry to care. "You're not making sense."

"You don't get it. You're smart, and confident, and, I don't know, have your shit sorted..."

"So have you."

"That's not me, though. You think it is, but I told you, I screw stuff up. Oh, jeez, Alana, I can't do this. I knew things were starting to go wrong when I ran the car off the road… I'm really, *really* sorry. Please say you understand."

He has his head in his hands. Suddenly I can't deal with this conversation. Maybe if I didn't have my own problems, I wouldn't feel so out of my depth with Liam and his insecurities. I've tried to help, to listen, to empathize, but he's a closed book. Issues or not, he let me down, he knew he was letting me down, and he did it anyway. That hurts. So does being told I'm some kind of status symbol. I thought Liam was different. I thought he understood me. I thought it was real. Now…

I don't know if I have the head space for Liam any more, not on top of everything else. "I'm going inside."

He lets me go without a word.

In my room, my thoughts turn to Xander. On one hand he was so convincing. On the other…

I grab the Post-its and scrawl down everything I know.

Esme found drowned in Witches' Pool (12.30). Head wound. GHB. Still think she was led away sometime around midnight rather than heading there herself (but message to Xander contradicts that).

Esme witnessed Halloween. She'd just realized who the rapists were. Person who drowned her cannot *have been Henry or Ozzie. Therefore – it was the third boy.*

<u>Who is third boy?</u>

Not Liam. Saved Esme's life.

Not Calvin. Was in Ursula's video, so alibi.

Not Blake. Not in Ursula's video, but was with Georgie, so alibi (unless she's lying?!).

Not Xander? Story about meeting someone in woods prob true – cocktail glasses, change of clothes etc. But. . .

How could the other person have lost him?

Did he really not see Esme's body in the pool?

Also, could have personal reasons for wanting to harm Esme too.

So it is Xander. Although . . . why would Esme ask Xander to meet her if she thought he was a rapist? Is there something – or someone – I'm missing?

I read over the Post-its again the next day, but end up going round in circles. Hoping to distract myself, I look at Marley's vlog. She only came back from Scotland last night, but the video we made earlier in the week is up. What's this in the blurb – *Watch me make over my model friend Alana*? I specifically asked Marley not to mention my modelling. It makes me feel so exposed – awkward and humiliated and illogically ashamed. And she knows how I hate it defining me. I click play. Marley pops up on the screen introducing the vlog. And she's done it again – called me a model, and name-dropped the campaigns I worked on.

I click stop. I can't watch this any more.

Marley doesn't pick up when I ring. I slam my laptop shut and go downstairs. I'll go for a bike ride, or a walk. Anything's better than sitting here fuming.

Then I see Mum come through the door, in her uniform and in tears.

TWENTY-FOUR

At first Mum snaps that nothing's wrong. Then she admits that she's been ordered to take the week off.

"I almost made a mistake," she says. "I'm so careful with drugs – never once have I got anything wrong, no matter how stressed or tired I was. . . Today I wasn't thinking."

"Did you kill anyone?" asks Seb. Mum gives him an acid look.

"No, Sebastian. I did not kill anyone. Another nurse spotted it before I gave the patient his dose."

She goes into the kitchen, slamming a plate Seb left out on the counter. Seb and I trade a scared look. Mum notices. I see her take a deep breath.

"I'm not annoyed at you two," she says. "I'm furious with myself. It was a silly, avoidable mistake that could so easily have ruined what's supposed to be a new life for us all. I'm not going to lose my job, but I am going to be monitored, which after twenty years is a bloody insult."

"Is there anything we can do?" I ask.

"Oh, I don't know, invent a time machine? That would be good. Oh, Christ. Sorry, love. I know you're trying to be helpful. Look, give me half an hour to do something mindless and cool down, all right?"

And she starts cleaning. I watch her on her hands and knees scrubbing the oven, then close the door.

"Cheer up, Ally," Seb says. "Mum will be all right. She always is."

Until now, I'd have agreed. Mum prides herself on being tough. But the last few months must have pushed her to the limit. Breaking up with Dad, moving houses, new job. . . The reason Mum chose Suffolk was to be close to her friends, but all that's happened is she's putting everything into supporting Esme's mum. Daily visits and check-in phone calls would drain anyone.

Suddenly I'm afraid. I feel young, naive, and completely useless. In a daze I go upstairs, where my phone is plugged in to charge. I look at it. Then I call Dad.

His phone rings for what seems ages before it's picked up. A slightly breathless-sounding female voice says, "Alana, hello. Your dad's in the shower."

Miss Parsons. Or Emily, as I'm supposed to call her. Great. "Can Dad ring me back, please?"

"Wait a sec, he's coming out. Nick, it's Alana."

I hear the muffled *um-mum-mum* of Dad's voice – Miss Parsons has covered the receiver. I wonder what they're saying about me. Is she there in the bathroom with him? I feel a little sick. I don't want to even think about my old science teacher seeing my dad naked.

"Sweetheart!" The sound of Dad's cheerful voice instantly twists my stomach into an achy, homesick knot. "I'm so glad you called. I've missed you. Everything OK? How are—" He sneezes. "Sorry, it's dusty here. I've been assembling furniture."

"Oh. What kind?"

He hesitates. "Things for the nursery. Not long to go now."

The word *nursery* is a stab to the gut. Dad fills the silence, babbling about my old school and trying to learn to cook. I lower the phone, staring at the picture I finally plucked up the courage to add to my pinboard. It's us at a fair, Dad dressed for jousting, me playing squire. I imagine Dad standing in the new house I haven't even seen with a towel wrapped around his middle, looking at Miss Parsons the way he used to look at Mum, baby junk all around him.

He's nervous, that's why he's talking so much, I get that, but finally hearing his voice, so familiar and yet so strange... Dad is gone. Really gone. He's having another kid. He's excited. The baby I've been pretending isn't happening is real.

Until now I never properly accepted that he'd moved on. Was that the reason I refused to pick up his calls? If we didn't speak, it could never become final.

A chasm of emptiness stretches inside of me.

"I can't do this," I choke, and disconnect Dad mid-sentence.

He calls back, but I mute the phone and curl on the bed and sob, pressing my face into the pillow to stop Seb and Mum overhearing. For weeks my anger's been a plaster, sealing the hurt underneath. Now it's ripped off, I can't hold those feelings in any longer – the hurt and confusion and fear and how horribly, achingly alone I am. I want to go back in time, to when I thought my funny, kind, loving dad was brilliant.

I start to cry again as I tell Liam everything. He puts his arms around me and lets me talk.

"And I guess it's finally sunk in," I finish. The skin around my eyes is puffy, make-up long ago washed away. Liam feels for the box of tissues on the coffee table. We're in the sitting room of his grandma's house, and I was so upset I remember nothing of the icy cycle ride over.

"Your dad's not gone, Alana," he says. "He and your mom aren't together, but that doesn't mean he can't be part of your life. He obviously wants to be. The baby won't make him care less about you."

"How can I trust him again? He hid the affair for months. I felt so stupid for not seeing it coming." I dab my eyes with the tissue. "The nice things Dad and I did feel fake, spoiled."

"Seriously, you should talk to him. Have you? For real, I mean."

No. Because I'm scared. Because it's easier to be angry. "Does it get better?"

"You'll get better at dealing with it. You're strong."

He gives me a hug. I press my face into his shoulder. Right now I don't care how angry I was at him yesterday. He's the only person I've really opened up to about Dad, and I need his comfort. We stay like that for a while. For the first time I take in the room. I've never been to Liam's house before. Like mine, it has beams across the ceiling and an uneven brick floor, but the windows are small and the furnishings dark, making it feel crowded. It's almost stiflingly hot. Liam doesn't seem bothered, but I'm sweating. I glance at the wall that connects with the house next door. Esme's parents are probably sitting a couple of metres away. I wonder if they're watching TV, trying to lose themselves in other people's lives.

"I would say we should go out," Liam says. "But a guy's coming to pick up furniture Grandma is selling, and she's at her book club so I need to stay in. I'll run you home before then, though."

"I don't mind helping."

"No, it's fine. I can always cruise by your place later."

Why can't I wait here? I wonder why Liam is being evasive. Now that I think about it, he didn't seem too comfortable when I showed up, but I assumed that was because he thought I was still angry at him.

Liam goes to the kitchen and returns with two mugs which he places on coasters on the coffee table. He starts fiddling with the strap of his watch. The grandfather clock in the hallway chimes four.

"You want to talk some more?"

I shake my head. Liam picks up the remote and turns on the TV, cycling through channels and settling on a gymnastics competition. He puts his arm around my shoulders and I lean in, hugging a cushion to myself. Something about the way he holds me feels tense. We should talk about Friday night, and the things he said in the car, but I don't have space for any more emotion. Right now, I don't want to think at all.

Instead we watch the gymnasts, sipping our drinks in silence. My eyelids grow heavy, and the warmth makes me want to close them. When the ad break comes on, Liam moves, taking my half-empty cup and placing it on the floor. He's barely touched his coffee.

"When's the furniture guy coming?" I yawn.

"Not for a while." Liam shifts round so he can kiss me. "I would say we should go to my room, but it's a mess," he murmurs. "Like, a real mess. I'm not expecting anything, don't think that, but if you want I could go tidy—"

"It's fine here." I'm not really in the mood, but I've had enough of gymnastics. I shuffle into a more comfortable position and kiss him back. After a while the usual warm feeling I get when he touches me seeps in, and my brain switches off. My hands end up under his top and his slide under mine, and at some point both come off. His hand hovers over the top of my jeans. Then the doorbell shrills, making us jump. Liam grabs his T-shirt and pulls it over his head as he hurries out.

By the time he returns, I'm back in my jumper, sitting straight-backed on the sofa clutching my cold tea and half wishing I hadn't come.

Liam clears his throat. "Um, the furniture guy's early. Do you mind waiting? We'll be in the garage."

I shake my head. Liam goes out, and a few seconds later the front door clicks shut. I turn the TV off. I'm feeling on edge. When Liam comes back I'll leave. Making out was awkward, like I was doing it to fill silence. Liam seemed into it, but maybe he was pretending. What he said about his room was mixed-messagey. Are we really as good a match as I believed? Sometimes I wish he was as strong at talking as he is at listening. And I wish I'd asked where the bathroom is. I'm starting to need the loo.

I go out into the hallway, but there's only a kitchen, junk room, study and walk-in cupboard. So I go upstairs. The bathroom door is open, but I pause before going in. The next door is ajar, revealing Liam's trainers lined up in front of a wardrobe. I peek inside and do a double take. Liam's room isn't messy at all. OK, it's not super neat, but there aren't dirty clothes on the floor, or plates encrusted with ancient food smears, and it smells fresh enough. In fact, it's nice – double bed, new-looking carpet, a big desk with Liam's textbooks, laptop, light-up headphones and gadgets on it, pretty view of the village from the window, more like a guest room than somewhere a teenage boy sleeps. The only personal touches are a couple of American-football posters, a big pair of speakers and a miniature skeleton not unlike Hector from the library. Why wouldn't he want me to see it? He clearly wanted to carry on what we were doing.

Then I stop. I've spotted something on the desk. Something I recognize.

Feeling like part of me is floating a long way away, I go and pick it up.

It's a photograph of Dad. My dad.

Stunned, I stare. It's quite an old picture, of Dad standing by a sports pitch. It must come from the doomed period he tried to encourage Seb into cricket. When I turn it over, Mum's handwriting is on the underside, with the exact date.

What the hell? I had a box of photos out last time Liam came over. Could he have picked this up by accident, and been too embarrassed to say?

No. He slipped it into his pocket. Why?

I put the photo down. I'm really feeling nauseous now. I inspect the rest of the desk. Under one of the textbooks is a phone, plugged into a charger. It isn't Liam's. At least, not the one I recognize.

The screen lights up when I press the main button. The wallpaper is standard, anonymous. Knowing what I'm doing is wrong but unable to stop myself, I enter Liam's regular passcode, which I know. It takes me right in. My finger hovers over the icons on the screen.

I'm snooping. I really shouldn't.

But Liam took a picture of my dad without asking me. That's not right either. And very, very weird.

The phone doesn't have WhatsApp so I look at the texts. There aren't many. All the people are nameless. I click on one conversation.

Sure I can sort you out, Liam writes.

Cool, cheers mate, the other person replies, with a thumbs up emoji.

Handy you havin a dark past lol. We wasn't sure how to get hold of stuff before. You gone up in mine and H's estimation.

He better keep his side of the deal

Yeah don't worry. Laters, matey

Drugs. I can't think what else this could be about. Is Liam still dealing? He said he wasn't. I believed him.

Laters, matey. I frown, then realize: that's something Ozzie says. Is the conversation with him? Is H Henry? Did Liam give them drugs? Henry mentioned Liam getting him what he wanted when I overheard them talking that time – and him doing something for Liam in return.

A nasty suspicion is forming in my mind.

Starting to feel like I'm falling from a very great height, but unable to stop, I open up the gallery. And my breath catches in my throat.

It's full of photos from New Year's. Photos of me.

TWENTY-FIVE

There are loads. Me chatting to Henry. His hand on my waist – I don't remember that. Us with Ozzie. Me and Henry leaving for the cinema room. Us going in. Even the closed door. Was Liam watching the whole time?

Oh my God.

A memory slides into my head. Me, hurrying out and almost colliding with someone who quickly stepped back into the shadows.

A boy.

Slowly, my brain links everything up.

Liam still deals drugs.

Liam is friends with Henry and Ozzie even though he told me he wasn't.

Henry and Ozzie use drugs to rape girls.

It doesn't need a genius to work out who got hold of those drugs. And who therefore must have known what they were going to be used for.

Liam, the very person who was standing outside the door when I ran out, about to come in.

I am the favour in return. He's the third boy. And I'm standing in his bedroom, where he didn't want me to go.

The front door slams. I freeze.

"Alana?" Liam calls.

Quickly I drop the phone. I meet Liam halfway down the stairs. He frowns.

"What're you doing up there?"

"Bathroom." I hope I sound casual enough. "You were quick."

"Yeah, well, I wanted to get back to you." He smiles. "Feeling better?"

I look past him to the front door. Just a few metres away, but it feels so very far. My head is spinning. I swallow.

"Yeah. I think I'll go home."

I try to squeeze past, but Liam catches my shoulders.

"You don't have to," he says. "We could—"

"No, I really should go."

For a second I don't think he's going to move. Then he steps back, looking disappointed. He follows me outside and watches as I wheel my bike to the road.

"Are you OK? I could give you a ride. It's still icy. Your bike would fit in the trunk if I collapse the back seat—"

"I feel like cycling. See you at school."

"Lana." He takes my hand. This time I can't stop myself from flinching. He's never called me anything other than my full name and there's something about the intimacy that makes my insides crawl. Somehow, I manage not to pull away as he kisses me goodbye, but I can't kiss him back, and he pulls away, looking confused. I leap on the bike and pedal furiously, putting as much space between us as I can.

The next morning I ghost through the bus ride into school, my first two lessons, break. Marley's back, telling us funny stories about Scotland, but I don't hear a word, and I can't even bring myself to care about her calling me a model on the vlog any more.

You need to go to the police, I tell myself. I don't know what's holding me back. Shock? Loyalty? The fact that I don't want to believe Liam did this, even though there's absolutely no other explanation for what I saw?

"Hello?" Marley's waving her hand in front of my face. "Earth to Alana! Hearing about my holiday can't be that boring."

It's impossible to play normal any longer. I hurry away into the cool of the corridor and find a quiet corner, leaning against the wall with my face in my hands.

This can't be happening. It can't.

But it is. And I know what I need to do.

*

I find the deputy head and tell her everything. Mrs Stannard calls the police. DI Underwood and another detective arrive. I repeat my story, no longer caring if I look stupid or paranoid. Mrs Stannard suggests I go home, but I can't face Mum right now and I'm too scared to ask for Marley to keep me company. What I've told the police is going to really land Henry in it. Will Marley be angry? Hurt? Or will she understand? If only he wasn't her brother!

I sit in Mrs Stannard's office by myself, trying to gather my scattered thoughts. Liam's the third boy. But does it follow that he drowned Esme too? He never had an alibi. He even admitted to speaking to her shortly before midnight – around the time she was heard arguing with a boy. Why did it never occur to me that the two conversations could be the same?

I picture Esme confronting him. Liam, realizing that Esme had to be silenced. He must have taken her to the pool directly before heading to the cinema room to have some fun with me. My throat tightens, and I feel hot and faint. I *dated* this guy. Let him kiss me, touch me, come into my home, told him private things about my family and feelings, and shared my stupid theories about Esme's death, when all the time he knew exactly what had happened.

He's a rapist, just like his friends. How could he keep up the caring boyfriend act like everything was normal? But then, Liam's clearly a screwed-up guy. You'd have to be to try to revive someone you thought you'd killed. Esme entered the water nearly an hour before I found her. Liam must have been confident the CPR would fail – and that doing it would make him look innocent. He must have nearly had a heart attack when she started to breathe. Also, driving her to the hospital was his idea. That was the wrong thing to do, Mum said so. Did he hope she'd die en route?

I can't explain the message Esme sent Xander, though. That's the one thing that still doesn't fit. Suddenly I'm hopeful I've got it wrong. Liam's always been respectful with me. It's so hard to picture him as any kind of rapist. But that doesn't mean he isn't one. Everything I've read makes this point again and again. Rapists aren't always shady strangers. More often than not, they're people we think we know, and trust. Regular guys like Liam, who pick their nails and pretend they don't follow geeky plane apps, who want to be doctors, who make sweet and thoughtful boyfriends.

Liam was miserable and lonely when he first came to Suffolk, he told me so. I could imagine him getting involved if that meant impressing the cool crowd. Henry would have told him it was just a game, that they weren't doing anything wrong, maybe taking the piss out of his awkwardness with girls. When you're on the outside looking in, desperate to belong, your logic bends so much you'd do anything to have someone to sit with at lunchtime and message in the evenings. Don't I know that myself?

And, oh! My stomach lurches. The key ring torch he had when I fell through the floorboards at Stillwater, the slim one I thought was a pen. . . It's metal, heavy, and even has a semi-sharp end. The perfect size for the puncture wound on Esme's head.

The missing weapon.

It is him.

I pace around for what feels like ages. Rain lashes at the window. Not knowing what's going on is driving me up the wall. Every five seconds I check my phone, but it remains silent.

There's a knock at the door. I badly want it to be Marley, but instead Ursula sticks her head round the door. She squeezes my shoulder.

"Hey. Are you all right? Mrs Stannard asked me to check up on you."

I wet my lips. "All I want is to know what's going on."

Ursula hesitates. "With Liam?"

"You know?"

"A little, Calvin's been messaging me, and. . ."

"What did he say?"

"Not much. But we could meet him, if you like. He has a free period now."

Ten minutes later Ursula and I are on the second floor of the library, which, while quiet, is a terrible choice because it makes me think of Liam. Hector the skeleton's empty eye sockets stare blankly across at me and I have to look away.

Calvin appears moments later, and insists on fetching drinks from the vending machine before joining Ursula and me on the sofas. I'm not sure I can stomach milky tea, but it feels mean to throw the gesture back at him.

"So?" I ask. "The police spoke to Liam, right?"

Calvin stirs his coffee, not meeting my eyes. "They're still speaking to him, for all I know. He left school in a police car."

Oh God. He's been arrested. "How did he react? Was he angry, or. . .?"

"I don't know. I didn't see." A pause. "Whatever you told them, you've made a mistake. Liam's a good guy."

Calvin doesn't speak accusingly – he seems bewildered more than anything else – but the thought of facing the rest of the rugby team sends butterflies sweeping through my stomach. How will Marley react? She hasn't even opened my messages. The rest of the gang aren't replying either. Are they blanking me? I twist the bracelet she gave me round and round. Am I going to lose my new friends as well as my boyfriend?

The idea of leaving the library and bumping into the boys makes me feel sick, so Calvin fetches sandwiches from the closest café. Mine tastes like cardboard and each bite is an enormous effort. We're preparing to leave when Calvin's phone rings. He snatches it up before I can see who's calling, turning his back to me and Ursula.

"They've what? No way. Did the police, or. . . Shit. OK. Bye."

I feel Ursula's hand squeeze my shoulder as Calvin ends the call. When he moves to face us, he's ashen.

"Henry and Ozzie are at the police station being questioned. Their parents collected them from school ten minutes ago."

My heart thuds. Has Liam confessed? Does that mean they're taking my story about New Year's seriously now? Even if Halloween Girl never comes forward, even if it's totally disconnected from Esme's murder, at the very least Henry and Ozzie might get done for possession of drugs.

Calvin hurries away, and Ursula and I return to school just as the bell announces the end of lunch. In history everyone is chattering excitedly. No one so much as glances my way; the full story hasn't spread, then. But if Henry's been taken out of school, Marley will know by now. Still nothing from her, even though she must have missed me at lunch. The foreboding inside me tightens a notch. I desperately need to see her. I've got to explain.

> Can you meet me by the vending machines after school?

Marley doesn't reply. When lessons end I hurry to meet her, ignoring the buzz around me. As minutes crawl without Marley appearing, my stomach sinks. After a quarter of an hour, I give up and leave – only to bump into Marley outside the sixth form block, on the phone.

"He didn't!" she snaps. "I was there and I would know. They can throw accusations about but they can't convict Hen without evidence. Mum! Are you even listening? Stop panicking. It'll be fine. I'm coming now."

She ends the call and stalks off in the direction of the small student car park. "Marley!" I call, catching her up. Is it my imagination, or does her face contort when she sees me?

"What do you want, Alana?"

"To explain." And I plunge in, telling her everything. I finish, "I know how tough this is going to make things for you at home, but, honestly, I didn't have a choice. This needs to stop. You get that, right?"

I wait, desperately wanting her to reassure me that she understands, but Marley barely even blinks.

"It's fine," she says shortly. "Don't worry about it."

And she gets into her car, slamming the door.

"Is that all you're going to say?" I cry as Marley winds down the window to get a clear view so she can back out.

"Alana! I don't have time for this."

"I still want to be your friend." My voice wobbles. "Maybe I never said it in words, but you matter to me, Marley. And if you want me, I'm here for you."

Marley leans out of the window, eyes sharp and bright. "If you were any kind of friend you'd have come to me first, not gone to the cops."

"I didn't want to put you in an awkward position. If Henry's done the things I think he has, then he deserves what he gets. Sorry, but he does."

"You know what, Alana? Your obsession with Esme's death is beyond weird. You didn't even know her! As for the drugs and whatever—"

"They're not a *whatever*, they're date rape drugs! They're sick, and wrong, and have no place anywhere, ever. Those boys nearly did it to me. They'll do it again! And I *did* know Esme. Maybe not like you, but she was my friend, and she mattered. That's why I care!" Unable to stop myself, I say, "You can't stand Henry, anyway."

"Don't tell me how I feel about my own brother. You know shit about us. Now leave me alone!"

Her car hurtles backwards and I have to skip out of the way. It's only when she's gone that I realize how badly I'm shaking. Marley's in shock, I understand that, but how can she not get that this needs to stop?

It seems black and white to me. But then, it's not my brother, or my family that's going to be destroyed. Maybe she's in denial, really thinks I've got this wrong. She never said in as many words that she believed my story about Henry and New Year's. I merely assumed she did.

If Marley turns her back on me, does that mean the other girls will too? Is that why none of them are replying to my messages? The thought I'll end up stuck on the edges like I was at my old school. . .

I can't bear it.

At home I message Marley, stressing that I'm here for her, as well as posting on the gang group chat. I don't mention Henry. There's no way in hell I'm apologizing for shopping him, even if it means having no friends. All evening I check my phone, but she doesn't reply. Neither do the others. I knew going to the police would have a ripple effect, but I never imagined everyone would cut me out. I so hope Marley's OK.

My thoughts turn to Liam. Is he spending the night at the station? I wish I knew what was happening. He's smart enough to have worked out I reported him. I wonder how that makes Liam feel, what he'd say if we could talk. Maybe the argument with Marley has numbed me out, because when I think about what Liam's done, the only thing inside me is a hollow numbness.

The next morning there are so many rumours whizzing round online that I have no idea what's true and what isn't. Everyone knows why Liam was expelled from his old school now – someone who knew must have blabbed. One of the rugby reserves is claiming the police found drugs, including GHB, stashed in Ozzie's room. Another says Henry's denying everything, pinning the blame on Ozzie and Liam. I have a horrible feeling that Henry is going to walk away from this. There's no hard evidence against him. Even the messages to Liam were sent by Ozzie.

People are gossiping about me too. At the moment it's stupid stuff – *she's Liam's girlfriend, do you think she had any idea?* – but how long will it be before everyone knows I'm the one who accused three popular, rich guys of planning to commit rape?

At break, Marley is nowhere to be seen, but come lunchtime I track her and the gang to The Hideout. Marley looks calm, but something about the way she sits is almost unnaturally still.

Everyone stops talking when I arrive. Great. Then Marley gives me a sheepish smile.

"Hey. Sorry about yesterday. I said things I didn't mean. Here. Peace offering."

She pushes a cardboard cup towards me. I stare at the tea, gobsmacked.

"You don't blame me?"

"You did what you felt you had to. Let's move on, eh, Lana? Want to share my fries?"

And she starts talking about something else, like it's just another day. I clutch the tea and sink down next to her, but I don't drink a drop. *You should be happy, she still wants to be friends*, I tell myself, but I'm not happy. Whatever happened with Henry is not the kind of thing you ignore. The air between us isn't at all cleared. How the hell can she feel it is?

I twice ask how things are at home. Both times Marley shuts me down. It reminds me of how she acted after Esme's funeral, when she asked if I wanted to go shopping. Marley barely mentions Esme now. It's like she never existed.

Someone bangs their hands on the table, making the cups teeter dangerously. We all jump. It's Xander.

"You," he says, and I realize he means me. "I want a word."

He looks like he wants to kill me. Maybe he does. Liam's one of his best friends. Determined to set him right, I get up, but Marley grabs my arm.

"How about you ask Lana nicely? Or is 'please' not in your vocabulary?"

"Get lost, Marlena," Xander snaps. "This is none of your business."

"Scared because your sidekick's been arrested? Or is it really yourself you're scared for? The police never cleared you of killing Esme, did they? Daddy's hot-shot lawyer won't be able to protect you for ever."

She's standing now, hands on hips.

Xander looks at Marley incredulously. "You're actually enjoying this. You really are a total psycho! I'd like to wipe that smug look right off your face!"

"Then why don't you? Because I'm a girl, and you're a gentleman? Don't make me laugh." Marley places her hands on his chest and gives him a little push. "Go on, Alexander. Hit me. You know you want to."

Xander's expression goes very tight, and for a second I think he's going to do it. Instead he kicks over Marley's chair. It crashes to the floor so loudly that people nearby stop talking. Xander stomps off. I stay frozen a second. Then I run after him.

"Xander! Wait."

"Don't come near me," Xander hisses. "I am this close to losing my temper, and you do not want to push me over the edge."

"You wanted a word."

"Not any more. Run back to precious Marley and her toxic lies. Now piss off. I'm busy."

He kicks open the café door and vanishes outside. I catch the door before it can slam in my face, and follow.

"What's happening with Liam? Have the police—"

Xander wheels round, his face white with anger. "Why should you care? You're the one who shopped him."

"For good reasons!"

He mutters something I don't catch and strides past the war memorial to the parking spaces on the other side of the town square. In a sea of greys and blues, his bright yellow Lotus is easy to spot.

"I need to know what's going on," I insist. "Tell me."

"Fine. Liam's vanished." The words are like a punch to my gut. "He was released on bail last night, but this morning his room was empty. His grandma doesn't have a clue where he is, and he doesn't have a phone on him. I know he's seen the online shitstorm because he told me so, in a message that made no sense whatsoever—"

He stops himself. I pick up on something else in his voice: worry.

"You think he might do something stupid?"

"Correct. I'm going to look for him." And Xander gets into the driver's seat. I stare at the steering wheel, remembering all the times Liam drove me places, and how he always listened when I had something to say. Something inside me twists. I run round and open the passenger door.

"I'm coming too."

"No, you're not. Get lost."

I'm already doing up the seat belt.

"If you want me gone you'll have to push me out. I mean it."

"Jesus!" He throws up his hands. "Get lost was a perfectly simple instruction! Last week you point-blank refused to get in my car, now you're desperate to. Make up your bloody mind."

I narrow my eyes at him. "You'd better get driving."

Xander narrows his eyes back. Then he snaps, "Fine. But don't you dare spill that tea."

He turns the key in the ignition, and the engine roars to life. As we speed down the one-way system to the fringes of town he says, "If you have any smart ideas where Liam might be, now is the time to share them. You're his girlfriend. I assume you had deep and meaningful conversations."

So that's why he wanted to speak to me. A voice at the back of my head reminds me to keep my guard up. Even if he did get me home safe last time, I still don't trust Xander.

"Shouldn't we call the police? They could track his number plate. It'll have been picked up on CCTV—"

"On country lanes? I don't think so. The police know he's missing already. His grandma rang them."

"Has she told his parents yet? I know Liam hasn't seen his dad for years, but surely he'll care enough about this to make contact—"

I stop. Xander's staring at me as though I'm speaking another language.

"Alana," he says, "Liam's dad is dead. Didn't you know?"

My mouth falls open. "He let me think his dad had

walked out. We talked about family all the time... He said..."

What did Liam say, exactly? Not much – I made assumptions, and he didn't correct me. With horror I remember that weird phone call after Esme's funeral. Me, saying Liam's dad would call one day. Liam replying he didn't think so. Telling me how he'd ring himself from the landline, just to see the word *Dad* on the screen. Saying my dad looked nice and taking that photo.

"Oh my God." How the hell did I miss this? "What happened to him?"

"He killed himself. It was sudden, unexplained, and Liam's never got over it. Who do you think owned that tatty jacket he wears all the time? He's a fucking messed-up guy, Alana. And that's why, whatever he might've done, I am very worried about him."

TWENTY-SIX

As we drive deeper into the countryside, I rack my brain as to where Liam might be headed. We spent so many hours together but I'm starting to realize, when it came to emotional stuff, we mostly talked about me. My head is spinning with the bombshell Xander dropped. When I suggest that Liam could be at his dad's grave, Xander says, "Where do you think we're going? It's not far – St Mary's, same as Esme's funeral."

Now I know why Liam was so strange that day! "Can I see the message he sent?"

Xander tosses me his phone.

I cant do this any more, Liam's written.

It feels all Iv ever done is screw up and I don't know how I can fix things moving here was supposed to be a new start I let mom down again i've said sorry but its not enough

"Crap," I breathe.

"Crap indeed." Xander pauses, eyes flickering to mine. "I think he's under the impression I'm angry at him too. And I was."

"What for?"

"Messing you around last weekend! He acted like a dick and I told him so. I don't even know why he did it. That's the thing that pissed me off most. He knows he's on to a good thing with you. It's very irritating."

"Why?"

Xander rolls his eyes. "Oh, I don't know, maybe because I think you should be making out with me instead? If you ignore the small fact that you hate me, we'd be great together."

"You're really killing the sarcasm there. I don't hate you. I just don't like you."

"Still think I'm a rapist and/or a murderer? I assume not, you are in my car, but feel free to correct me."

I'm not ready to answer that. "Do you know what I found in Liam's room?"

"Uh-huh. I can't explain the photos. They're weird.

The texts... I'd guess he put Henry and Ozzie in contact with some dealer. Henry thinks he's edgy, which is both hilarious and untrue, but he wouldn't have a clue how to get anything harder than weed." He glances in the interior mirror as we turn off for St Mary's. "Liam was stupid to do it, but he probably thought they wanted ket or whatever. I'm a hundred per cent sure he doesn't deal himself any more."

I swallow, really hoping I've made a mistake. Xander pulls up outside the church, but a quick walk round reveals that it's empty.

"Great," Xander mutters. "This was our best bet. Any ideas?"

"What about the nature reserve? Liam told me he used to go there as a kid, I guess with his dad."

"Are you certain? We could be searching there for ages."

I bite my lip. Then I shake my head. "If you were him, where would you go?"

"Somewhere quiet? If he really is suicidal, he'll want to be alone." Catching me wince, Xander says, "We might as well use that word. It's what we're both thinking, isn't it?"

"Do you think he'd really do it?"

"I don't know."

Xander's words hang there. Starting to panic, I look around the graveyard. How can the two of us really have no idea where Liam would go? We're supposed to be his friends! I open my mouth to say we should talk to the police. Then something obvious comes into my head. I grab Xander's arm.

"The Witches' Pool."

Xander frowns at me. "I don't think so. My mum was down that end of the estate an hour ago. No one's there. Trust me, Liam hates that place. Won't go near it."

A tiny whisper of a memory creeps out from the back of my mind. "What did Liam's dad do?"

"He was a pilot. But—"

"He's there." I set off in a run.

Xander catches me up. "How can you be so sure?"

"If I remember right, before Thea Keats, the last person who died there was a man, around the time Liam's dad died. I think that was him. And if we're not really quick, Liam's going to do the same thing."

Seconds later we're screeching out of the car park.

"We'll be there in five minutes if I step on it," Xander says as the Lotus gathers speed. "I'll drive right up to the pool. It's possible he arrived in the last hour. You're right that it's where Liam's dad died, but I'm not convinced that means Liam's there now."

I am. Liam told me he used to draw his dad pictures. I've seen several tied to the trees, all of aeroplanes. I should have realized earlier. Liam mentioned his dad travelling for work and calling him from abroad. What other reason would Liam have for knowing about that geeky plane app? And he visits the pool more than he let on to Xander.

We hurtle down the narrow lane, way over the speed limit. Each time we near a bend I brace myself, but Xander slams on the brakes, screeching round like he's on an episode of *Top Gear.* The only car we meet pulls over and we fly past without even slowing.

Near Stillwater, Xander swings on to a dirt track I didn't realize was part of the estate and ploughs straight across a grassy field so overgrown that we can barely see through the windscreen. I yell for him to slow down, but the engine's roaring so loud he doesn't hear. Then the grass clears and I realize Xander knows exactly what he's doing because we're right by the cluster of trees that border the Witches' Pool. He stops, and we jump out and run to the pool. The water is as serene as ever. Liam isn't there.

"No," I gasp. Then I realize we've arrived at the pool from the path, like I did on New Year's. Liam would have cut through the woods. Xander clearly clocks this too, and together we wind through the woods to the other side, leaping over stumps and nettles. Colour flashes through the branches: red. A T-shirt. Liam's sitting at the edge of the water, half-hidden by a holly bush, hugging his knees to his chest, eyes closed. I kneel down and shake his shoulder.

"Liam! Are you all right?"

He mumbles something, half opening his eyes. His forehead is sweaty despite the cold, and he's shaking uncontrollably. I feel for his pulse. It's pounding.

"How many of these counts as an overdose?" Xander holds up an empty pill packet. He doesn't wait for an answer, just takes out his phone. As I hear him ask for an ambulance, I feel a deathly sense of déjà vu.

Even though help arrives quickly, the minutes we wait crawl. Liam's conscious, but barely responsive. The paramedics get him into the ambulance, then speed off.

I look at Xander, who's talking to his dad. He rang his parents after calling 999. His mum is on the phone to Liam's grandma.

Now the adrenaline has worn off, I feel dizzy with horror. A few minutes later and Liam might have been dead.

And those pills weren't painkillers. They were antidepressants. Why the hell didn't I know Liam was taking them?

Xander comes over. He's pale, his usual self-assurance gone. "Are you all right?"

"Not really. Are you?"

"No," he admits, and, for the tiniest moment, I want to hug him.

We go back to the house, but I quickly start to feel uncomfortable and ring Mum to pick me up. Only a few days ago Xander was my number one suspect. Even if I don't believe he's a rapist any more, he's still a knob who tries it on with girls, and sitting next to him on a sofa while his mum and dad ask questions I don't know the answers to puts me on edge. When Mum arrives I put down the tea Xander's parents made me, untouched, and hurry out.

*

Later that afternoon, my phone starts pinging. I've been lying in bed since getting home, doing very little except thinking, thinking, thinking. I keep coming back to how Xander and I couldn't see Liam when we arrived and had to run round to the other side of the pool. It plays over and over in my mind, like a broken cinema reel. I feel sure it's important but can't figure out why.

I pick up my phone.

Apparently he's responding well to treatment

We'll know if there's any lasting damage tomorrow

It's me by the way

Me as in Xander

Just in case you elected not to save my number

I feel less tense with Xander on the other end of the phone than I did in his house. How depressing is it that he's the only person I want to speak to right now?

Me: I knew it was you.

Xander: Because you're Inspector Alana, obviously

But yes

That's the news

I assumed you would want to know

Me: Thanks

I've been so worried

Xander: Ditto

Me: Did the hospital call you?
I thought they weren't supposed to give information out if you aren't family

Xander: They aren't
I rang up pretending to be Dad and threw my weight around
He sits on the hospital's board of governors so they like to keep him happy

I'm surprised the nurse fell for it. Pulling rank is a crappy thing to do, but for once Xander's done it for a good reason.

Me: Thanks. Hope your dad isn't angry when he finds out.

Xander: Meh
My dad is perpetually angry at me these days
Anyway
How are you?

Three small words, yet so very big. I shift into a comfier position.

Me: Kind of numb
Today doesn't change what I think Liam did so why does it feel like it does?

Xander: Because finding him there was scary?

I sigh. Another person might say Liam overdosing is a sign of a guilty conscience. I'm not so sure. He's not been right since Esme's funeral. I'm no shrink, but I'd guess that brought back the unresolved feelings he has over his dad. Being arrested pushed him over the edge.

Me: I feel like I should have been a better friend

Xander: Don't you mean girlfriend?

I pause, wondering if Xander meant it when he said he thought I should be with him. One thing is clear: on some level, I still have feelings for Liam. Wanting to find him earlier was instinctive, something I didn't think twice about. How can I still care about someone who is a rapist, maybe even a killer? Someone who probably knew about me being threatened?

The way I feel makes no sense. Up until now I felt so certain – rape is rape. Evil. I should hate Liam. And yet all I could think about this afternoon was whether he was going to be OK.

Eventually I type, Don't know

Xander: Do you want a cute fluffy dog picture (Xander not included) to cheer you up?

Me: I think this goes beyond animal therapy

Xander: What about a photo of the ancestral sword?

Me: Stop going on about that bloody sword!
You could have called you know
Kind of a long conversation to have by text

My phone rings immediately with a video chat. I hesitate, then pick up.

"Hi." Behind Xander I can see a panelled wall and the corner of some kind of tapestry. The flickering light makes me wonder if he's sitting by a log fire. "Just FYI if this becomes a habit, I massively prefer talking to messaging. Also, I will shut up about the ancestral sword. Not one of my better jokes."

"Noted." I'm too tired to feel self-conscious about my messy hair and lack of make-up. "How are you doing?"

"Honestly? Not great. I keep fixating about how I had a go at him last weekend, even though he deserved it. It feels like I should have noticed how low he was. I had no idea he was on antidepressants."

"It's not your fault. If you hadn't gone looking it might have been too late."

He sighs. "He always seemed so OK."

I thought the same. But I guess that never means someone really is OK. A lot of guys still don't admit feeling down in case people think they're somehow less of a man.

The one time Liam did try to tell me how he felt I was angry and didn't want to listen.

"Haven't your parents ever thought of draining that pool? All it seems to bring is misery."

"They tried to fence it off a few years ago, but a public footpath runs nearby, and in the end it was too much hassle. The priority was keeping the area by the folly off limits. There are ancient mantraps lurking around there. They're dangerous, not to mention illegal." He sighs. "I guess Liam lied about visiting because he wanted to keep those notes private. Don't tell people about his dad, please. I don't think anyone else at St Jules or Fairfield has connected Liam to the guy who died seven years ago."

"I won't."

"Good. Finding Liam today really brought back what happened to Thea."

First-name terms. "What was the deal with you and her, Xander? Really."

For a few seconds I think he's not going to answer. Then he says, "I'm only telling you this because you've caught me in a low moment. Here goes: for all my big talk and expensive tuition, I, Alexander Rupert Octavian Montgomery Lockwood, am a bit shit at school. My predicted grades were a real kick up the backside. Dad paid Thea to give me extra tuition. She saw me in the house rather than at school to spare me the humiliation. How this mutated into us banging each other, well. Blame the rumour mill."

"Oh." This explanation is a lot more ... ordinary than I was expecting. So much so that it never occurred to me.

Xander rolls his eyes. "Wow, really deep response, Alana. I'm so glad I confided in you."

"Sorry. I'm just surprised. You're so articulate."

"Using big words is a cunning ruse to con people into thinking I'm bright."

"Come on. Not liking school doesn't mean you're stupid. There are other things you're good at. Don't you rank at county level for fencing?"

"Oh, my non-scholarly talents are endless. Unfortunately they don't impress my parents much. Anyway. Thea. I had nothing to do with bullying her, in case you wondered. Not my style. It was funny, though."

"What was?"

He hesitates. "Thea killing herself. She hated St Jules, but she was leaving. In a couple of months all that shit would have been history."

"What? How do you know that?"

"She gave my parents notice on the cottage. Told them she was moving back in with her mum and dad. Rather her than me. Some of those villages along the Norfolk-Suffolk border are really tragic. Still, it sounded like she was looking forward to it."

The county border is maybe an hour from Attlingham. Somehow, I'd always pictured Thea as isolated, her support network far away, and that being another reason for her unhappiness. "Everyone just accepted her death as suicide?"

Xander shrugs. "Who knows what was going on in her head? We didn't know what was going on in Liam's, did we?"

I glance down. Xander isn't seriously suggesting Thea didn't kill herself. So why am I having doubts? People are complicated. Thea being excited to go home doesn't mean other things weren't wrong in her life.

The important thing here is that some seriously nasty boys made Thea's life hell – the same boys threatening me. And one of them killed my friend. My heart hardens. Xander and Liam excepted, the rest of the rugby team were in Thea's classes. No doubt they clocked she was out of her depth and decided to have some fun – probably for no better reason than just because they could.

Xander and I talk more, the conversation veering back to Liam. When I hang up I'm surprised to find out that we were on the phone for well over an hour. A ping tells me I have a new message. Xander's sent me a photo of Bella lying on her back, legs in the air. I half-smile. Just then it was easy to forget who I was talking to.

The mood at Fairfield the next day is sombre. New rumours keep popping up but I can't bring myself to care. I deliberately cut it fine getting in so no one can mob me before lessons, and at break and lunch I vanish to the history classroom. When Marley finds me I say I want to be alone. Once upon a time she'd have put an arm around me and asked how I was feeling, but today she just nods. She turns to go, then looks back.

"I got that sponsorship deal. The online retailer? The video I did with you cinched it. So thanks, Lana."

"Congratulations." The word sticks in my throat.

"If you ever want more modelling, let me know and I'll pull some strings. They thought you were great."

"I don't."

"Just offering." And Marley leaves. She hasn't even mentioned Liam, though she'll know what happened. If she has any reaction, she's keeping it to herself.

Hurt wells up inside me. Without me wanting them to, things have changed. I can't see our friendship ever being the same. Marley once made a joke about boys getting between us. One has. Her brother. And he's been there from the start.

The day stretches out, ends, and another begins. Instead of Marley and her gang, I hang out with Ursula and the others from history society, but I'm not sure if they want me there or not. Most of them are in the year above anyway. In a few months they'll be gone.

Then I get a call from Liam's grandma, and I forget about worrying over friends.

He's out of hospital and wants to speak to me.

TWENTY-SEVEN

Liam's grandma answers the door when I knock. She doesn't say much, just tells me to go up. It's unsettling meeting her again like this. I never got the impression that Liam was very close to his grandma – he spends enough time out of the house – but he's clearly told her all about me. And her red eyes show she cares about him, maybe more than he believes.

Liam is on the bed when I enter his room, propped up by pillows. There's a biology textbook on his lap, though the angle suggests he isn't really reading. He looks tired and pale. I hover in the doorway, suddenly not sure I'm ready for this. Then I tell myself, if Liam can be brave enough to talk, I can be brave enough to listen. I close the door and perch on the end of the bed. Hoping I can handle this sensitively, I ask, "How are you feeling?"

Liam doesn't answer. His eyes are downcast.

I try again. "You wanted to see me."

He swallows. Then he mumbles, "I don't blame you for going to the cops. The stuff on that phone looks hella bad, but I didn't hurt or mess around with anyone."

He sounds so flat, so unlike him. Despite everything, I badly want to give him a hug.

"You don't have to tell me this now. You should be resting. What happened didn't do any, erm. . ."

Lasting damage sounds wrong. I'm hyper-aware that even if overdosing didn't do any harm, it's going to take longer to heal his deeper, unseen scars – if that's even possible. Liam gives a tiny shake of his head.

"Why did you take those photos of me?" I ask softly.

Liam rubs his hand across his face. "I should have told you everything before. I almost did, lots of times. Only I promised I wouldn't, so. . ."

"I don't understand."

He sighs, leaning back on the pillows. "I knew about Halloween. Esme told me."

I stare at him.

"She didn't plan to. When I came to ask if she wanted to leave the party, it all came out. I was shocked, obviously. Esme thought the guys were outsiders, like, from another town, but she wasn't sure who. And the girl either didn't know or wouldn't say, so there wasn't much we could do." He pauses. "At New Year's . . . Esme realized she'd got it wrong. The rapists weren't outsiders. When Esme ran off, she found me. That's what we were talking about, last I saw her. It got pretty heated. She was so upset."

I suck in a breath. Esme's comment about boys from outside town. Liam insisting Esme hadn't been raped. Both of these now make sense. So does the argument Georgie overheard. It *was* Esme and Liam. Only, it wasn't an argument at all.

"Esme was scared Henry and the others were going to do something to you, and she wouldn't be able to stop them. So I said I'd make sure they didn't."

Finally, Liam looks my way. His eyes are so sad. "I really did notice you the moment you arrived. I know I've lied about other things, but that was true. I was so stoked that you were interested in me. I want you to know that."

My chest goes so tight that all I can manage is a nod.

"When I found you, you were chatting with Henry and looked . . . I don't know, but you clearly weren't drugged. Suddenly I wasn't sure Esme had got it right. I didn't want to accuse Henry and look stupid . . . so I photographed you together. I thought if he did attempt anything, it would be useful to have evidence. It sounds so dumb when I say it like that."

Another pause. "Even when Henry led you off I wasn't sure it was anything shady. So I hovered outside the cinema room. I was about to bail when Ozzie came along. Esme couldn't be certain who the third boy was, but I wasn't going to wait for him to show, not with both of them in the room with you." He makes a noise that I realize is a very unhumorous-sounding laugh. "I was all ready to bang in and be a hero and then you ran out. The rest, you know."

Without thinking I take his hand. "Why didn't you tell me before? Whoever you promised not to . . . they can't have wanted this."

It sounds like Liam's fighting tears now. "I was scared."

"Because you got Henry the drugs?"

"You won't get it, but when I moved here everything was bad. Mom was barely speaking to me, Grandma had all these rules, and I was angry and confused and that made everyone think I was weird so I had no friends. The only time I felt OK was when I was on the rugby field, but there wasn't a space on the team. Then Henry said. . ."

Suddenly, the favour Henry did Liam in return is blindingly obvious – and nothing to do with me.

"He'd drop someone and put you on the team instead if you helped him out?" I guess. Now Liam really does start to cry.

"I was so lonely and miserable I couldn't think. Somehow he knew why I'd been expelled. I thought he'd tell everyone. All I did was find him a dealer. I didn't know he wanted GHB! Mom, oh man, Mom will be so disappointed . . . I'll probably be expelled again, maybe banned from med school. I've screwed up my whole life."

I tighten my grip on his hand. "You haven't been

charged with anything, Liam. It looks bad, but you need to tell the police everything. Who is the person you promised to keep quiet for?"

"The girl," says Liam, as though it's obvious. I stare at him.

"The girl they raped?"

He nods.

"You know who she is?"

"Esme didn't want to leave her at the Halloween party. So I drove her home too." He rubs his temple. "She wants to forget it happened. I can't explain why, it's complicated. . . I promised I'd keep her secret. So, you see, I couldn't tell you. However much I maybe wanted to. Then the cops arrested me. Stuff's been bad so long and it was too much." His shoulders slump. "All I could think about was finding a way out."

I look at my fingers linked through his. "Do you still want a way out?"

He doesn't answer.

We're silent awhile. Everything I can think of to say sounds silly or flippant, and I don't want to make this about me by wishing out loud I'd noticed how bad things had got. I sense now is not the time to bring up the unresolved feelings Liam has about his dad's suicide, or point out that honouring someone else's secret nearly left him dead, and had everyone believing he was a rapist. I'm burning to ask who Halloween Girl is, but somehow I know Liam won't tell me, or the police. And I should respect her privacy too.

"If you'd talked to me I would have listened, you know," I say eventually.

"It didn't feel like I could. I wanted to impress you. Guys don't talk about this stuff."

"Liam! Saying you feel low doesn't make you a wuss. Neither does taking antidepressants. People care about you, even if you don't think they do. *I* care."

He doesn't look like he believes me. "You should have the photo of your dad back. I didn't mean to take it, but he reminded me of my dad a little, and I guess I wanted to pretend. . ." Liam stops. His eyes are swimming again. "I'd give anything to have him back. A day, even an hour. . . If I could just hear his voice one more time. . . Your dad. . . He let you down. It hurts, it's hard, it's not OK, I get that, but he's alive. And he loves you, Alana."

A lump wedges in my throat. I turn my back as I take the photo, wiping my eyes. Then I whisper, "I know."

Liam swallows. Then he says, "Sorry."

"What for?"

"Us."

Maybe my head is full already, or maybe it's not obvious, because I ask, "Us?"

"I always knew it wasn't going to work."

"You didn't know that."

"No, I did. Listen, don't argue. . . You were out of my league from the start. You seemed to think I was someone I wasn't, someone better. . . Don't get me wrong. I liked that. You made me feel good. But it was a lot of pressure after a while. And you have so much more in common with Xander—"

"What? Liam, I don't even like the guy."

"—but I couldn't make myself end things. Not when everything else was wrong. And I still thought you were cute, so . . . I didn't mean to string you along."

"You didn't. You really helped me, Liam. Everything at home – it meant so much that you listened, and understood. And you were kind. Thank you."

Liam closes his eyes. Eventually, he opens them again.

"That's nice," he whispers. "Maybe we can be friends."

Now it's my turn to swallow. "Of course we can. I . . . I think I knew too, really. That we weren't right. But I was scared to admit it. To you, and myself."

"It's OK."

And it is. For a few seconds, we stay as we are. Then, slowly, he takes his hand from mine.

TWENTY-EIGHT

Liam is evidently exhausted, so I don't stay much longer. As I wheel my bike on to the road, the tears finally spill. I don't know whether I'm crying because it hurts to see someone I care about in pain, or because I've finally accepted we're not right for each other, or because I want so much to hear my dad's voice.

I pull out my phone. My fingers are shaking a little as I tap on Dad's name. It rings once, twice, three times. Four, five. What if he doesn't want to speak to me? I hung up last time, and never plucked up the courage to listen to his voicemails. Six, seven. What if he's changed his mind? He'll have a new kid soon. Maybe he won't feel the same way about me. Eight.

Then Dad picks up, and even though my voice is so choked I can barely speak, I tell him I love him.

The call lasts the entire walk home, and then another hour in my bedroom. We only touch on the big stuff, but that feels weirdly OK. Mostly, it's nice to chat, and feel like he's part of my life again. It's not easy, but it's not as difficult as I'd worried either. We laugh a little. I cry some more. When Dad says he loves me whatever happens, I don't immediately think *lie*. We finish with him promising to visit whenever Seb and I are ready.

I still wish none of this was happening. I still hate what Dad did. I'm still angry. But I'm not *only* angry now. That's a start, I guess.

The next morning, my thoughts return to the third boy. I believe everything Liam told me, so it must be someone else. Piecing together alibis for Halloween is impossible, so all I have to go on is New Year's. Calvin has a firm alibi, Blake was with Georgie, and Xander, well, Xander's definitely holding something back, but after yesterday I'm struggling to picture him being in on this – though there's no evidence to prove he wasn't.

Could Georgie be giving Blake a false alibi? I hunt for Georgie at lunch and find her lounging on the grass round the back of The Hideout with Blake's arm around her shoulders, Faith hunched opposite. I watch them a moment, thinking how mismatched they seem as a couple, Georgie streetwise and cutting, Blake creative and flamboyant.

"Can I speak to you in private, please?" I ask.

Georgie arches an eyebrow. "That sounds ominous."

"Please?"

"I'm comfy. Whatever it is, you can say it in front of Blake."

Out of the corner of my eye, I catch Faith glance downwards. Even her friends seem to treat her like she's invisible.

"It's sensitive."

"So am I," says Blake. "Exceptionally sensitive."

He and Georgie laugh. But she does get up, and follows me to a quiet spot. When I ask if the alibi she gave Blake really is true, she pulls a face. "Erm, yeah?"

"Are you sure about the timings? He didn't slip off at any point?"

"Totally sure. What's this about, Alana? I thought your boyf, sorry, I assume *ex-boyf* attacked Esme?"

"He didn't. Whoever did is still out there." And I explain about the date rape, the third boy, and Halloween.

"And you think it's Blake?" Georgie's starting to look angry.

"Look, I'm not trying to ruin things, but you could be in danger—"

"Get lost, Alana! Who the hell do you think you are? You've got a real nerve pointing the finger at my guy, making out it's for my own good."

"I genuinely can't see who else it could be—"

Georgie shoves her phone at me. On the screen is a

selfie of the two of them, clearly taken in a car. In the background, I can see the edge of the manor house. The timestamp reads 00.20 on 1 January.

I piece things together. It would take over ten minutes for Blake to get from where he's parked to the Witches' Pool. He could have driven, but I don't think that would be much faster, and tyre tracks would have shown in the mud.

Crap. There's no way it's him.

I hand Georgie back her phone. "Sorry."

"You should be." Georgie stalks back to Blake. "You need to get a life. Find Halloween Girl if you're so desperate to know everything."

"She doesn't want to come forward. That's her choice, and I respect it."

Georgie shrugs as she settles back under Blake's arm. Faith suddenly speaks up. "How's Liam?"

Not one person has asked me that and sounded like they've cared. "Pretty tired."

"He'll be OK, though?"

"Physically, yeah. Beyond that, I'm not sure."

Faith looks frightened. It strikes me that she must have had a pretty horrible time this week with the gossip flying around about Henry. I should ask how she's doing, but I don't know how to speak to this girl who's loved up with a toxic rapist, so I walk off.

This time I really have hit a brick wall. What the hell can I do now? My only choice, as Georgie said, is to track down Halloween Girl, but that feels wrong. Unless. . .

There's another simpler option. A few days ago I wouldn't have even considered it, but a lot has changed.

I take out my phone. A few swipes is all it takes to find Ozzie on social media.

I need to talk to you, I type.

I meet Ozzie by the duck pond outside the castle. It's late afternoon and getting dusky, but the car park is busy, and several groups are enjoying beers on picnic tables outside the nearby pub. I'm not scared of Ozzie exactly, but I have no idea which way this chat will go. If he does get angry and lose it, much safer to have other people around.

Ozzie appears late, shoulders hunched, looking miserable. I'm both relieved and a bit surprised he's shown up.

"I shouldn't be here," he says as he joins me on the bench. "I promised Mum I wouldn't talk to anyone. She thinks I'll say something stupid. What d'you want?"

I watch him closely, wondering if he feels bad about what he's done, or just about getting caught. I've never had a conversation with Ozzie. All I know is he's Henry's mate, which I hope means he'll be feeling hurt, humiliated and betrayed. Doing my best to ignore how even being near him makes my skin crawl, I say, "Believe it or not, I can help you."

Ozzie suddenly looks suspicious. "Are you recording this? I'm not saying anything if you are."

I show him my phone's blank screen. Knowing how important it is to pick my words with care, I say, "Henry's stitched you up, hasn't he? He made you get the drugs and keep them so that if anyone found out, you'd be in trouble instead of him. He's going to walk away while you take the flack. Some best mate."

Sullenly, Ozzie says, "I don't have to talk to you."

"The police have been asking you about Esme drowning, haven't they?"

Ozzie's cheeks flare. My guess is correct.

"She had GHB in her system. They found GHB in your room," I press on. "Doesn't take a rocket scientist to do the maths. I know Esme being drugged was an accident, but the police don't."

"I've got an alibi. You saw me."

"No, I *think* I saw you. I never said to the police I was one hundred per cent sure." I pause, aware this next part is critical. "It was dark. I was new. And I don't think you can trust Henry to back you up any more, do you?"

I wait. I can almost hear the cogs turning in Ozzie's brain. Then his worried expression clears. "You'll say I was definitely there if I talk?"

Bingo. Hiding my excitement, I nod. Ozzie stares across the duck pond.

"Henry won't like it. Neither will my mum."

"Your mum would want you to take any help you can get."

"Guess so. I dunno if you can still get into cavalry if you get done for stuff." He fiddles with his cuff. "I haven't even thought about a plan B."

I lean closer. "Henry's set you up, Ozzie. People joke about you not being very bright, but I think you know when you've been taken for a ride."

An expression that might be hurt crosses Ozzie's blocky features. A father with a baby in a sling gets up from the bench next to us. We're alone now, and the car park is thinning out. I need to move this on.

"The GHB was Henry's idea, wasn't it?"

A tense few seconds pass. Then Ozzie says, "It started last summer. Henry gets bored easily. Shagging Faith wasn't doing it for him any more, but he couldn't be bothered putting the work in with someone new. Lots of girls around here really think they're something. You buy them stuff, spend hours taking them out, then they piss off, giving you nothing in return. I've had enough of girls laughing in my face when I make a move, like they're so much better than me. Maybe I don't look like, I dunno, Xander, but the bitches acted like I was a joke. Henry said we should put the joke on them. It seemed a good idea the way he said it. They had it coming really."

And that's how he justifies it to himself? It's a real effort to keep the disgust out of my voice. "So you'd, what, pick a girl, drug her, then find somewhere quiet to rape her?"

"People use that word too much. We only chose the girls who were up for it."

"I chatted to Henry for five minutes in the village shop. How on earth could he think I was 'up for it'?"

Ozzie shrugs. "Everyone knows models are sluts."

Is that what people really think when they look at me? Before I snap back, something sinks in. Summer. Ozzie said this started in summer.

A chill creeps through me.

"How many girls have you done this to?" I whisper.

Ozzie doesn't say anything. He doesn't need to.

Jesus.

Halloween Girl wasn't the first.

And Esme knew. *She's not the only one* – that was the single specific thing Georgie remembered Esme shouting at Liam. I'm not sure I can stomach sitting here any more. I honestly don't think Ozzie believes he's done anything wrong.

"How did you slip the drug into their drinks?"

"Dunno. Henry handled that."

"When did the third boy join in? Halloween? Before?"

Ozzie looks a little surprised. "I know there was one." There's a real edge to my voice now. "Who is he?"

"If I tell, will you promise you'll say I was in the cinema room at half twelve?"

I clench my teeth. I don't want to help this guy. I want him to pay. But . . . there's a killer out there who needs to be stopped.

It briefly crosses my mind that yet again I'm playing with fire, putting myself right in the danger zone. I don't trust Ozzie to keep this conversation secret. A coolness that might be fear prickles my skin. But the heat of needing to know, needing this to end, overpowers it.

So I nod, and Ozzie tells me who the third boy is.

TWENTY-NINE

The only sound at Stillwater is the squeak of wheels as I pedal up the driveway and take the turning to the health club. Even though the lights are on, the empty car park tells me no one is here. As I prop my bike outside I check my watch: a quarter past eight.

Reception is deserted so I peek through the glass of the door to the gym. Nobody's there. But I can hear the beat of music from the end of the corridor where the pool is. I pause outside. Ever since I finished talking to Ozzie, a tense knot has lodged itself in my stomach. What I'm about to do could be a very bad idea. I should call the police, let them deal with this. I already know I'm not going to, though. I push the door open.

There's just one person in the pool: Xander, cutting through the water with a quick, neat front crawl. When he gets to the end of his length, I cough loudly. He swivels round, looking surprised.

"Oh. Alana. Hi. Hang on, I'll come out."

Without speaking, I go to where his phone sits on the docking station and turn the music off. Xander picks up a towel and joins me, pushing wet hair off his forehead.

"So," he says. "What's up?"

I tilt my head, looking at him. What must it be like to be a boy who never hears the word no, and can't deal with it when he does? For the first time I feel sorry for Xander and his friends living in their unreal little bubble.

"This is becoming unsettling," says Xander. "You didn't come just to stand there looking at me. At least, I assume not. Feel free to contradict me. Has something happened?"

"I've had a chat with Ozzie."

"Ozzie? You must have been desperate. He's got zero banter."

Xander finishes towelling his hair and sits on one of the sunloungers. When I don't do the same, he stands up again.

"All right. You clearly want me to ask, so I will: why did you speak to Ozzie?"

"He told me the identity of the third boy."

Does the side of his mouth twitch? "Did he?"

I can see the swimming pool reflected in the glass of the window behind Xander. The way light dances across the water reminds me of the moon on the Witches' Pool, glimmering across Esme's body. I look away.

"Ever since you told me your story about that night, I thought something didn't gel. I want you to tell me what you're holding back."

Xander remains silent. He's watching me closely, though. Very closely.

"Well?" I ask.

"How about you say what you think I'm holding back and then I'll tell you if you're right?"

"No. We're not playing one of your stupid games. I think you know who the killer is."

"You need to get to the point." Xander's voice is cold now.

I watch him a second more, then decide I've seen enough. I really didn't want it to be his name when Ozzie opened his mouth. Having Liam's back doesn't make him a nice guy, but I can't dislike Xander in the way I used to. Ever since, I've struggled with the idea that he could be a rapist. But I guess if I'm honest, I always knew he was the prime suspect.

I draw a deep breath. "When Ozzie said the name, I didn't believe him. All along I've been so sure the third boy and the killer are the same person. But I was wrong." I sigh, shoulders slumping. "The third boy didn't kill her – because he has an alibi. It's Calvin."

I thought I'd misheard when Ozzie said Calvin's name. He seems such a good boyfriend to Ursula, and he's been kind to me too. Once he appeared in the video I stopped suspecting him. Third boy = killer was deeply rooted in my head by then.

"Henry was the one who got him in on it, just to mix things up," Ozzie told me. "Before Halloween it was us two. Didn't think Cal would have the guts, but fair play, he did."

What Henry and Ozzie did is disgusting, but I'm almost angrier at Calvin. He knew what they were doing was wrong but he didn't stop or shop them. For whatever reason, he must have got cold feet on joining Henry and Ozzie in the cinema room at New Year's after all. I wonder what was running through his head as he listened to the speeches in the barn, knowing that his friends had taken me away somewhere quiet. How can he live with himself?

Xander narrows his eyes. "I don't think I believe you. This is my friend you're accusing, remember."

"No. Sorry."

"Cal's a good guy. There's no way he'd do something like this."

But Xander doesn't sound one hundred per cent certain.

"It's true," I say. "Ask Ozzie yourself."

There's a long moment. Then Xander runs his hand over his face. "Shit. I knew Cal and Ursula weren't getting up to much, and he was pretty frustrated, but I didn't think he'd. . . Shit. Sorry, not very articulate right now. And there I was thinking you were going to accuse me again! Jesus, Alana. Did you need to be quite so dramatic?"

I join him on the lounger. Sheepishly, I admit, "I was trying to gauge how much you knew."

"You think I'd have kept something that sick secret? I do have some integrity. I can't believe you thought it might have been me!"

"Your reputation confused me. I thought you might have been . . . er. . ."

"Desperate for some action? No. Seriously, no! Until you started going on about those photos, I had no idea why those girls dumped me, all right? None of them gave me a proper explanation. I assumed my personality was just repellent, hooray."

The sarcasm he lays on doesn't fool me. This has hurt him. Not just his pride. Something deeper. Maybe I got it wrong. Xander doesn't have it all.

"Did you really only send me the first anemone?" I ask.

"Haven't we already had this conversation? I swear on Bella's life that's true. The others must have been Henry or Ozzie. They're the ones who wanted to scare you. Henry knew I'd pranked you with the first flower, so I assume that gave him the idea."

"How did he know I'd been nosing around in the old wing? Did you tell him?"

Xander nods. I swear under my breath as I realize how easily I fell into the trap, just as Henry planned, right down to blaming Xander. "You didn't help yourself by acting so suspicious!"

"You make it sound like I did it on purpose."

"This isn't funny. Where did you even get the anemone? The florist in town?"

He shakes his head. "We have a walled garden full of greenhouses. The gardeners cultivate all kinds of flowers off season. I just went in and picked one. Henry won't know that, though. I imagine he used the florist."

There haven't been any more flowers since I spoke to that grumpy woman. Maybe she passed my message on, or, more likely, Henry realized the anemones can be traced to him and backed off. This should reassure me but it doesn't. Threats can take other forms. More dangerous forms. As I found out with my bike, and in the old wing.

I ignore the chilly tingle that runs up my spine.

"Look, Alana," says Xander. "Why exactly are you here? I wouldn't have thought I was your first choice for this conversation."

I'm too embarrassed to admit that it feels like he's the only person I can trust. "Because I need you to tell me what you know. I've been so distracted by obsessing about the third boy that I've missed something. Maybe there *isn't* a connection between the date rape drugs and Esme's murder. None of the rapists could have done it. Perhaps I've been wrong from the start."

"Why do you think I can help?"

"Because I think the killer is the person who threw the drinks over you in the wood. The timing fits – they were heading back to the barn after the attack when you came along. Why else would they hide? But I don't buy you losing them in the trees."

Xander leans backwards. He's looking torn. I wait, heart thudding.

"All right, you win," he says. "I did see the person in the woods. Not their face, but something pretty important. You won't believe me, though."

"Try me."

His eyes flicker to mine. "It was a girl."

I stay very still as this sinks in. Then I let out a long, slow breath.

"I guess there's no reason now the killer has to be a guy. Did you tell the police?"

"Of course. Guess what? They didn't believe me! Cocky rich boy with no alibi claiming the killer's female? I was laughed out of the room."

I know how humiliating *that* feels. "They did the same to me. I'm still not sure how seriously they're taking my story."

"Indeed," says Xander, and for a second I'm distracted by just how posh that sounds. "So. The girl in the woods. Four girls weren't in the video Ursula made. You were in the cinema room, Georgie was with Blake. That leaves two." He pauses. "Faith and Marley."

THIRTY

"Marley wouldn't do something like this," I say immediately. "Esme was her friend."

Xander shrugs. "I'm not saying she did it. I'm saying she's a suspect. Surely you see my logic?"

Yes. No. I don't know. I look away. "It wasn't her."

Xander gets up, tossing his towel on to the lounger. "Course not. I suppose you're going to insist it was Faith."

"Doesn't that seem more likely? She's obsessed with Henry. Maybe she pushed Esme into the pool to keep his secret from coming out. If she loves him – can't see a future without him – that's a pretty powerful motive." Suddenly, I'm excited again. If I'm right, it means there *is* a connection between what Esme knew and her murder – but not as obvious as I'd thought. "Ozzie would have done anything for him too. Maybe that's what he does, picks on weak people and gets them to do what he wants."

"And that's not what Marley does?"

I stare at him, speechless for a second. "What?"

"Esme worshipped her. So do her other friends. Marley loves it! That's what her channel is about as well. She has a massive ego. Haven't you noticed?"

"Well, you'd know. Are you calling me weak too?"

"No, but didn't it strike you as odd how quickly Marley cosied up with you after so recently losing Esme?"

"We got on, all right?" I snap. It comes out sounding childish, even to me, but the way he's echoing my own thoughts gets under my skin. "Sometimes that's just how it is."

Is that true, though? Marley and I got on when I didn't challenge her. When I started asking difficult questions, she wasn't so friendly.

"You look angry," says Xander. "You can push me into the swimming pool if that'll make you feel better."

I glare at him. "Don't tempt me."

"Look, I'm not trying to piss you off, even though I realize I am. I'm simply saying there are two girls who could have drowned Esme and you can't overlook Marley. Right now, both of us need to find out the truth. Until this is solved, I'm still a suspect. Here's a suggestion for you to throw back in my face: how about we work together?"

"Why would I throw that back in your face?"

"You don't like me. You think I'm a liar. That means you don't trust me."

My anger fizzles out. I remember Marley describing how bitter Xander was when she dumped him, then Xander claiming it happened the other way round. I play with the zip to my coat, not speaking. I know what Xander's going to say next. And sure enough, it comes.

"Marley and I can't both be telling the truth. Who do you believe?"

My heart is hammering away. I want to tell him that of course I believe my smart, switched on, feminist friend, despite how weirdly she's been acting. If she says he messed her about, he did. Privileged guys like Xander have had things their way for too long.

And yet. . .

Marley has lied before. OK, outing me as a model on the vlog isn't important, except to me, but it wasn't something a friend would do. And I'm starting to wonder if she really dislikes her brother as much as she claimed.

If Xander dumped her . . . maybe she made up the story about him sharing her pictures to make him look bad. His story about the photos coming from one of the team subs could be true. If they've been deleted, there's no evidence to prove who sent them.

Suddenly I have a horrible feeling I know why Xander keeps getting dumped. It's Marley's revenge. She tells every girl he dates exactly what she told me. If she can't have him, no one else can either. People remember the team getting suspended over some nudes. The girls have no reason not to believe Marley. No girl would admit to something this embarrassing if it wasn't true. I didn't think twice about trusting her, or keeping the story secret. When Xander denied it, I automatically assumed he was the liar.

Another thing's fallen into place too. When Xander first told his story about reaching the Witches' Pool and not seeing Esme's body, I thought it wasn't true. The timing meant she'd already drowned, and I spotted her easily when I arrived. But Xander and I didn't approach the pool from the same side. I entered by the path. He arrived through the woods. Completely different views of the pool. That was why when we were searching for Liam we didn't spot him at first. Did whoever attacked Esme take her round to the path side of the pool before the attack? Or did they arrive that way? Either way, it figures. They wouldn't want to give away that one of the few people who knew about the short cut did this.

Xander's waiting. For a passing second, I feel irrational fury. It would be so much easier if he was all the toxic things I once thought he was.

Hating myself just a little, I whisper, "I believe you."

We don't talk much longer, but we agree to meet the next day, and when he says he'll drive me home, I let him. As he turns the key in the ignition, he tosses over his phone.

"Read my WhatsApps with Nell and Amelia. Kaitlin too."

Nell is one of Ursula's friends. The other two must also

be from Fairfield. I do as he says. Each chat follows the same pattern: flirting, dates, then Xander suddenly being dumped without explanation. There's no evidence of him pestering the girls for photos.

I feel sick. "Did you really not know what they believed you'd done?"

"One of them said something about photos, but I was pissed off and didn't really listen. The others just told me I was a shit." He glances over as he pulls into my driveway. "Not Esme, though. Turned out we . . . well, you don't need to know the details. We were both OK with things ending, that's what I'm saying. I'm guessing Marley never told her the photo story. Esme would have known it was a lie."

Esme. How did I forget she and Xander dated? The messages I saw on her phone made it clear that they broke up on good terms. Stupid! That was a massive clue that Marley's story was a lie. If the nudes really had been her, she'd have confided in Esme – and Esme would never, ever date someone who'd hurt her best friend.

I hand the phone back and slide out of the car with a mumbled goodbye. Xander's given me lots to think about, none of it nice. *Was* I needy when it came to making friends with Marley? She's fun and made me feel so welcome, but would we have gelled if I hadn't been desperate for a friend? Did the same thing happen with Liam? He made me feel better about the things I was most self-conscious about, but how much did we really have in common? There were silences, times we kissed because I couldn't think of what to say. Even so, I really wish he was here. Without him and Marley, I feel isolated.

If it wasn't for remembering Esme's chat with Xander, I'd still be holding on to a tiny flicker of hope that I'm wrong about Marley. In my heart, though, I know I'm not.

So Marley's a liar. Does that make her a killer too?

Xander appears at my house the next morning forty-five minutes earlier than we'd agreed, which means I'm still in pyjamas, eating breakfast. When, irritated, I ask what he's playing at, he shrugs and says, "My plans changed and I got bored waiting."

"So you just decided to show up without asking?"

"It's hardly early. I assumed you'd be up, not lazing around. I've already swum thirty lengths and taken the dog out. Nice PJs."

And to think I was warming to the guy. I swallow my last mouthful of toast, then shower and get dressed. After a moment's hesitation, I put on some lipstick. When I return downstairs Xander is chatting to a bemused-looking Mum with an easy confidence I'm sure must come from growing up in hotels, and being so rich. I was going to suggest we found somewhere quiet in town, but maybe it's best not to be seen together. So instead I take him upstairs, trying to ignore how uncomfortable I feel as he looks around my room, taking in the heap of dirty clothes on my chair, hastily made bed, the box of junk I still haven't sorted from the move. Fortunately he's most interested in my crime scene wall.

"The Inspector Alana thing was a joke," he says. "What the hell is this?"

"It's called visual mapping. It helps me think."

"It gives me brain ache. You need to get out more."

"Ha ha." I pick up a fresh pad of Post-it notes. On one I write *Faith* and the other *Marley*, ignoring the face he pulls when I slap them on the wall. "Who shall we talk about first?"

Xander looks at my computer chair. "Is this crap special, or can I move it?"

I toss the clothes on to my bed, and he sits down.

"Faith," I say. "What do we know about her? One, she has no alibi from midnight onwards. Therefore, opportunity. Two, she's devoted to Henry. Like, when he did break up with her, she begged him to take her back."

"Huh. I don't remember that. But then I don't give a crap about Henry's love life."

"Does he really like her? I've never been sure."

"He likes her hanging on his every word. She's pretty. Her dad does admin for the county rugby club. Free tickets aplenty. For Henry that's probably enough."

I pull a face. "Pretty funny relationship."

Xander starts swinging the chair from side to side. "If Faith did this to protect Henry, she must know everything. Does that sit well with you? It doesn't with me. If she loves him, she's not going to like him banging other girls, is she?"

I think back to the only real conversation I've had with Faith, at the pool party, when she said she hadn't minded Henry flirting with me. "Extreme as it sounds, I think she'd do whatever it took to keep him happy."

"Even commit murder?"

Neither of us say anything. It seems fantastical. And yet someone killed Esme. Our list of suspects is very narrow. I can think of plenty of famous killers whose wives and girlfriends knew they were doing terrible things and carried on loving them anyway.

"It's hard to imagine Faith doing anything violent," I say eventually. "She's always so meek."

"You'd be surprised," Xander says. "She had a massive catfight with Georgie before Christmas. Nails, swearing, everything. Even whacked her with a reusable coffee cup, which is so hilariously first world."

I almost drop my pen. "Is that a joke?"

"Nope. Georgie bitched about Henry not really being into her, and Faith blew a fuse. Which I suppose backs up our theory. And" – Xander nudges the Post-it notes with his foot – "it was an attempted drowning. Not exactly brutal."

"You're forgetting the wound on the head."

"Oh. Yes. I am. Shit."

We still haven't figured out what the killer used to hit her with. "Anything else you can think of on Faith?"

"Not really," Xander says after a moment. "We've hung out enough, but I wouldn't say I really know her. She's not the kind of person you notice."

"On to Marley." My voice dips as I say her name. "One, no alibi. She told me she left the barn because the speeches were boring, but she's never said where she was other than outside. I don't know if anyone saw her, or if the police even ruled her out. What's the motive, though?"

"Same as Faith's. Protecting Henry."

I shake my head. "There's no way she'd be OK with what Henry was doing. Her channel is all about girls feeling good. Other things about her might be fake, but that isn't. And Esme was her best friend."

"Marley was annoyed with her, though."

"About you two dating? Marley didn't know. She told me Esme never had a boyfriend."

"Haven't we already established Marley's a massive liar? I happen to know that after we called it quits Esme felt bad and confessed. Apparently Marley was furious! She'd calmed down by New Year's, but I bet she was still seething. As for motive . . . principles get forgotten when someone you care about is in trouble. You'd do whatever you could to protect Simon, wouldn't you? Even if you thought he'd done something wrong?"

"If you're talking about my brother, his name is Seb."

"Seb, Simon, same thing. I don't pay thirteen-year-olds much attention."

"He's fifteen."

Xander waves a dismissive hand. "Whatever. Can we get back to Marley, please?"

I swallow a snappy reply. "Look, I love Seb, but I

wouldn't kill someone for him. I guess Marley *might* have helped Henry to protect their mum and dad. Adoptive mum and dad, I mean. Do you know what happened to their birth parents?"

"They're dead. I don't know any details, but I'm guessing it was traumatic. Henry plays the poor-little-me card whenever he wants to get out of something and our head of year lets him get away with it. What? Don't look at me like I'm being nasty, it's true."

Despite myself, I feel sympathy. Scars like that never quite go, even if they fade. What Liam nearly did proves that. If Marley remembers losing her family before, her protecting Henry becomes more believable.

"I don't think I like your crime wall," Xander says as I stick up the new Post-its. "It shows us we basically know nothing. Let me guess, you poking around my house was playing detective too?"

I nod, and tell him I'm sure someone tampered with the floorboards. Xander immediately looks furious.

"They could have killed you! Not to mention landing my parents in a mess, and me with a shit half-term cleaning up filthy cellars and sheds! This makes the Faith theory more likely. She was there that afternoon. Marley wasn't."

"There's one final thing." I explain what Mum said – or rather, didn't say – about the night Esme died.

"Whoever attacked Esme needed to make sure she didn't get a chance to talk. It was a massive risk, obviously, but hospitals really aren't that hard to walk into. But, oh!"

I give a start. "Mum said whoever went into Esme's room was a boy."

"Is she sure?"

"There was CCTV. The police have been concentrating on boys, so I guess it was pretty definitive, even if that lead's gone cold. . ."

I trail off. I don't need to say that both Faith and Marley are slight, impossible to mistake for boys.

"Annoying," Xander says eventually. "That seemed like just the kind of thing Marley would do. She has a really cool head."

I've only seen Marley lose it once, when Jennifer Liu's comment about Bramford popped up on her vlog. I wonder why that was. Maybe I'll drop Jennifer a message later, if I can find her on social media.

Xander checks his watch. "I have to go soon. We need to decide what to do next, as much as we can, anyway, with the bloody fair next weekend."

"Could we confront them?" I ask. "They might give themselves away."

"There's no way that'll work with Marley. Faith, maybe."

"All right. I'll speak to her."

"Fine. And I'll have a word with Calvin. I've known him a long time. If I'm nicey-nice he might 'fess up about Halloween. And then I'm kicking them all off the team." There's a dangerous edge to Xander's voice. "I'm not playing with rapists. Liam better get his backside into gear and come back or else we're screwed."

"Don't you dare tell him that. The last thing he needs is any pressure."

"I'm not a total bastard. And on that note, I'd better get round there."

"Oh. That's where you're going."

"Don't sound so surprised. He's probably sick of me showing up all the time. We don't do much apart from watching films and kicking a ball about in the garden. No idea if it's helpful but it seems to distract him."

Xander's clearly read up on how to support Liam. I'm not sure why this makes me feel funny. Their friendship's stronger than I realized. Xander asks if I want to come, adding ungraciously that he's sure Liam would like to see me. Clearly Liam hasn't said anything to him about us, not that us is even a thing any more. I shake my head. I've sent Liam several messages since Thursday to check in but he hasn't replied. Despite telling myself it's OK if he needs space, I can't help but feel hurt he's cutting me out.

I walk Xander to his car.

"You'd better get back on friendly terms with Marley so she doesn't get suspicious." He opens the door, then pauses. "I really think we're close to cracking this. Be careful, all right? If anything happens, even if it's just a weird noise in the night, call me. I mean that. I know where our groundsman keeps the shotgun."

"Not the ancestral sword?"

"Sadly it isn't sharp enough to be of much use. Ditto my

fencing épée. And I'm not joking, Alana. Whoever did this might well try to harm you again."

He's probably right. A shiver goes through my body. But I know I can't give up now.

THIRTY-ONE

At school I make a big effort to be myself. Sure enough, Marley soon thaws. By the afternoon she's acting like everything's normal, and the rest of the gang follow her lead. I have no idea what's going on in her head. Maybe Jennifer Liu can tell me more if she replies to the message I sent at the weekend.

Faith is away on a German trip, so, frustratingly, I don't see her until the middle of the week, queuing in The Hideout with Georgie and Blake, who are more interested in eating each other's faces off than ordering lunch. A meaner person might think it serves her right for the times she and Henry have been all over each other in public, but

Faith doesn't just look miserable today, she actually looks ill. Her cheekbones jut, and the bags under her eyes are ashy grey. When I ask if she fancies sitting with me, she shakes her head.

"I'm supposed to wait outside for Henry."

I don't like the way she says *supposed to*, like she has no choice. Perhaps I stand a better chance when Henry isn't around. Everyone involved with the fair is heading over to Stillwater after school – she can't say no if I ask her for help getting into my Elizabeth costume, can she?

Sure enough, Faith agrees. All the costumes are being stored in the barn – far enough away from where everyone else is to be private. I keep up neutral chatter, hoping to relax her.

"It's not as bad as I expected." The dress is quite plain – no ruff, just a square neckline lined with fake jewels, full skirt and lace cuffs that drape over my hands. The wig has fortunately died a sorry death in storage. "Hooks and ribbons on this corset seems like overkill, though. Historically inaccurate too."

Faith doesn't reply, concentrating on lacing the back of the corset up. Rare end-of-February sunlight blazes through the skylight. It seems impossible to believe the girl behind me could be a murderer. All the same, I messaged Xander to tell him where we are, and he replied to say he'd be nearby. I'm not taking any chances.

Here goes. I take a deep breath.

"Can you believe it's been almost two months since Esme died?"

Something clatters to the floor. Faith's dropped her phone.

"Did you like Esme?" I turn so I can see her properly. Faith mumbles something that sounds like, "Everyone liked Esme." Her hair covers her face as she stoops to pick up her phone. What I can see is chalk white.

Maybe it *is* her. A strange sensation runs through me – a mix of excitement and surprise and disbelief. Keeping my voice level, I say, "I think you know more about Esme's death than you let on. Keeping a secret that important must be eating you up. Why don't you tell me about it?" I pause. "I know the killer wasn't a boy. And you don't have an alibi."

Faith stares at me. The expression in her big blue china-doll eyes is one of pure terror.

"Esme was about to accuse Henry of rape," I press on. "She witnessed what he did at Halloween. I'm guessing you know all about that."

She opens her mouth. A single word comes out: "No."

"Protecting someone is a pretty powerful motive. Was pushing Esme into the pool his idea or yours, Faith?"

"No." Faith is actually backing away from me. "You've got it wrong."

"Put me right, then. Talk to me, Faith."

She runs out. I blink after her, too startled to follow.

I'm struggling to undo the corset when Xander strides in.

"Faith rushed past me sobbing," he says. "She hasn't joined the others so I guess she's gone. What happened?"

I fill him in. Xander's frown deepens.

"So, either she did it, or knows who did?"

"I'm not sure." Brilliant – now I'm confused as well as unsettled. "Maybe confronting her wasn't such a great idea. It feels like I've kicked a puppy."

"A possible killer puppy. Look, do you need a hand? Watching you trying to undo that thing is painful."

I turn round, and Xander comes over. His fingers brush my bare back as he tugs the ribbon loose, then starts unhooking me. I feel my cheeks colour. Thank God he can't see. "Have you spoken to Calvin?"

"Not yet. I've a free period with him tomorrow afternoon. We usually sports coach some of the younger boys then but that's cancelled. I can fill you in before Henry's crappy gathering. You're going, aren't you? I'll give you a lift."

Henry and Marley are having a get-together at their place so everyone can chill before the fair the next day. I can't believe Henry feels comfortable hosting just a week and a half after narrowly dodging drugs charges. He really believes he's untouchable. "Thanks. Um, I can manage from here."

He steps back, and there's a weird silence that might be awkwardness, if Xander was the type of boy who got awkward.

"Pretty big design flaw, not being able to get undressed yourself," he says. I wonder when he's going to leave so I can get fully changed. "The dress is less extravagant than I was expecting. Didn't Elizabeth have hundreds of jewels sewn into her outfits? My ancestor was one of her ladies-in-waiting. We still have some of her letters. One describes being shocked by how heavy the dresses were. I wish I could remember the exact quote; it was funny."

I raise my eyebrows at him. "You know what, Alexander Lockwood? I think you're a closet history nerd."

He raises his eyebrows back. "I prefer to call it taking a healthy interest in my family's history."

"Of course you do. You're right, though, this dress is a bit of a let-down. If I was still friends with Marley I'd ask to borrow her necklace."

"What necklace?"

I show him a picture on my phone.

Xander shakes his head. "That got nicked ages ago. My mother has some prop jewellery somewhere. Want me to ask her if there's anything suitable?"

"Yeah, go on – wait. What do you mean, the necklace got nicked?"

"I took her to the beach on a date. Someone went through our stuff while we were swimming. Marley kicked up a huge fuss. Insisted on showing everyone we met a picture of it on her phone and asking if they'd seen it, then sulked the whole way home. Wins a prize for worst date ever. And I've had a few."

"How certain are you it's the one in the photo?"

"Pretty certain. Is this important?"

"It could be." I tell Xander about Marley wearing the necklace when I turned up at her house. "Esme had a matching one – and she definitely wore it to your party. Perhaps Marley somehow got hold of it. She did show me a photo where they both wore the necklaces, but that was kind of old."

Xander looks at me, not saying anything. And I realize. Feeling the colour drain from my face, I glance down at my wrist, and the friendship bracelet I can't quite bring myself to take off.

I can't hide any longer. So I say it. "Marley must have been at the pool that night."

"There's no other way she could have got the necklace. Esme was wearing it when she left the barn. We've got to find it. Any idea where Marley keeps her jewellery?"

"On the dressing table. But there's no way Marley will let me in her room alone if she thinks I'm suspicious."

"She will if I distract her." Xander smiles. A little distracted myself by holding up the corset, which, now undone, is doing its best to slide off, I look at him.

"Marley won't fall for that. She hates you, remember?"

"I can be very distracting if I want to be. Even to girls who think they hate me. Just you watch."

He looks back at me like this is some kind of challenge, and I know he's not only talking about Marley. I glance away. If he thinks this is going to get some kind of reaction he can forget it.

"Fine," I say. "Tomorrow. You do your thing, I'll find the necklace. Hopefully, anyway."

"Definitely. I have total faith in your abilities to rifle through Marley's jewellery. Finally we'll have evidence we can take to the police."

"You think she did it, don't you?"

"It explains the message Esme sent asking me to the pool." When I look blank, Xander sighs, his smile falling. "Look, I didn't want to say until we were sure. . . But what function did that message serve, other than landing me in the shit? Esme was probably already in the water by then. I'm guessing it was faked, probably typed as the killer walked back through the woods. That's where you found Esme's phone, isn't it?" He pauses. "And who hates me enough to do that?"

There's only one answer. Feeling a traitor, I whisper, "Marley."

I'm buttoning up my jeans – Xander having finally left – when my phone pings. It's Jennifer Liu.

> Hey, sorry I took a while to write back. I'll talk to you but only face to face. I'm around Saturday morning if you want to chat? Can you come to see me?

I swear. Saturday is the fair. I'd suggest another time, but Jennifer's message sounds kind of twitchy. I don't want to scare her off. I google Bramford. It's up near the Norfolk-Suffolk border, and by bus the journey takes about an hour.

If Jennifer is happy to meet first thing I could see her before the fair opens. It'll mean skipping setting up and pissing people off. But this is urgent.

Finally, everything is falling into place.

Xander's car appears in my driveway at exactly half six on Friday, the time we agreed to head over to Henry and Marley's. Relieved to be going out, I grab my bag. The house feels empty without Seb. He and Mum left straight after school. I don't think Mum's looking forward to the cat show, even though she's hating being stuck at home, but I know she'll enjoy seeing him happy.

The moment I open the passenger door I can tell Xander's itching to tell me something.

"I confronted Calvin." He doesn't even bother with hello. "First I was nice, and he denied everything, so then I got nasty, and he caved. I now know more about Halloween than I ever wanted to. Cal said he was drunk, and the others were jeering at him so he went along with it. Have you ever heard such complete and utter shit? I told him to own up. And I think he might."

My eyes go wide. "Why? He's got away with it!"

"Cal's terrified. He thinks Ozzie will rat on him. His eighteenth isn't until August. Much better he confesses now, when he's still a minor. His parents are lawyers, he knows how this works."

Which no doubt means Calvin is aware that even if he does confess he'll probably get away with it. Glumly,

I remember how staggered I was when I read how few people are actually convicted of sexual assault. No wonder boys like Calvin, Henry and Ozzie think they're invincible. In many ways, they are. "Did he name the girl?"

"Nope. I think he believes he's being honourable, which would be laughable if it wasn't so deadly unfunny. He feels awful, or so he says."

"Should have thought about that before he raped someone." I bite my lip, thinking of Ursula, who's been nothing but kind to me. It isn't in her nature to gush, but I get the impression she's pretty into Calvin. Just another person who the truth is going to hurt.

"At least I got him to talk," says Xander. "It wasn't easy. Perhaps I'm not thick or lazy after all. Or maybe this is my calling, playing sidekick to your detective." His eyes flicker my way. "I dare you to be impressed."

"Shut up," I say, but, secretly, I am.

We decide it's best not to arrive together, so I walk into Henry and Marley's alone while Xander waits. Everyone's standing in the sitting room chatting. There are fewer people than usual: no Liam, Ozzie or Faith. I'm a bit worried about her. She hasn't been at school or posted anything online since I confronted her.

Marley's over the other side of the room handing round drinks. As she passes Henry a beer, I swear she leans in to whisper in his ear. Henry rolls his eyes and Marley laughs, mock-smacking his shoulder. My skin prickles.

Surely they're not always this friendly? Then, with a start, I realize that I wouldn't know. The only time I've ever seen them together is the first time I came over, when Henry walked into Marley's room. And that could have been staged.

Starting to feel on edge, I go to hang out with Marley's gang. Marley soon joins us. She starts telling everyone about the latest product she's been reviewing, a bronzer with shocking red undertones. It's a funny story and she tells it well. Again, I'm uncomfortably aware how easy she is to like.

Later, when the music is louder and a few people have left, Xander appears.

"Marlena," he says. "May I borrow you for a moment, please?"

Marley looks at his hand on her arm suspiciously, but doesn't immediately snipe back – perhaps because he's wearing a dazzling smile. I down the rest of my juice, and say I'm going to the loo. The hallway outside is empty. I hurry upstairs to Marley's room and go straight to the mirrored cabinet where she keeps her jewellery. Inside, earrings, bracelets and necklaces are sorted into different boxes. I lift up the top compartment – and there it is, half-hidden under a velvet pouch. Hardly able to believe my luck, I turn it over in my palm. Antique teardrops, dark gold collarette. Bingo.

I slip the necklace into my pocket and hasten downstairs. Xander is still with Marley. I can tell from her expression that whatever he's saying, she's not buying it. Deciding I'd better break them up, I ask Marley if there's any apple juice. As I follow her to the kitchen, I lock eyes with Xander and give a tiny nod.

"I don't get that guy." Marley sounds flustered. "He's been a total bastard for months, now suddenly he's all Mr Nice Guy."

"Maybe he feels bad about how things ended between you?"

"I doubt it, babe. He's playing some kind of game. And I heard he was getting cosy with you. Helping you out of your costume the other day ring any bells?"

She looks directly into my eyes, and I flush. Someone must have passed by the barn and seen us. "Nah. Not my type."

Marley doesn't say anything else, but back in the sitting room, she keeps glancing my way, expression calculating. Soon after, she leaves the room. Relieved I don't have to keep up an act, I turn to talk to someone else.

Ten minutes later Marley returns, face white. She makes a beeline for Henry.

"Hen." The urgency in her voice makes me stand up straight. "I need to speak to you."

"What?" Henry sounds annoyed.

"Not here. Alone."

Henry's expression changes. He places his bottle of beer on a shelf and follows her through the open windows to the patio, his hand on her back. They go, round the side of the house, out of sight. I search for Xander, only to see him vanish outside.

He's going to eavesdrop. I sip my juice, only with great effort stopping myself from glancing at the windows every two seconds. My throat is dry, my palms clammy. The necklace feels like it's burning a hole in my pocket.

A hand grabs my arm.

"We're leaving," Xander hisses in my ear. "Now."

Too startled to protest, I let him pull me outside and down the road to where his car is parked.

"What's happened?" I whisper.

Xander doesn't answer. He drives up to the edge of town, pulling over at the entrance to a farm. He turns off the ignition, breathing rapidly. Then he says, "They know we're on to them."

THIRTY-TWO

My eyes widen. "How? We were so careful."

"Obviously not careful enough." Xander flicks off the headlights. "Maybe Marley worked out I was distracting her. She was rattled as hell. 'It's not there,' she kept saying. Henry had to ask what she meant. He didn't know she even had Esme's necklace! When Marley told him, he looked like he wanted to kill her."

"What happened next?"

Xander doesn't answer immediately. Then, very slowly, he says, "Henry gave her a hug. And then he said, 'We've dealt with worse.'"

I stare at him. He stares back. After what feels like ages,

I say, "They're in this together. They've been lying about not getting along."

"No shit, Sherlock. More importantly, we're officially a 'problem'. I don't think that means everyone has a friendly chat and makes up, do you?"

I realize we've landed ourselves in it, right down to clearing off so suddenly. Marley will know exactly who took the necklace, and why. I lean back heavily in my seat, trying not to spiral into total freak-out mode.

"What do we do?" I whisper. "Tell the police?"

"And have them laugh in my face again? No, thanks. I'm still a suspect, remember? And you're a hysterical drama queen. They won't believe either of us. Marley will only say we're lying. What does the stupid necklace really prove, anyway? Nothing!"

Xander swears, smacking the steering wheel. He's right. I feel myself pale. When I speak, my voice trembles.

"I'm seeing Jennifer tomorrow. You know, the girl from Marley's vlog. I think they were friends. She definitely knows something. Maybe something key."

"Maybe? That's not very reassuring, Alana. The psycho siblings might have killed you by then. I'm deadly serious. The moment Esme became a threat, she was dealt with. They're ruthless. And you, you're a massive threat."

"So are you."

"I'm not the one they've warned multiple times already," Xander snaps. "My house is CCTV and burglar-alarmed up to its eyes. You're going home to an empty cottage."

I'd forgotten. Of all the nights for Mum and Seb to be gone! My stomach plummets. I picture home – the creaky stairs, the lack of neighbours, the lock on the back door which wouldn't be hard to break. Who am I trying to kid? I won't be all right. I'll be huddled in bed too terrified to sleep, with the knife block on my bedside table.

Perhaps my silence gives me away, because when Xander speaks, his voice is much calmer. "I think you should stay at mine tonight."

My eyes flicker to him. "Won't your parents mind you bringing a girl back?"

"Why would they? You're not sleeping in my room. Sorry. Even if they did, so what?" He pauses, then says a word I don't think he uses often. "Please?"

I'm super nervous about rocking up at Stillwater, which I know is silly considering the alternative. Xander's parents look surprised when he announces I'm staying over, but both make me welcome. His mum takes me to a guest room, probably so Xander's dad can sound him out. I didn't take much in when I was last here, but the inside of Stillwater House is a lot less grand than I'd expected, worn looking, even, and everything creaks. The Lockwoods only live in a small section.

I put the bag I hastily packed at the foot of the bed, looking round at the room with its narrow windows, low, decorative ceiling but otherwise modern decor. It's a relief to be safe, but I still feel shaky, and very aware of how isolated we are here. The seriousness of the situation is only slowly sinking in.

Xander comes in, tossing a clean towel on to my bed. "Not as opulent as you were expecting, I'm guessing." He sounds a little off. I wonder if his dad gave him a hard time downstairs. "Don't get me started on the disadvantages of living here. Crappy reception, for starters. There are acres of land that haven't been touched for decades. We found an unexploded bomb in the grass once, not to mention the mantraps."

I think he's only talking to put me at ease. I don't feel like banter but I play along. "If you're trying to make me feel sorry for you living in a beautiful Tudor manor with an on-site gym and swimming pool, it's not going to work."

"How about if I tell you there are mice?"

"If you were a cat person there wouldn't be any mice." That reminds me of Bruce, alone in the cottage, and I swallow. He wound himself around my legs when I quickly grabbed my things, but I was too worked up to even stroke him. "Oh God. I hope Bruce is OK. What if Henry and Marley hurt him? My brother will be devastated!"

"I think it's you they want to kill, not the cat." Xander pauses. "You feel safe here, I hope?"

"Yes."

"But?"

I sigh, shoulders falling. "I want this over."

"Funny, so do I. Oh em gee, we finally have something in common." He says this in a Valley girl voice which sounds so wrong in his accent that any other time I'd laugh. I look at him, remembering the first time we met, and what an entitled jerk I thought he was. Before I have time to second-guess myself, I say, "I'm sorry about what I said about not liking you. I had you wrong. You're all right really."

"Oh God, it's all coming out now." Xander pulls a face, but there's an intense kind of feeling in the air now, one I can't ignore. Suddenly I wonder what will happen when – if – this is all over and Xander and I have no reason to hang out any more. Could we be friends? Somehow, I can't see it.

We linger where we are. We should say goodnight, but I don't want him to go. Not yet. And maybe he doesn't want to leave, because he asks, "What's going on with you and Liam? I promised myself I wouldn't ask, but who am I kidding? Feel free to tell me it's none of my business."

"It is none of your business. But, as you asked, we're over."

"How do you feel about that?"

I tuck a lock of hair behind my ear, thinking. After a moment, I say, "Sad. I liked having a boyfriend. We had a good time together. But I wasn't as into him as I thought. It feels weirdly OK, ending things. Even a bit of a relief. I think we could be really good friends."

Xander nods, expression blank. "Just so you know, I realize the way I acted when you first showed up wasn't helpful. I don't have any excuses, other than being an arrogant rich boy who spends most of his time with other arrogant rich boys." A pause. "But even then I would never have thought what Henry and the others have done is OK. I'm annoyed I haven't been calling out the shit I've heard other guys say over the years. From now on, I will. It shouldn't be up to you."

"No," I say quietly. "It shouldn't."

Xander glances away. "For some reason it felt important to say that. Blame darkness and mortal peril."

Is he embarrassed? It can't be easy to rethink things you've accepted as normal for years. "Well, I'm glad you did," I say. "Even if was awkward." I pause, fingering the cuff to my top. "If we're doing confessions... I judged you and the other rugby boys as being all the same and I shouldn't have."

I'm expecting a sarcastic response, but Xander just looks at me. Then he nods.

"We should get some sleep," he says. "This bed isn't the one Charles I supposedly slept in, by the way. Just in case you were getting excited."

I almost smile. "Right."

"There are extra blankets in the cupboard if it gets cold. And if you need anything in the night..." His voice softens. "Wake me up, OK? I'm only two doors down."

His hand brushes my shoulder. It's only a second, less, even, and my top has sleeves, but, just as it did weeks ago, his touch sends electricity running through my whole body. My hand reaches towards him before I check myself.

"Night, then."

"Night."

He turns. Before he can go, I say, "Xander?"

He looks back. I lean in and give him the quickest hug. "Thank you," I whisper.

The next morning the skies are bright and clear. Everyone involved with the fair will be beyond relieved, I think as I dress. Despite the bed being comfortable, worrying kept me awake. Xander knocks on my door as I'm brushing my hair. It doesn't look like he slept well either.

"What time are you meeting Jennifer?" he asks. "I'd come too, but there's no way I can dodge fair prep."

"Half nine. Once I'm on the bus I'll be fine."

He checks his watch. "Do you want to check your cat isn't dead? If you don't mind eating on the go we'll have time."

Stupidly touched, I grab my bag. It turns out that Bruce is fine, though the dirty look he gives me makes me wonder why I cared. Xander drives to the end of the lane that leads to Stillwater, and waits with me by the side of the road until the next-to-empty bus appears. I hail it and sink down on the closest seat. On the other side of the window, Xander mimes a telephone, and I nod. But as the bus meanders through fields and narrow roads dotted with cottages, I realize calling Xander if I need to might be impossible. Reception is patchy at best. I really hope this meeting is worth the risk. Else we're screwed.

Bramford is a village not unlike my own, though poorer looking. It's only as I press the button to get off that I realize Thea Keats must have grown up nearby. Didn't Xander say her parents lived in one of the villages on the Norfolk-Suffolk border? She must have felt so out of place at St Julian's, not to mention intimidated by her students' privilege.

I step off the bus and look around, shielding my eyes from the sun. A few metres away a slim Chinese girl is waiting on the footpath: Jennifer.

I join her. "Thanks for agreeing to meet me."

Jennifer shrugs. Her face is carefully composed, giving nothing away. I follow her down the road and into an empty play area. We perch on the swings.

Jennifer scuffs her heel in the dirt, then looks up. "Do you think Marley had something to do with that girl drowning?"

Jennifer's heard about Esme; that isn't a surprise. What's more of a surprise is that she's come straight out with it. "What makes you ask?"

"No reason."

But Jennifer's watching me closely. I decide to start with something neutral. "Were you two friends?"

"Kind of. Back then I was really introverted, and Maya seemed, I don't know, so cool and confident, the kind of girl people noticed, even if they didn't like her."

"Yeah. That sounds like Marley— Wait. You called her Maya."

"Just a nickname," says Jennifer quickly. "Her brother was the same, only moodier. People weren't drawn to him in the same way and he didn't like it. Thought because he was clever people ought to treat him differently." She laughs. "God, I sound so sad, like I was watching them all the time. I really wanted Marley to be my friend. But she didn't seem to need any."

"Why was that?"

"Because of—" She hesitates. "Henry."

I had a feeling Jennifer was going to say that. "They were close?"

"Hell, yeah. You almost never saw one without the other. They even had their own secret language. It was them against everyone else. Even their parents. Which they often were."

"Why?"

Jennifer glances over her shoulder. "You won't tell Marley you spoke to me, will you?"

"Of course not. Tell me about their mum and dad."

"Well, Marley said once that their parents were ordinary, like it was a bad thing. She looked down on them, Henry too. Their mum and dad were nice, but they couldn't keep up with their kids intellectually, and there wasn't the money to give them the things Henry and Marley thought they deserved. They acted like their mum and dad were disappointing children, and they were the parents. It was really weird."

A chill is settling on me. "Their parents died, didn't they?" When Jennifer looks confused, I frown. "Isn't that why they were adopted?"

"You don't know?"

"Know what?"

"Henry and Marley's parents were murdered."

THIRTY-THREE

According to Jennifer, Mr and Mrs Pendleton – I hadn't known that was Henry and Marley's original surname – were downstairs watching TV, and their children asleep when the house was broken into. No one knows what happened next, but by the time twelve-year-old Henry called the emergency services, both parents were dead.

"It was bloody." Jennifer's voice is barely audible. "Whoever did it used gloves – no DNA evidence. Gave me nightmares for years. I was terrified my parents would be next."

My hand is in front of my mouth. Jennifer's pointed out the house where it happened, a little cottage painted grubby white, shrouded by thick evergreen trees. "Didn't Henry and Marley hear anything?"

"I'm not sure. They were taken into care. I only saw Marley once afterwards."

"How was she?"

"Excited. She said something about getting new parents, like they were a phone she was upgrading. She did cry, but—"

"You weren't convinced she was very sad?"

Jennifer glances downwards. "Maybe it was her way of coping."

Like hell it is, I think, remembering Marley's heartfelt speech at Esme's funeral, and how minutes later she was off shopping.

"Why did you message me?" asks Jennifer nervously. "May— Marley's doing fine now. I found her online ages ago, but she never replied to my messages. I guess she wants to leave the past behind. That's why I wasn't sure whether to talk to you."

Out of the corner of my eye I spot my return bus trundling along the road.

"Jennifer," I say. "If I told you I suspected Marley had killed someone to protect Henry, what would you say?"

Jennifer doesn't answer for what seems ages. Then she murmurs, "I'd say Marley and Henry like to get what they want."

Jennifer hurries off and I jump on the bus, flashing my

ticket. My feet walk me to a seat, and my eyes stare out of the window, but my brain is too busy wrapping itself around what Jennifer's told me to take anything else in.

Xander answers immediately when I ring, sounding short of breath. I pour everything out. To my frustration, the line starts cutting out before I can finish, then goes dead entirely. Xander must have lost signal. Bloody countryside! I tap on Chrome and type *Bramford Suffolk Pendleton murders*. It takes an age for the results to pop up. Most are news reports. One, close to the bottom, catches my eye.

Conspiracies UK: were the Bramford murderers close to home all along?

I wait as, agonizingly slowly, it loads. "Come on!" I mutter. "Come on, come on, come on."

The 4G icon vanishes. I almost scream in frustration. Then I catch sight of a road sign, and realize I'm almost at Stillwater. At least there I can pick up the wifi. I need to read this!

But I don't get a chance. The moment I near the manor house I'm grabbed by a group of anxious girls and swallowed in a bubble of pre-event stress. Someone snatches my coat, bag and phone and bundles them into the room in the barn where everyone's stuff is being stored. Georgie appears with my costume. Everyone's in meltdown. Ursula looks on the brink of a heart attack, and I can hear Blake yelling about a sign with a typo in it. Furious, but not seeing what else I can do, I pull on my costume, and Georgie starts lacing up the corset. Then a new voice says, "Let me do that, babe."

"Go ahead." Georgie steps back. The corset ribbons are yanked so sharply I cry out.

"Too tight? Sorry." Marley's voice is as sweet as sugar. A deathly feeling creeps over me. I stand rigid as she does me up.

"All done!" Marley sings, and I turn and stare into the expressionless eyes of the girl I'm now sure attacked Esme. She raises her eyebrows.

"What's wrong, babe?"

"Nothing," I mumble.

"Take a seat, I'll make you up. Can't have a queen with a naked face, can we? I've done everyone else. Let me get my gear."

She vanishes through the doorway. I lean against the wall, feeling dizzy. This can't be happening. But it is.

By the time Marley returns, chirpily complaining that her mascara had rolled out of her bag, Faith has joined us. I half-thought she wouldn't show. I don't know what Faith's deal is, but I'm grateful not to be alone with Marley. When we hurry out of the barn a few minutes later, the first visitors are wandering into the field.

If I wasn't desperately trying to work out what to do, I'd be bubbling with joy over how brilliant everything looks. The field is full of colour, bunting tied across trees, and rows of stands selling crafts, gifts and locally made jams and cheeses, with plenty of space for falconry, archery and the mock joust. Further along, there are food carts, and hay bales and benches nearby for people to sit and eat. Over the far side of the field is a stage, the kind you'd see at a music festival, set up for the play and fencing display which Xander decided he could be bothered to organize after all. Already there's a good crowd. That a bunch of sixth formers have pulled this off is incredible.

Fanfares blaze when I appear, and people bow and curtsy. I do my best to look regal as the fair gets busy, somehow smiling and making small talk. It should feel like I'm in my element – normally I get a real buzz from events like this – but I can't concentrate. All the time I'm aware of Marley sticking to me like a shadow. She and Faith are my ladies-in-waiting. I realize she's not going to leave me all day, even if I go to the toilet. Sweat breaks out on my forehead. I spot Xander over the other side of the field, dressed in a knight's costume with his fencing sword in a scabbard, which on another day I'd be incredibly distracted by because that outfit ticks all the boxes of my weird historical crushes, but he's busy, helping clear the crowds for a catering trolley to come through. There's no way we can talk properly here. I haven't seen Henry yet, but I'm sure he'll be watching too.

I feel trapped, even in the middle of a crowded place. All I can think is that the murderer's right behind me.

Then I see someone I'm not expecting. Liam is standing

by a hay bale, clutching a coffee. With him is his grandma, and a chic woman who must be his mum. He sees me around the same time as I spot him. There's a funny moment when neither of us react. Then he gives me a tentative smile, and walks over.

I wet my lips. "Hi. I didn't think I'd see you here."

"I decided to come last minute." He clears his throat. "You look nice. But then you always look nice."

I ask him how he is. Liam shrugs.

"Oh, you know. OK. Mom's been here a few days. I thought she'd be cross, but she's really shook up. We never talked much about, you know. . . My dad. Turns out there's a lot I never knew about him. Not just the obvious things, like him and Mom not getting on. He was struggling at work, and moving to London made him lonely and unhappy, plus he was finding sleeping hard and taking meds for that. . . Lots of things." He pauses. "It's tough to hear. But, yeah. We're talking."

"Good. I'm really glad."

"Sorry I didn't reply to your WhatsApps. I read them, though." Liam's gaze flickers over my shoulder, and I guess Marley is rolling her eyes impatiently. "I'll let you go. I might not be sticking around. Mom's talking about getting me a private tutor in London until the exams, but if I stay, we could hang out." A pause. "As friends, I mean. That is, if you want to."

I nod, racking my brain for how I can somehow give him a message to pass on to Xander. Then Liam does something surprising. He takes my hand, giving it a squeeze, just the way he used to. In his palm is a scrap of paper.

"I saw Xander earlier," he says. "Didn't get the chance to say more than hi. He's ridiculously busy. Anyway. See you later."

The words sound totally innocent, but they're enough. I let go, closing my fingers over the note.

"Come on, Queenie." Marley pokes my back. "You've duties to perform."

Reluctantly, I say goodbye to Liam. He frowns as we walk off, and I wonder how much he knows. I'm desperate to read the note, but I wait ten minutes before saying I need a toilet break. Predictably, Marley comes too, but she can't watch me in the actual cubicle, and there, with trembling fingers, I unfold the scrap of paper, which looks like an old receipt. On the back, in the jagged handwriting I recognize as Xander's, is one word:

SUSPECTED

And underneath are two stick people, one clearly intended to be female. My breath catches in my throat.

Xander has managed to google what Jennifer told me. He's read that link. And he's thinking the same as me.

The Pendletons' house didn't look big from the outside. If they didn't have anything of value, why would someone break in, let alone kill them? And how lucky would the murderers have to be to leave no DNA behind at all?

It feels unlikely.

Something else feels unlikely too: that two children

whose parents were killed so dramatically would, years later, be involved in another murder.

Way too coincidental.

What if Henry and Marley know exactly how their parents died?

What if . . . they did it?

The next two hours are agonizing. My head is all over the place, and I'm sure Marley's noticed. It all fits. Did the police ever seriously suspect Henry and Marley, or is that just a conspiracy theory? There can't have been any real evidence if they were cleared for adoption – and given new identities. Jennifer called Marley *Maya* earlier, didn't she? And she hesitated before saying *Henry*.

I need to speak to Xander. Yet each time I glimpse him he either doesn't see me, or something stops me going over. When fanfares announce that the play is about to begin, we head along with everyone else to the stage. As we're finding seats Faith says, "They won't start for a few minutes. Does anyone want to get food while it's quiet?"

Those are almost the first words that have come out of her mouth all day. "Good idea," I say. Marley purses her lips, then asks if we can bring her something. I can't believe she's letting me out of her sight. Then I remember. Xander's in the play, the fencing display immediately afterwards. Even if I get backstage, our chances of talking are nil.

I'll have to wait until the fair is over. Still on edge, but beyond relieved to get a break from Marley, I go with Faith to the food carts. She's fidgeting, obviously not really interested in eating. Then she blurts out, "Do the police still think Liam did it? He wouldn't tell me."

I hide my surprise. "When did you see him?"

"Thursday."

So that's where she went after running away from me. How weird – Faith and Liam aren't friends. Although . . . she did say he was a "sweetie" at the pool party, and asked how he was.

"I had to see him," Faith's saying. "He wasn't feeling great but he was so lovely. He told me it would be OK, that I didn't have to do anything I didn't want to—"

She stops, swallowing. I stare at her, deaf to distant applause as the play begins.

"What are you talking about?"

Faith doesn't meet my eyes. "You've always been nice to me. Not many people are. What you said to Georgie, about Halloween, and respecting the girl's privacy. . . I. . . I don't know how to say this." Beads of sweat cluster on her forehead. "It's me. I'm Halloween Girl."

THIRTY-FOUR

My first thought is *no*. Faith's outfit was a classic witch one. Not a red feather in sight. But then who said the feather came from a girl? I don't have my phone to check, but wasn't Calvin wearing some kind of headdress? The feather must be from that.

My second is *shit*. Henry and his mates raped his own girlfriend.

Faith's eyes have started to swim. I take her shoulder and guide her to a quiet spot away from the food carts.

"Liam's right, Faith," I say gently. "You don't have to talk about this."

"I do though. I didn't realize Liam would get into trouble because he was protecting me."

"Why did Henry do this to you? You're his girlfriend. It's not like you're . . . unobtainable."

"We weren't together at Halloween. I'd broken up with him." Her lower lip wobbles. "Everyone thinks he ditched me, but it was me who ended things. He was possessive and it was freaking me out."

That's not what Marley said. Another lie. Even if she hadn't, I'd have assumed Henry dumped Faith. It seems so much more believable that way round – just like the lies Marley told about Xander.

"I take it he didn't like being dumped."

"I think it was the first time in ages something hadn't gone his way. He couldn't believe it. He kept saying, 'You don't get to dump me.'"

So this isn't just about sex. It's about power.

Faith glances at her feet. "Esme and Liam kept telling me it was, you know, that I should go to the police, but I was too scared. I even lied to them and said I didn't know who the boys were. If Henry found out I'd grassed him up. . . And it's not like I said no, so really it's my fault. At least, I don't remember saying no. I only had one drink, but it must have been stronger than I realized. I was really drunk by the time Henry took me upstairs. He was being sweet that evening, making me remember why I liked him in the first place. . ."

As gently as I can, I say, "If you don't clearly give consent, then it is rape, Faith. It's one hundred per cent not your fault. And I think you were drugged. Listen, this is important. Did Henry give you that drink?"

She shakes her head. Crap. I still can't tie him to the drugs. Not quite able to hide my disbelief, I say, "How can you stand hanging around him? Everyone still thinks you're his girlfriend. . . I don't know, are you?"

"It's safest to keep him happy. If I don't. . ."

She doesn't need to complete the sentence. Her face is wearing the blank look I'm used to, but it doesn't make her look vacant any longer. Just sad and scared.

"You're the only person I've told about this, apart from Liam," she continues. "No one else would care. My friends drifted away when I got with Henry. He didn't like me spending time with them when he wasn't there. I thought it showed how much he liked me, so I was happy to do what he wanted, and then it was too late. . ."

She falls silent, then bursts out, "I hate him! He's taken everything from me. I used to be a fun, happy person. Now I feel like I'm invisible. Just a thing that belongs to *him*. I keep telling myself there's only a few months of school to get through, and once we go to uni he'll leave me alone, but I'm terrified I'll never get away."

"Of course you will!" My voice is fierce. Inside, my heart is breaking for Faith, and all the times her pain went ignored. "The bastard is going to pay, I promise you. I'll make sure of it."

She wets her lips. "Do I need to tell the police?"

"I don't know. Probably." My voice is almost drowned out by a cheer from behind, and it brings me back to reality. There's a killer in the audience waiting for her burrito, and unless it comes quickly she's going to get suspicious. "Thanks for confiding in me. I promise I won't talk about it to anyone else. Have you got my number? Think about what you want to do. Whatever it is, I'll help. You're not alone or invisible. And you are going to get away from Henry, Faith, really soon." I squeeze her hand. "I'm so sorry about what I said to you the other day. I had it all wrong."

She attempts a smile. "It's OK."

"Are you absolutely certain Henry didn't give you that drink?"

"Positive. Marley did."

For a second, my heart stops. "What?"

"She asked if I wanted something when I arrived and chatted to me while I drank it. I remember because I was so grateful to have someone to speak to. Alana? Is this important?"

I can't speak. Suddenly I'm back at New Year's, taking that dodgy punch from an outstretched hand. All this time, I couldn't remember which girl gave it to me, the new faces a blur. Now I'm sure. The girl who fetched that punch was Marley. And she slipped the GHB in it. So her brother could rape me.

The rest of the fair drags. It feels like months have passed when, eventually, the field clears. Apart from the pre-opening meltdown it's gone smoothly. Everyone is in a jubilant mood. It takes ages to pack up and take the props and outfits to the barn where they're being stored until they can be taken back to school next week.

"I bet it feels like you can breathe again now," the girl who helps me out of my corset says. Wrong – I'm not going to be able to breathe until Xander and I are telling the police everything. Quickly I change into my ordinary clothes. My WhatsApp is full of pictures Seb's taken of the cat show. I fire off a quick message to say I'm glad he's enjoying himself, and that the fair went well. Then I find Xander helping Ursula and a couple of others take down the signage.

"We need to talk," I say.

He nods. "Let me finish this and get changed. And don't worry. I've just seen a blue Mazda with a very particular number plate leaving the estate."

Henry and Marley's car. She's leaving with a friend, but at least this means he's gone. I blow out a long breath.

"Good. Be quick, OK?"

In the barn I help with the last few bits of tidying. The others leave. I pace around, unable to keep still. Then Ursula sticks her head round the door. "Hey, Alana. Message from Xander. He wants you to meet him at the pool."

What the hell? Is he seriously suggesting a swim, right now? Then I realize Ursula means the other pool.

The Witches' Pool.

Even thinking of that place makes me feel uneasy. I'd hoped never to go there again. Xander must have a good reason, though. Perhaps he's found something he needs to show me, or maybe he's parked down that end of the estate.

Henry and Marley aren't here, and I trust Ursula, so, too tense to feel annoyed, I zip my coat up and head into the woods.

> You'd better have a good reason for dragging me to this horrible place, I text Xander.
> Setting off now.

Five minutes later, I step out of the trees.

"Xander?"

"No. Sorry," says Marley's voice. I cry out and whirl round, and she pulls a *sorry I startled you* face as she moves out from the tree she was hiding behind.

"You and I need to have a little chat," she says.

Panic swells inside me like a balloon. The only thing that stops me bolting into the trees is the knowledge that Henry has left. By herself, Marley isn't a threat. She doesn't have a bag, or coat, so there's nowhere for her to hide a weapon. I'm stronger than she is. There's no way she'll be able to hold me underwater – if that is her intention. And there's a good chance Xander will work out where I am from the message I sent.

So I act calm, inching round so my back is to the woods rather than the water.

"All right. What do you want to chat about?"

"This." Marley takes a strip of paper from her jeans pocket. It's a bus ticket. My bus ticket, from this morning.

"You went through my bag!" I exclaim.

"You were looking at me funny when you arrived, so I investigated."

There's no point lying. "Fine, I went to Bramford. Want to guess why?"

"To dig into my past. That's obvious." She pauses. "Tell me, babe, I'm curious. When did you start to suspect I did it?"

Is that a confession? If I can just guide the conversation in the right direction...

"I'd ruled out the boys. Xander told me he met a girl in the woods. It was either you or Faith."

Marley bursts out laughing. "Faith? She's hopeless! Won't even swat flies! Xander didn't see my face, then. Good. That's been worrying me for weeks."

"So it was you."

"Lana! You're a bit slow tonight, aren't you? Of course it was me! Keep up."

She sounds so casual, as though we're discussing lip gloss. She's totally psychotic. How did I not realize? Unable to play it cool any longer, I burst out, "Esme was your best friend! How could you kill her?"

"She'd pissed me off. If she hadn't, maybe I'd have thought twice, but going out with Xander was a real betrayal. Accidentally-on-purpose dyeing her hair a crappy colour didn't hit the spot as far as revenge went." Marley sighs. "If I'd had time I'd have been more careful, but I had to act quickly once Esme realized about Hen. I could tell the moment she rushed off that she knew."

"So you decided to murder her."

"Of course. I have Hen's back, he has mine. I was hoping the police would write it off as an accident. They did pretty quickly with Miss Keats. Turns out the Witches' Pool is a good place to get rid of people. Who knew? Your drinks switch messed that up, though."

I stare at her, mind whirring. Is Marley hinting at killing Thea too? Why? I don't have time to figure that out now. "I bet that annoyed you. Instead of covering up your brother's sick game, the police started looking into it."

"I thought Esme was drunk, not drugged! Henry was furious I drowned Esme without telling him. Normally we do things like that together."

Suddenly I wonder if their parents and possibly Thea are the only other people they've killed. "Why did you help him, Marley? Turning a blind eye to him drugging and raping girls is one thing. Actively helping him – drugging the girls yourself – that's another."

"You've worked that out? I'm impressed. It's simple, babe." She flashes me a smile. "No one would suspect a girl. Easier for Hen to cover his tracks. Most people think in a very linear way. I've already told you why I helped him. He's my brother. You get that, right?"

"That's a crap reason. You know rape is wrong."

"Yeah, sure, in a general sense, but Hen wanted girls. And what Hen wants, I help him get."

"You're a twisted fraud." Hurt tumbles into my voice; I can't help it. "How could you make out you were my friend? If your plan had gone smoothly, your sick brother would've raped me."

"You should be flattered, babe. He thought you were hot. He's probably pretty good in bed by now. He's had enough practice."

I can't look at her any longer. She really means all this. I think I'm going to be sick.

"If you ask me," Marley continues, "it was stupid getting his mates involved, but he said it was more fun that way. At least Ozzie was a good fall guy."

"Like you planned Xander to be?"

Marley's eyes sparkle. "I would have loved it if he'd got done for killing Esme! Serve him right for the way he treated me." A second later, the look fades. "I was obsessed with him once. I hated that. So many girls fancy him, and I don't like being obvious. I tried so hard. Went all over social finding out what he was into, hung out where he did, even took up bloody fencing. Hen tried to set us up too. I don't know why Xander wasn't interested."

"Maybe psychotic murderers aren't his type," I sneer, but Marley laughs.

"You're fun when you're angry! Have you worked out what I hit her with yet?"

"No," I admit. "Tell me."

"I'll give you a clue. That night I was dressed to kill."

She pauses, but I look blankly back, and she sighs.

"It was the shoes! My killer heels! God, another pun, I'm on fire tonight. I thought Esme would drown when I pushed her in, but she bobbed up and tried to climb out. I panicked and hit her round the head. The shoe was in my hand anyway. It'd been rubbing. Do you want to know a secret about those shoes? I've still got them! Hen told me to bin them, but they're vintage. I don't see why I should throw them out just because of this."

She's showing more remorse for losing a pair of shoes than for killing the girl she was best friends with for years. From somewhere in the woods, I think I hear a twig snap. Xander?

I need to keep her talking. "How did you pull off creeping into hospital to finish Esme off? I slept in the same bed as you that night. I'm pretty sure I'd know if you'd left."

"Oh, that wasn't me. Hen did it. We thought that was best, as I'd done everything at the pool. Keep the police guessing."

Of course it was Henry. Mum almost recognized him, that time he dropped Marley off at mine. Marley continues, "He was the one who orchestrated your accident in the old wing too. The flowers, they were a joint effort. We hoped you'd blame Xander for everything. Shame you didn't get the message and back off. I don't want to have to kill you, but what choice do I have?"

And she smiles. Even though I anticipated this, a jolt runs through my body. "What?"

"You don't think I'm letting you walk away after I've told you everything, do you? You'd tell the police. Even if they couldn't prove anything, being arrested would send my sponsors running. I'm really sorry, babe, but visiting Bramford was a step too far. No one here knows who we are, or suspects us. Not any more, anyway." She pauses. "I've been watching you closely and I'm pretty certain you've not told Xander, which is just as well. The rugby team would be really screwed if we had to get rid of him too."

Somewhere to my right there's a muffled thump. Someone is definitely in the trees. I force myself not to look round. As sarcastically as I can manage, I say, "I suppose you 'had to' kill your parents too. Tell me about that."

"Them?" Marley makes a dismissive noise. "We deserved better. People used to ask what they'd done to get two such clever children and they always looked so confused. Our new parents are a bit wet, but at least they're rich."

I glance around and catch a flash of blue. Unable to help myself, I shout, "Xander!"

A figure steps out of the trees. But it isn't Xander. It's Henry.

He raises his eyebrows when he sees me, looking unimpressed, but underneath his glasses his eyes are dark with anger. In his hand is a kitchen knife, at least thirty centimetres long. Fear hurtles through me: what if Xander didn't even get my message? The coverage out here is patchy. I didn't check it sent.

"Are you still talking?" Henry asks his sister. "You'd better not have said anything stupid."

"Oh, shut up, Hen. You were ages!" Marley huffs. "How long does it take to drive off, loop round and park at the other end of the estate?"

In the second they're distracted, I seize my chance and plunge into the woods, leaping over the brambles. If I can just put enough distance in between us – then my legs fly out from under me, and I slam to the earth, breath knocked right out of me.

"Good tackle, Hen!" Marley calls. "I take back everything I ever said about rugby being a shit sport!"

Henry grabs my shoulders and yanks me up, one arm round my waist. The blade of the knife gleams. He's not as tall as I am, but he's far stronger. I do my best to writhe away as he half drags, half pushes me towards the water, but he doesn't budge. It's as though suddenly he's made of steel. I open my mouth and scream as loudly as I can.

"No one can hear you, Alana!" Marley calls. "Sorry, but everyone's gone. How shall we do this, Hen? I know you want to use the knife, but—"

"Let's just get rid of her." Henry forces me to my knees, pinning my arms behind my back with one hand and clamping hold of my head with the other. And then he plunges my face into the water.

THIRTY-FIVE

I'm going to die.

The thought flits through my head as cool water closes round me. All of the stuff Seb looked up after Esme was attacked comes shooting back. Thirty to sixty seconds before the agony of not breathing becomes overpowering and I open my mouth and water floods inside, cutting off oxygen entirely. Under a minute to somehow overpower Henry. I kick and jerk, but it's hopeless. There are two more hands on my head now. Marley. She's helping. As though the thrill of drowning me is something they need to share.

My lungs roar. Esme's face swims through my mind.

Then Seb, Mum, Dad, Bruce. The home I'll never see, the things I'll never do. I can't die. Not now.

My eyes fly open. All I can see is dirt, and endless, terrifying blackness. My body screams for me to breathe. Stubbornly, hopelessly, I hold out. But my strength is ebbing away. I can feel darkness closing all around me, and I know I can't win. I need to open my mouth and get this over with. . .

The pressure from behind suddenly relents, and I drop forward. Instinctively, my hands whip out and hit mud. The next second, I'm splashing about at the edge of the pool, gasping in sweet, fresh air.

"Alana! Run!" someone shouts. Disoriented, I drag my limp body on to the grass. My lungs burn. Then pain explodes from the back of my head. I see Marley raising a sharp stone to whack me again. I roll to one side just as her hand flies downwards. Marley overbalances and falls.

If I don't move, everything's over. Adrenaline kicking in, I somehow scramble up, legs almost giving way. A few metres away Xander's on top of Henry, fighting in the mud.

"Run!" he shouts again. I stumble into the woods. I'm woozy from the lack of oxygen and my lungs feel like they're full of lava. But a desperate need to survive makes me move. I make it a few paces before my stomach heaves, and I'm on my knees again, throwing up. Someone shouts, and there's an almighty splash. I must black out for a few seconds because suddenly arms close around me, and I can feel firm ground beneath my feet.

"Move. Now," Xander's voice says in my ear. "I'll help you."

I try, but my legs aren't working. Xander drags me forward, then changes his mind and scoops me up. My face lolls against his chest. The next thing I know, everything is dark, and I'm sitting on a cool, smooth surface, my head and back supported by a wall.

There's a scuffling noise, then light from the torch on Xander's phone. His fingers press the back of my head.

"Shit," he mutters.

"Am I badly hurt?"

"I don't know, but it's bloody. And I can't call for help. My phone's dead in here. Shit, shit, shit."

"Where are we?"

"The folly. It's safe. I've bolted the door."

I don't know where he means. Then I remember. The little house in the overgrown part of the estate.

Nowhere near the manor.

"Do they know we're here?"

"Not sure. They're out there, though. He's still got the knife. I wish I'd killed Henry, not pushed him in the pool!"

"He didn't hurt you, did he?"

"No." His hand closes round mine. "If I'd been just a few seconds later—"

"I'm all right. Xander, listen. It's both of them. Marley told me everything. I think they killed Thea to keep her quiet too. She's from a village close to Bramford. Something Marley said implied she knew their old identities, and—"

My body folds, and I'm retching again, though there's barely anything to come out now. I clutch Xander's hand, groaning.

"I feel awful. How bad is the bleeding?"

"Bad enough. Should I bandage it? I can rip my T-shirt up. It's a favourite, but if it means you not dying I'm prepared to make that sacrifice."

I laugh weakly. Xander turns on the torch and pulls off his top, ripping it into strips. "Fresh on half an hour ago, in case you're worried about hygiene. My hoodie's going straight on again after this, so if you want to check me out, now is your opportunity."

"No joking. Laughing hurts."

"Stop being hilarious. Noted. Right, scream if this hurts. Actually, don't you dare scream."

I stay still as Xander bandages my head. I have no idea if he's doing it right but the pressure comforts me a little. Outside, it's silent, but these stone walls are thick. At least Henry and Marley can't hear us. Problem is, we can't hear them either.

"Will anyone notice we're gone and call the police?" I whisper.

"Nope. Sorry. My parents think I'm at the after-fair party, and I didn't tell Liam anything when I asked him to deliver that note. Your mum? Brother?"

"Still in Birmingham." I close my eyes, concentrating on steadying my breathing. Then Xander's saying my name, shaking my arm. I groan. "What?"

"You passed out. I am really not happy staying here. If you can walk, we should go."

I nod, then wince and wish I hadn't. "How close are we to your house?"

"Not very. This is the part of the estate where no one goes. Even I don't know it very well. Listen, when we open the door, head uphill, as fast as you can. You should get an emergency signal. Ring for help. I'll catch you up."

"What? Xander, no – Henry's got a knife—"

"So? I'll knock it out of his hand. They might not know we're here. Even if they do, I bet I can take Henry out. Do you know how much time I spend in the gym? Marley, well, she's five foot nothing. Easy."

"You'll still be outnumbered. She's done self-defence classes. They're fighting to kill. No. We're not doing this. No way. I won't let you."

"Alana! If we stay here you'll pass out again. Maybe you won't wake up. I'm not having an argument about this, all right? We're doing it."

"This is a terrible plan!"

"It's a great plan," Xander says firmly, and I choke back a snappy reply. He helps me to my feet. All my limbs feel shaky, almost elastic, but my feet hold my weight more steadily than they did. I even think I can run.

"Ready?" Xander whispers.

I feel I should say something deep, something he'll remember. But my brain is in too much of a fuzz. So I whisper back, "Yes."

And he opens the door.

Henry is right outside. Xander reacts a split second before Henry does, foot flying out and sending Henry tumbling down the folly steps. We climb round him. Xander makes a grab for the knife, shouting at me to run. I make it a few metres before something whacks the back of my legs, sending me crashing to the ground. I roll over and see Marley, armed with a heavy branch, turning to lunge at Xander. Before I can warn him, somehow Henry's on top of me, face furious, knife gleaming in the moonlight. I grab his wrist and we grapple a few seconds before my arm gives way. The blade embeds in the earth, centimetres from my shoulder. As Henry yanks it out I do the only thing I can think of: I rip off his glasses, tossing them into the undergrowth. Then I dig my fingers into his eyes, pressing down as hard as I can. He yelps in pain. The pressure of his body on mine relents. I scramble out from under him, and stumble towards the hill, but I realize I've no hope of outpacing anyone. To my side I spy long, overgrown grass, rippling in the wind. Grasping a sudden idea, I duck down on to my hands and knees and dive into it.

"Alana!" Xander catches me up. Blood streams from his nose. He tries to pull me towards the hill, but I crawl deeper into the grass.

"Henry can't see," I hiss. When I risk looking round, hope surges through me. Henry's pursuing us, still armed, but the way he moves is slow and cautious even with Marley beside him, sweeping her phone torch across the field. Realizing the breeze will make it hard for her to pinpoint where we are, I crawl forward, whispering to Xander to follow. If we can just get to the road, or one of the rented cottages, or even far enough to call for help without alerting Henry and Marley—

"Watch out!" Marley shouts. A second later there's a vicious snapping noise and a scream.

Xander and I whirl round. Marley is rooted to the spot a few metres away. She's dropped her phone. The torchlight shines upwards on her face, a bloodied, muddy mask of horror. But she's not the one who's screaming. It's Henry. I can't see properly but he's sprawled on the ground. I don't think he can move. Marley falls to her knees by his side. Henry roars something that might be, "Get them!" and slumps forward.

"I'm not leaving you, Hen," she cries. "Let them go. They don't matter. Only us."

She struggles with something I can't see, putting all her weight behind her. I catch a flash of blood.

"Oh shit," Xander says suddenly. He leaps up and sprints over to Henry, grabbing the knife before kneeling beside Marley. I follow. When I see what's happened, my hand flies to my mouth, because there's not just a little blood, there's blood everywhere. Henry's lower leg is caught in the sharp jaws of some kind of rusty metal contraption. I think I can see bone. His face is contorted in agony.

Forgetting for a second what a monster this guy is, I pull out my phone.

*

We try, all three of us, but the ancient mantrap is heavy and stiff. We haven't managed to free Henry by the time we hear sirens blazing. He's in so much pain that he keeps passing out. Marley's beside herself, clutching his hand and crying so hard she can't talk. Neither Xander nor I comfort her.

The next few minutes pass like a film montage: paramedics checking my head and breathing, an ambulance, the hospital, sitting in a white, sterile room as my wound is cleaned and stitched up. I don't see what happens to Henry. Dad appears as they're taking me into a ward. I realize he's raced up from Chelmsford. He sits by the bed, face ashen. By the time Mum and Seb arrive a couple of hours later my eyelids are drooping. My last thought before I fall asleep is, I really hope Xander's finally gone to the police.

When I wake, my lungs still burn, but thanks to the painkillers I feel human again. I can't hear movement so it must be early. I find my phone, which Seb thoughtfully put on charge. There's a message from Xander.

> Alana,
>
> Firstly, I hope your head/lungs are OK. You owe me one T-shirt (Abercrombie and Fitch, £26).
>
> Secondly, I had a lengthy chat with the police. Before you were rushed off you

gabbled something about killer heels (thanks for being so opaque, how very annoyingly you). You'll be pleased to know I did work out what you meant. If she's kept the shoes (knowing Marley I bet she has) I think we've got her. Tbh I have a feeling she'll confess anyway. She was in pieces after Henry was taken to hospital. Thirdly, in case you cared, Henry's going to be OK. It doesn't sound like he's going to need his leg amputated but he won't be playing rugby anytime soon. I can't BELIEVE the team is basically me and Blake now. And we have a match next week, ffs.

I'll call later. Glad you're not dead.

X x

And the guy claims he can't write essays. I lean back on the pillows, smiling. Then I call him.

Over the next few days, it all comes together. I don't know whether seeing Henry so badly injured has broken Marley, or whether she wants everyone to know how clever she's been, but she tells the police everything. Together, I'm hoping the heels, necklace and confession will be enough for a conviction.

What I can't prove is that they killed Thea too.

Somehow – maybe through local gossip – Thea knew Marley and Henry were suspected of killing their parents, and when she turned up at St Jules they realized she'd recognized them. Perhaps they were worried she was going to spread it around, and the bullying was originally about scaring her into silence. Then, for whatever reason, Henry and Marley decided she was better off dead. The theory's pretty sketchy, but feels like it fits. Maybe I'm wrong, and Thea was driven to suicide by a whole host of other reasons. Somehow, I have a feeling I'll never know for sure.

The police are looking properly into Henry's date rape game. Perhaps because of our chat, or perhaps because he's less stupid than people think, Ozzie cracks and talks, and so does Calvin. The police won't get anything out of Henry when he's well enough to speak, though, of that I'm absolutely sure.

"Faith went to the cops too," Liam says when he comes to visit me at home. I've been discharged, but I'm feeling nowhere near OK enough to go to school. "Hearing about Henry trying to kill you made her decide she had to. It's a real brave thing to do. I hope she'll be OK."

I do too. I'm glad telling her story was something Faith chose, not something that was forced out of her when Ozzie and Calvin owned up. Maybe she'll tell me about it when I see her next. "It was kind of you to protect her, even when you were arrested. Not many people would. You're a good guy, Liam. Maybe you don't believe that now but it's true. So what's happening with you?"

A resigned look comes on to Liam's face. "I'm not

denying I hooked Ozzie up with that dealer. I don't know if that counts as being an accessory or anything. Mom thinks I'll get a sympathy pass because of, well... But I don't know. It's not like I don't have previous."

I want to say everything's going to be OK, but as I don't know that for a fact, I reach out and pat his arm instead. "You're going to London, then?"

"Yeah. Maybe I'll do better somewhere Dad's ghost isn't hanging over me. I'll message and whatever. Just in case you worry about me."

He gives me a half-smile. The joke isn't funny, but I play along.

"You better. I'm your friend, remember."

Friend comes out sounding funny. Adjusting how I act around him is still a work in progress. Liam was my first boyfriend, and such a big part of the last two months. So was Marley. With both of them gone, I'm going to feel like a new girl all over again.

"What about you?" asks Liam. "Are you OK?"

It feels like I should say yes. The honest answer is I don't know. There's an emptiness inside me that wasn't there when I was so focused on finding Esme's killers. "Mum's made me promise to see the school counsellor. She keeps saying I've been through a lot. I don't really know how to process it all. Before I had anger and grief fuelling me, now. . . The world isn't the way I thought it was. Bad things happened. Bad things almost happened to me. I've got to confront all that, haven't I?"

Liam nods encouragingly. "My mom's making me see someone too. We can compare notes."

I give him a hug. "I'll miss you."

He hugs me back. "I'll miss you too. Do you regret coming here?"

I think back to my old life, with the friends who forgot me the moment I moved, and the dad I used to think was wonderful.

"No," I say eventually, and it's the truth.

Liam and I chat some more, and he promises we'll meet up before he leaves. I hear his car stall in the driveway, and even though there's nothing endearing about his crappy driving, I tear up. I think it's only just dawning on me that things really have changed.

At the weekend, a group of us meet at Stillwater and go to the Witches' Pool. It's mostly Fairfield kids, but there are a bunch of St Jules boys too. With Marley gone, I've got closer to the other girls who were Esme's friends, and discovered things in common. Naima has such similar book and TV taste to me it's uncanny; Tash also grew up in Essex; and Daisy is into archaeology, which sparked my interest in more ancient history. Marley was such a dominant personality that I never got to know them properly before. They feel hurt and upset and betrayed too, and that helps. And the history society are making plans to watch Blake perform in some play at the end of the month, so I've got them too.

What would have been Esme's seventeenth birthday is in

a few days. I guess tonight is a kind of vigil – one Marley can't hijack or make any fake speeches at. I can't believe I'm going back to that place after nearly becoming its latest victim. As we walk through the woods, my chest is tight and anxious. But when we arrive the feeling eases. It's only water. It has no power over anyone here, not any more, and there are no new blue anemones.

All the same, I don't go too close to the edge.

Most of us have already written messages to Esme, and someone has brought ribbons so we can tie them to the branches. We light candles and sit by the pool for a while. No one seems to know what to say. Esme's dead. She'll never experience all the things we have waiting for us, because Marley and Henry have taken that away. They can't steal our memories, though, and that's important.

Will anything change as a result of all this? I'd like to believe so. There's been a lot of talk at Fairfield and especially St Jules about consent, and drugs, and what can be put in place to prevent anything this awful happening again. The boys I've spoken to are still in shock, and seem to want to do better, or say they do. And maybe I'm imagining it, but the recent interviews I've had with the police have had a gentler, more open tone too.

One thing that is definitely happening is a memorial to commemorate the historical victims of the Witches' Pool. Xander's parents are letting the history society take the lead on that. It won't change the inequalities of the past, but it might be a positive force for the future.

After a while, someone makes a comment that has nothing to do with Esme. The mood shifts as people relax. Life, I guess, goes on.

"So, Inspector," says a voice by my shoulder, "I've been thinking."

For a second, I smile, though when I turn round, I make sure I'm not. "You know that nickname annoys me."

"Which is why I keep saying it." Xander grins, and I roll my eyes at him.

"Whatever, Constable Lockwood."

"Ouch. Don't I at least get to be a sergeant?"

"Don't push your luck."

"Oh, come on. We made a good team. Even you have to admit that." He pauses, daring me to disagree. "I supply the muscle and the misplaced humour. As for you. . ."

"If you dare make a smart comment about the Post-its, you're in trouble."

"Would I?"

"Yes."

"So suspicious." He sighs, but I know he's not really annoyed. I look him up and down, dimly aware we're standing much closer than we need to. "You're wrong. I was going to say something flattering about your shining future career as a detective, but I've changed my mind. I'm sure you could persuade me to unchange it, though."

The old flirty look in his eyes is back. The one I used to mistrust.

I give him a glare that says I know what he's up to.

"Nope. But if I do stumble upon any murders and need a sidekick, you'll be the first person I call."

"So we did make a good team. You admit it."

I open my mouth, then stop. Xander saved my life. He deserves this, at least. I look him up and down, and decide he's definitely two, not one, inches taller than I am.

I smile. "All right. We made a good team."

Xander gives a nonchalant shrug. Of course he's too cool to show he likes this. "I'm not bad to have around. Maybe you'll find that out if you decide to carry on hanging out with me. Which, judging by all the WhatsApping we seem to be doing, I'm guessing wouldn't be unwelcome." I open my mouth, and he holds up his hands. "Not so fast. Note, I used the word *guess*. I would hate to be an arrogant rich boy and assume. I'll give you a fencing lesson, if you like. Free of charge. Historic costume and massage afterwards optional. Anyway. Your call, Miss Ashman."

There are a lot of things I could say to that. But I don't get a chance, because Blake wanders over, and the moment passes.

We start to walk back towards the house. I'm conscious that I don't really know the people around me, but without a murder investigation hanging over us, maybe I soon will. Tomorrow, life returns to normal. Whatever normal is now.

I have no idea what happens next, but I'm looking forward to finding out.

Acknowledgements

I have so many people to thank for this one!

Firstly, all the publishing professionals who have worked tirelessly and with such good humour to bring this book to the shelves. A HUGE thanks goes to my agent, Lydia Silver. Lydia, thank you for believing in this book and me as an author, and getting what I was trying to achieve from day one. There's a popular saying that good things come in threes, and that certainly applies to this book's editors – thank you to Yasmin Morrissey, Ruth Bennett and Sophie Cashell. Thank you also to Jenny Glencross, who ironed out a lot of inconsistencies previous edits created. And thanks to Kiran Khanom for publicity, Ella Probert for marketing, Jess White for copyedits, Sarah Dutton for proofreading, and Jamie Gregory for that fabulous cover.

This book had a number of readers before any of the people above saw it. I'm so grateful to my beta readers – Heather Chavez, Margot Harrison, Valerie Ward and Kali Richmond. You are all brilliant. I am also (weirdly) grateful to everyone who totally savaged my original Chapter 1 online – can't lie, it was brutal, but I'm not sure the book would have got anywhere if I hadn't ditched that bad beginning. Thanks also to Lizzie Huxley Jones, Winnie Li and Tessa Lyle who acted as sensitivity readers and whose comments were so insightful.

Thank you to the friends who've supported me over this book's long journey, even if you weren't aware you were doing it. Particular mentions to: The Kalettes, Nina Kelly and Melanie Griffiths, because you're great, and Grace Carroll, particularly for support when the book didn't even have an agent.

I also want to thank my family, starting with my husband Hugh. I'm sorry "your" title didn't make the cut, but, as always, your tolerance and patience is appreciated. I know you don't always "get" fiction (shame on you), but you get me, and that counts for more. Nicky and Toby, my feline companions. Rosemary Pattenden, for the nursery days. David Blaxill, not so much for this book, but for always supporting my writing. Luke Blaxill, even if I'm not sure I took onboard many of your suggestions this time (sorry!).

The biggest thanks I've saved for last. This book would be nothing without the MANY discussions with my mother, Sheila. Mum, this one is as much yours as mine, right from the lunchtime chat about suffragettes that sparked the initial idea. This book has been a total rollercoaster of emotions, and no one else could have supported me like you have, or been so brilliant to brainstorm with. We did it!